Druid Lake Inc.

www.druidlakeinc.com

for Leigh & Korbyn

TETHER

PART ONE

CHAPTER ONE
2021, Thursday June 17th

What do you talk about when the end is near?

The Vermont weather?

Work?

How all the zucchini at the supermarket appeared rotten?

Peter watched his wife take a bite of pizza and place it back down on the paper plate.

He quickly looked away as it hit him that she may have wanted a much more glamorous last few days. Posh restaurants, big spending, going out with a bang.

Instead, they juxtaposed their luxurious kitchen, very expensively renovated shortly after they purchased the home, with take-out pizza on plain white paper plates. They sat at their reclaimed wood dining table across from the marble island that rested between them and the commercial gas stove. The walls a shiny Italian tile complemented by hanging luscious green plants.

But he couldn't bring himself to be in a position that felt celebratory, to cook or even do dishes.

This whole damn thing mutated from his original intention.

Lila reached over and took his hand as if to say *it's okay*. Her gaze a pressure felt on his skin as he looked at her, only to see her release her grip.

She folded the disposable dish around the half-eaten slice and stood, rounding the island to pull the drawer for the trash and toss it away.

Lila left the kitchen for the front of their home without a word. He figured she would head upstairs to bed. With hope now lost, Lila always retired early and no longer exercised, read, or paid him too much attention.

Peter gave the silence he found himself with company. Sat with it as if to say to the emptiness that it was not alone.

He turned his body to stand from the natural wood bench and followed the same path to the garbage to rid himself of the food.

Unlike his wife, though, he went to one of the two tall and arching back windows framed with dark stained wood.

With the sun set and in the bright room, he couldn't see anything out there. *Perhaps that's for the best*, he thought.

But against his better judgment, Peter reached for the light switch between the twin windows and the door to the yard and flicked it off.

The blackness embraced him until his eyes adjusted and he could see his small backyard, the standalone two-car garage off to the right, and the trees beyond.

The moon just a few days from being full, now offered enough illumination to see clearly.

He hesitated and looked down a moment before raising his head again. Resolute in facing what was to come.

Just into the tree line he made out the distinct shape.

The white nightgown glowing softly, the pale skin, and dark hair.

From where he stood he could not make out the features of her face as shadows shifted slowly across. But Peter knew it was his daughter standing there in the night.

She haunted him.

CHAPTER TWO
2021, Friday June 18th

The glass tower loomed over Dallas. And on a hot day like this one, the haze and sunshine beating the city's residents into submission, made Kristin's office building feel like a stalagmite in some cavern of hell. On occasion, in the infrequent weak moment, she would slip and start thinking of it that way. The oppressive heat. The tall buildings. The mass of people and debilitating traffic that mocked you as you tried to deal with all the real challenges in life. Hell.

But she never let those moments last longer than a fleeting second. She knew to entertain them was to risk the thoughts becoming something more. Instead, the transplanted Vermonter, accustomed to being surrounded by mountains, trees, and disparate seasons, focused on her career. It was how Kristin Fuller rose from unpaid intern at age 22 to Lone Star Equity Partners' young star at 29.

In those seven years she never did get entirely used to the heights. Standing a few feet from the floor-to-ceiling window that looked out at the city, she still felt uneasy. Even if the window were to fall suddenly, she stood plenty of distance away to be safe. *But,* she thought, *maybe there would be some pressure difference that would push me out.*

A silly thought for sure, but that's what she needed right now.

She looked up to the almost full moon, the ghost-like image ominously hanging in the blue sky. Looking at it she understood why past civilizations both revered and feared it. It sat at the virtual center of the window frame she stood in front of as if it watched her. As if across hundreds of thousands of miles it peered down on her and waited, biding its time…for something.

Kristin turned in place to face the boardroom. Opposite the windows to the city, equally imposing frosted glass to the offices and natural wood panels completed the room. Eight men and one woman sat around the long rectangular table, with the empty chair at its head opposite the screen she presented from — empty because Mr. Wilmington had to step out for a minute to take a call. Most of the leaders in the room were old white men, save for Mrs. Hawthorne, who had taken her under her wing years ago. While Kristin thought the executives as old, she realized the feeling came from the stereotypical image the group of primarily males mimicked.

In reality, Mr. Cooke couldn't be more than 50. He was the most slender of the bunch and still sported a full head of hair. He sat on the left side of the table, closest to Kristin.

On the right, between Mr. Schneider and Mr. Cordova, sat Mrs. Hawthorne. She looked good for early sixties, with her graying blond hair up and wearing a neatly pressed deep purple suit.

All the men wore either blue or gray, standard and conservative ties, and shirts a shade of blue or white.

The table they sat around had a center of wood that Kristin couldn't identify, but it had a beautiful natural light color. Framing it was a gray marble with veins of silver. A small lip between the materials allowed hidden LED lights to glow a faint blue for no apparent reason but to be showy. *If I ran the company*, Kristin thought, *I'd find nice-looking things that were not quite so extravagant. Maybe a lovely maple from Vermont.*

The group sat quietly, either typing calmly on their thin laptops or flipping through the binders she had passed around about an hour ago. They patiently waited for Mr. Wilmington's return.

Behind her, the sixty-inch monitor displayed her last slide. On it, the lonely *300%* text is in bold and green. She developed the entire presentation to lead to this figure, the impact now shattered as the Vice President of Investment Strategy's cell rang just as she had clicked to it.

She hated these moments. She never was one for small talk, and here sat nine of the firm's most important, most influential members. Should she entertain them? Tell a story? Ask about their plans for the weekend — God, she hated that question, just as bad as *how about the weather?*

Mrs. Hawthorne caught her eye and gave Kristin a thumbs up just in the crook of her elbow for only her to see.

She appreciated the nod and reciprocated with a smile.

Kristin saw herself as the firm's best weapon. Many of their fine southern clients enjoyed the opportunity to treat her like a lady, all the while she impressed them with her acumen. Today she had her dirty blond hair down and wore a silky-white buttoned blouse with a knee-length deep blue skirt. She always got compliments from Mr. Wilmington when she wore that type of outfit. She realized it both fitted her slender frame well and displayed the necessary professionalism.

The executive re-entered the room, thoughtfully moving quickly to his chair at the head of the table and across the room from Kristin. Those on their computers quickly shut them.

His large figure stretched his expensive dark blue suit as he sat. The sides of his head sprouted thick white hair, but his scalp shined. Mr. Wilmington, at age 72, refused to retire. Kristin wasn't sure if he loved the position too much to leave, or made so much money that he had become addicted to the collection of wealth.

He looked up kindly, "I apologize, Ms. Fuller, that was one I needed to take. Please continue." He smiled, warmly.

She had to make a joke, she thought, to change the tone of the moment.

"Not a problem at all, Mr. Wilmington, I think the room needed the break from my voice."

The group chuckled lightly.

Now, as many likely have been lost in other work, she needed to pivot. Instead of driving home her estimated 300% return on the investment, she needed to summarize how she came to the conclusion. She needed her best elevator pitch.

"To summarize. AviCare is led by Leban Carter, the prior CEO of HarborPharm. AviCare's single drug is a molecule that showed promise at HarborPharm. Leban left the pharmaceutical, purchasing the rights to the molecule shortly after he left. So, he is very familiar with it and personally invested in its success."

Kristin took a breath and stepped closer to the table, "Phase two for the drug was beyond successful with a *p-value* less than point zero zero one. Phase three testing has been very specifically designed to mimic phase two. Safety is not a question, and efficacy is stronger than any drug in its comparative market including the current standard of care."

"With a worldwide market in the range of 600 million, sales potential eclipsing one point five billion, secondary indications already identified, enough cash-on-hand to complete phase three, and no debt means low likelihood of an offering in the near-term. A current stock price of only $2.13, a market cap of one point two billion, and a 300% return in 24 months is not only possible but in my opinion a conservative estimate."

"It's biotech. Not exactly our forte. The inherent risks in biotech don't make this attractive, and it seems what you presented could apply to any pharma stock." Mr. Wilmington, always direct, had his hands on the pages of the open binder and his eyes locked on Kristin.

"No offense, but that isn't the case. Most never make it to phase three. And for AviCare, ninety-three percent of phase two participants specifically requested to re-enroll in the phase three trial. If they did not directly experience the benefits of the drug, without harmful side effects, they would not have requested in such high numbers. Also," she paused for effect, "the company only has 35 employees, and they believe with their wallets. Not just by direct investment, but 40% of those employees have purchased new homes in just the past year, and 74% new cars. I follow all employees on Twitter and have managed to connect to some of their friends on Facebook. While they are of course careful not to disclose, reading between the lines has them ready for something big."

"You are also suggesting," Mr. Wilmington continued, "a not insignificant investment, however."

"I am. With an opportunity like this, it doesn't make sense to just dip our toes in the water. The returns are too great."

He huffed and the others looked at him as he paged through the documents again.

"Your research is quite thorough," Mrs. Hawthorne called the group's attention to the large binders.

"Thank you, I've put quite a bit of time into it."

Mr. Wilmington closed the black cover and looked around the room, then at Kristin, "You're supposed to be going on vacation, are you not?"

"That's correct, visiting my parents for a week. Leaving tomorrow morning." She worried she might have to postpone, which she would no doubt do if he specifically asked.

He nodded, "And you're asking for 60 million dollars."

"That's right."

Mr. Wilmington smiled and billowed a laugh that came up from his belly, "Oh, Kristin, I have to say your balls are bigger than anyone's in this room."

The men looked to the VP, and Mrs. Hawthorne's eyes got large. It wasn't like the old man to use such colorful language, but he let it rip.

"To come in here suggesting we drop 60 million into a fucking biotech the day before you hop on a plane for fuck-knows-where…"

"Vermont," she interrupted.

"Vermont! Right! For Vermont! Well, then," he lowered his voice, "I'd say with the guts to do that, and what you've put in front of me, I'd be the dumbest man alive to not approve it."

Kristin smiled as Mr. Wilmington stood and the remainder of the room followed suit.

He turned to the slightly younger man on his left, "Ian, get us in this game."

"Sure thing."

He spoke to Kristin and raised his pointed finger to the ceiling as he exited, but without looking at her, "And you better be right!"

All but Mrs. Hawthorne followed their Vice President out.

The woman, her smile wider than ever, approached Kristin and gave her a hug, "You're brave."

"Not really," Kristin didn't fully understand her mentor's response, "I believe in the investment and it's my job to identify the opportunities and bring it to the panel's attention. I didn't do anything outside of my duties."

"True, but it's 60 million."

"No, it's a lot more than that. We just can't collect it yet."

Mrs. Hawthorne nodded, "Proud of you."

With that, she pivoted on her purple heels and left the room.

Kristin went to the door and shut it, then turned to the long table, sat in the closest chair at its center, and plopped down. She crossed her arms in front of her, the sleeves of her white blouse hiking up her forearms, and dropped her head to them.

How many nights did she lay in bed, her eyes

closed, and visualize her presentation? Walking through her main points, and anticipating where questions would be asked and she'd be challenged. She even played out how she'd handle technical issues with the monitor.

But she didn't consider this moment. The sudden success.

She got what she wanted, the green light, and Ian McClellan, who led the firm's team of traders, had his marching orders direct from Wilmington.

And tomorrow vacation started.

It all seemed so...anti-climactic.

Sure, she got an *atta-girl* from Hawthorne, and Wilmington's comments added a feeling of increased empowerment to her, but no fanfare.

A sudden and sinking feeling hit the pit of her stomach. She did get what she asked for, but if the biotech failed she'd not only be out of a job but probably completely flushed her career down the toilet.

That feeling was quickly accompanied by an intense fear that pulsed through her as she remembered her research into the biotech began with an anonymous email that contained a concise and compelling case for her to look further into the company. A half-dozen emails followed, all from the same untraceable address, with trial data, personnel files, and projections.

She shook her head. All those materials she verified, corroborated, and did so three times over. The information checked out, so there certainly was no good reason to tell anyone where it came from or to worry about its validity. Regardless, she worked her ass off and now the true reward would come when AviCare proved successful.

Kristin raised her head to the surrounding city and those binders she spent hours late at night printing and compiling. The room's large presentation screen still displayed that big green number. Looking out at a million people she felt entirely alone. The survivor of a catastrophe, the evidence of the past civilization scattered around her. Kristin focused on pushing all those terrible feelings away. Today was a good day.

She needed to feel connected, needed to wrap up and get home to Emil.

Kristin stood and turned off the monitor, the imposing number now gone.

One by one she made a pile of the materials and then opened the door.

With the thick binders stacked high in her hands, reaching her chin, she walked the hall of glass offices to her own, where she dropped them on the small sofa against the right wall. They bounced and collapsed into a mess.

Kristin closed the door and pulled shut the blinds that offered a view of the inner sanctum of the firm, now largely empty as five o'clock passed, and on Fridays the place tended to quiet early.

She dropped herself into the Herman Miller office chair behind her black shiny desk that sat by the left wall. The chair, easily worth twice as much as her first car, felt good after standing for so long. Leaning back as far as she could she allowed herself to exhale.

She spun the Herman Miller to the windows that brought the natural light of the day in, stretched her feet out, flicked off her heels, and pressed her bare feet against the frame of the cold metal floor-to-ceiling windows.

Again finding herself looking out at the city, from the 45th floor of her downtown office, now made her feel on top of the world. She felt the muscles in her face flex for the irreversible smile. *This is how I should feel.*

"AviCare," she said aloud to herself, "you better fucking pull through."

"Oh, I'm sorry ma'am."

Kristin heard the familiar voice behind her and quickly turned back around to see Ingrid, the cleaning lady, had entered and had one hand on her cart just outside the office door.

Startled and a bit embarrassed, Kristin sat upright and began straightening her blouse. She hoped Ingrid wouldn't notice her bare feet or lonely shoes by the windows.

"Ma'am?" Ingrid's pale and wrinkled face turned red, posing the single word as a curious question as if to ask if everything was all right.

Kristin smiled at her as she gained composure, allowing the silly nature of the moment to be realized, "Oh, it's okay, Ingrid. And please, no 'ma'am' here."

Ingrid grinned thankfully and went for the trash can at the side of Kristin's modern desk, "Good day, Kristin?" She picked up the stainless steel and likely over-priced trash can and went toward the door to dump its contents.

Kristin wanted to share all the exciting details with Emil first, so she just kept it high level with Ingrid, "Really big thing happened. I'm...excited."

Kristin knew she was the only one at the firm that ever meaningfully interacted with the woman...or any of the janitors. As well as Kristin did professionally, as hard as she worked, she never allowed it to impact her treatment of others. Kristin found Texans to be very polite, but she felt she brought a genuineness from Vermont that helped her connect to people like others might not. She got to know Ingrid, though admittedly a bit superficially, as a kind and funny woman in her late fifties. Married, with two children now working construction outside the city.

"Big deals made?" She returned with the empty trash bin, placing it right back where she had found it.

"Big deal indeed."

Ingrid brought a hand up and stretched it out to Kristin, "High-five, girl!"

Kristin obliged, happily slapping the janitor's hand and making a note to herself to use the Purell in her drawer. She felt a little guilty for the thought, but given the woman's profession, she thought it prudent.

"Thanks, Ingrid."

"You've always been the nicest of them, I hope you run this place one day."

"Well, that would be exciting. If that happens, what position could I offer you?"

Ingrid blushed again, "Oh, Ms. Fuller…"

Kristin interrupted, "Kristin."

"Kristin, I don't have the smarts like the people here."

"Well, I'm sure there's something else you could do."

"I'm afraid I'm doing it."

"What's something you'd like to try or do? Since we're playing make-believe here, might as well enjoy it." Kristin laughed a little to lighten the mood.

"Okay, well, I guess anything during the day so I can have dinner with my husband."

Ingrid's request hit Kristin hard. One of those moments where she understood her privilege, saw it in front of her.

"Consider it done."

"Your vacation is coming up, yes?" Ingrid changed

the subject as she went to the door and positioned herself behind her cart.

"Leaving in the morning."

"Safe travels then." Without waiting for a response Ingrid pushed her supplies down the hall to the next office.

Kristin sat a moment, reflecting on the past couple of hours as she flexed her now-free toes against the soft fibers of the rug. She withdrew the sanitizer from her drawer, dabbed a bit on, and rubbed her hands together. When she returned, she thought, she would look for opportunities to help Ingrid.

She flipped open the black laptop at the center of her desk, typed in her password, and opened her email.

Sixty-four unread messages.

Five-fifteen PM.

She set her out-of-office reply to *On* and began chipping away at her email, answering questions and noting to everyone that while she would be out the following week she was available as needed at her included cell number. *A vacation*, she thought, *but still need to be connected.*

Kristin hadn't seen her parents much the past few years, generally only for the Christmas holiday, and typically only for a few days at a time. A couple of months back her father called, which he rarely did as he delegated communication to her mother, to ask Kristin to come visit for the week. The lunar eclipse would be occurring late on a Sunday, and Vermont was poised for perfect viewing. She could fly up Saturday, enjoy the eclipse the following evening, and spend the week catching up with family and friends. It would also relieve her of the damn Dallas heat for a bit.

It sounded nice and being able to see the lunar eclipse also gave it a sense of adventure, so she took the rare time off from work. Unfortunately, Emil, her serious boyfriend whom she had been living with for a couple of years now, had his own commitments and wouldn't be able to make the trip.

At about 6:45 she replied to her last email and gathered her things, closing her office door behind her.

She walked the dimly lit row with cubicles on her left, and the offices on the right. Over one shoulder she had her laptop bag, in the other arm hung her small purse and the jacket that went with her skirt in case some of the meeting rooms got cold from the blasting air conditioning.

"Kristin."

She stopped in her tracks and jumped at the unexpected and deep voice.

To her left, over the cubicle's half wall, she could see Brad Unger leaning back in the chair, his feet up, and hands behind his head.

She immediately realized that it wasn't his desk, he had an office like hers, so he must have been sitting there waiting for her.

"Brad, you scared me."

She never really liked Brad, he rubbed her the wrong way — like he always had an agenda. He dressed sharply, always in a pressed suit, but didn't place much attention on his beard. She figured Brad took advantage of the beard fad to hide his complete lack of a chin.

Kristin's parents taught her to be kind, even to those she didn't care for, so she stepped closer to the fabric-lined wall and rested her arms on them. "What's up?"

He didn't budge, didn't even drop his feet from the desk, which were now just a few feet away from her. And, of course, no apology for the start.

"I heard about your big win."

"Well, not really a win for me. Just hopeful it's a win for the firm."

"Hmm," his tone skeptical and eyes unblinking.

He finally sat upright, his tie loose and top button unbuttoned. "I did a little research, you know, out of curiosity."

"Oh yeah?"

Though confident she had turned over every rock prior to presenting her proposal, she still didn't like where he was going.

"Yeah. And I noticed that AviCare recently posted a large number of sales positions to a job board. Not only that, but these positions all come with stock options. I think the company is going to have an offering, that would dilute the shares."

"I took all of that into consideration. They have the cash, stock options are the norm for sales, and those shares are already represented in my calculations."

"Oh, well, that's good. I know you're thorough, but still it's a curious thing that you didn't share this in your presentation. At least that's what Ian said when I talked to him about it."

"I didn't cover all the material I reviewed, I had to prioritize the most important items to consider."

"Of course, of course. I just want to make sure Wilmington has the necessary information to make a decision. You understand I'm sure, Sweetheart."

Kristin understood just fine. And that *sweetheart* remark was his cherry on top. Brad didn't like the fact that Mr. Wilmington approved her proposal, that she secured 60 million for an investment…probably twice his biggest win.

Putting on her best face became exhausting.

Misogynistic assholes like Brad were a fact of life, and in no way was Brad the first she had encountered. But certainly one of the most brazen.

Kristin wouldn't let him ruin her day, "You do what you feel is necessary, Brad."

"Good," he slapped the gray desk with one hand and leaned back again. "It's agreed, while you're out I'll wrap up a little risk analysis."

She removed her arms from the wall and pivoted around, taking the first step toward the elevators, "Have a good evening!"

Though she no longer looked at him, Brad raised his arm in a dramatic wave, "Please, enjoy your vacation. I'll hold down the fort."

Fuck you, Brad, she thought. Not just because of his unwarranted challenge to her professionally, but also for the impact on her vacation. She'd have to put some extra time in an effort to play defense.

She pushed him out of her mind as she passed through large glass double doors to the floor's foyer and elevators, which took a few minutes to arrive.

The thought of AviCare snuck back into her mind while she waited, and she ran through the elements of her presentation to set her mind at ease. The science was solid, their leadership team experienced, and the financials sound. She had no need to worry.

The elevator buzzed and opened empty. Kristin entered and hit the button for the third garage level.

Leaning against the back wall and shifting her weight from one foot to the other for some relief from her high heels, she rode it down to where she had parked her car that morning. Another reason to hate the heat. She preferred to bike to work. It was her way to fit exercise into her busy life, but when the temperature read 95 degrees with high humidity she just couldn't stomach the ride. So a good portion of the year she drove, along with seemingly everyone else in Dallas. At least her typical habit of working late meant missing the worst of it.

She began her evening routine to set work behind her, allowing her to be more present in her personal life. As she exhaled she felt her muscles relax and tension leave her body.

Again the elevator buzzed as it reached its destination, as was typical on a Friday it hadn't been interrupted by any other passengers.

The door opened and Kristin started walking the fifty or so yards to her car, a brand-new Jeep Grand Cherokee. Only a few vehicles remained in the garage.

Unlike most of the other employees, she preferred to park by the entrance and exit ramps. It made for a long walk to and from, but she felt better not driving through the cramped space. And she thought the fewer vehicles there would mean less of a chance of getting her nice new car dinged by some jerk not paying close enough attention.

The tapping of her heels echoed off the concrete floor, ceiling, and pillars as she walked the distance. She shuffled through her purse for her keys and positioned them so that one stuck out between each finger in her fist, which clutched the key fob. Her dad taught her to do that in conjunction with their driving lessons. "If some weirdo ever comes up to you and tries anything," he'd say, "you just punch 'em like that." She thought it an odd lesson being in Vermont, seemingly the safest place in the world, but this small thing made her feel safer in the city. Her new Jeep didn't even require putting the key in the lock to open it, much less retrieving them from her purse, but her makeshift metal knuckles had become a habit.

As she walked she became used to the rhythm of her heels, the direct sound followed by the reverberations off her concrete surroundings. *Click click, click click.* Then, as if some dubstep DJ were hiding in the shadows, she began to hear what sounded like other heels tapping behind some row of thick pillars off to her left. They sounded…different. Like women's shoes but much more solid. Larger. Even heavy. And not just a pair, but a *clickety clickety* of 2 sets of stilettos worn by friends so used to each other that they walked in unison. *Clickety clickety.*

She stopped and leaned a bit forward to look between a sedan and support column to the row beyond, but as she did the sounds stopped as well.

Kristin started walking again, slowly, listening carefully as she went. The odd noise returned and then faded off into somewhere unknown as she reached her SUV as if whatever it was had retreated. She opened the door and quickly got in to shut and lock it. She shivered from the odd experience, started her Jeep, and drove out into the Dallas sun.

She slowed as she reached the top of the ramp to look for pedestrians on the sidewalk, then took a right turn out of the garage. About a block further she flipped the left turn signal on, slowed, and took the turn onto Main street. She came to a stop after another two blocks as a delivery vehicle positioned itself just right to block traffic, and the row of a half dozen vehicles waited.

Kristin turned the radio on to some atmospheric chill electronic music, the kind with no discernible beat but calming and just right for moments without company.

She turned her attention to her right to see Dallas'

Giant Eyeball, the large blue-eyed sculpture in a small park, staring at her just over the low metal fence. The sun reflected off the tall glass building behind it, making the thing look like the heavens beamed it down with purpose. The blackness of its pupil like the entrance to another realm, or portal to a mysterious and unexplored region of our universe. One with creatures, probably not too dissimilar from Cthulhu, that held mythical powers and control over time and space.

For some reason feeling uneasy, she turned away from its artificial gaze, her hands tight on the wheel, and for the next fifteen or so seconds forced her attention to remain forward until the truck moved and traffic started again. She stayed close to the Mercedes coupe in front of her, leaving that ocular gateway behind.

* * *

Kristin drove down US-80, a narrow two-lane road with snaking pavement repairs and patchwork band-aids. The poster child for the country's inability to invest in infrastructure. Somewhere a mile or so to her left was Lake Ray Hubbard, minuscule compared to her Lake Champlain back in Vermont, and home to the Yacht Club she sometimes visited for corporate gatherings.

She turned off by the grouping of fast food joints and headed down the suburb's artery, lined with homes that have seen better days, busy utility poles, and empty lots.

Another mile and she took a left, and two miles later reached her neighborhood. If she had continued further she would have reached that Yacht Club she had just recently become a full member of. Though she hadn't yet purchased a boat and doubted she would ever make such a poor investment, membership had other benefits — like the use of their health club, pool, and access to the restaurant overlooking the lake.

Kristin parked her SUV next to Emil's hybrid Toyota hatchback in the driveway of her two-story Tuscan-style house. They had too much stuff in storage in the garage to utilize it for its intended purpose. At the top of her priority list of things to do at home was to clean it out, if only to prevent the sun from turning her car into a sauna.

She purchased her home three years prior, and about a year later Emil Gifford, her boyfriend for the past four, moved in. As a nutritionist he didn't make nearly as much money as she did, so they made a deal — he wouldn't have to pay rent, but he needed to make dinner four times a week, and take her out to eat at least once. For Kristin, the deal was far better than money. She enjoyed not having to cook after a long day, and as a nutritionist, he made great meals. Because of his job, Kristin rarely found herself making any food at all.

The two were not much alike. Kristin's type A personality benefited her professionally. Her drive and intelligence made her the success she was. Not that Emil wasn't successful, he was, but his compass guided his efforts toward his passions. Emil often said he just *went with the flow* and she saw that in him. He didn't make planning a habit. He didn't think about what was next for his career. He loved what he did, he helped people, and that made him happy. For all of her stress, he was her peace. Her Zen.

Kristin exited the car and opened the door to the back seat where she grabbed her bag, purse, and jacket. She followed the flat-stone walkway to the small front stoop, took the two concrete steps up, and opened the unlocked yellow door of her home.

She opened it to reveal the small entry area within

the living room. Kristin regretted not having a true foyer, but she recognized the house as a great starting point for her and it quickly became home. The bright room held a small television in the far left corner, next to the large windows, and a white leather couch. An Ansel Adams photo hung on one wall, an early work of his, called *Aspens* she thought, which reminded her of Vermont for some reason. The almost square photo depicted tall and slender trees, just a light enough gray to be seen against the sheer black of the forest behind. Their stalks barren of branches or leaves until a few emerge toward the top. In front, one lone and shorter tree, brighter than the rest and fully bloomed. Next and a bit behind it a similar one — smaller, more sparse. It haunted the larger tree.

On the longest wall, an abstract and colorful painting by a local artist dominated. It splashed with red, blue, and yellow, complementing the colors of the pillows on the couch.

Kristin dropped her keys in the large oyster-shaped dish that sat on the entry table. Next to it stood Emil's replica of the statue of Gandhi at the Pacifist Memorial. He wanted it there as a reminder whenever he left the house and returned home. Kristin admired Emil's pacifism, though admitted to herself at times that she wished Emil demonstrated more traditional masculine strength. But, she would always conclude, then he wouldn't be her Zen.

She slipped off her shoes and flexed her toes on the plush carpet, refusing to have tile in the living area like so many do in hot climates. It's a habit she started as a child. After being in shoes all day at school, or in sneakers while out playing, she loved the feeling of coming inside, kicking them off, and having the sensation of her nerve endings coming alive as she rubbed her feet on her parents' living room carpet. Today the same holds true, but she also uses it as a way to ground herself. For Kristin, it's a way to say *okay, I'm home now, out of work mode and into Kristin at home mode.* Much like Gandhi was for Emil.

After a moment to appreciate her toes' new freedom, she passed through the open doorway straight ahead to the kitchen at the rear of the house. She could see Emil through the back windows, sitting on the porch reading. He didn't mind the weather so much, used to it as a Texan.

Kristin had the kitchen remodeled just five months prior. Contemporary in style, it had big windows looking out at their backyard, beautiful white and gray granite countertops, stainless steel appliances, and bright white cupboards. While she loved the room, she didn't spend much time in it and Emil likely appreciated it more.

The island between the windows and the cooking space, which also held the refrigerator, had a sink, the dishwasher, and a small built-in mini-frig specifically for liquor. She opened it and pulled out her favorite brand of lemon vodka. Into a small drink glass she mixed it with ice and pomegranate juice.

The A.C. felt good but did make the kitchen's hardwood floor feel a bit too cold. She wondered how she seemed to easily tame multi-millionaires, convince them to invest ungodly amounts of money into something speculative, but not be able to handle temperatures outside of a relatively narrow range. For her, Texas really was the opposite of Vermont as back home she hated the winter months, the cold made her hurt. She'd be happy with Vermont summers, and Texas winters. *One day...* she thought.

Next Kristin pulled her dinner from the refrigerator,

where Emil always placed it for her unconventional and irregular times of returning home. A plate already made of baked chicken breast with rosemary, a small serving of brown rice, and green beans. She slid it in the microwave, set it to two minutes, and went out to Emil who sat stretched out on one of their lounge chairs under the dark awning.

The backyard looked out at a vast and undeveloped field, she was lucky to find a home where she had some space and didn't feel completely surrounded. Along each side extended her neighbors' natural wood fences, but straight back was open to the large grassland, with a lone and ragged oak a hundred yards or so away.

Just over the oak and a bit to its right, the large moon hung bright in the dusk sky.

The night smelled like cut grass.

Kristin bent down and gave Emil a kiss before sitting in the fabric deck chair next to him, and slid her drink onto the small coffee table between them.

"Hey."

Emil put his book down to give her his full attention, "Hi, Sweetie."

They met through mutual friends, no great story to recount to the kids they talked about possibly, maybe, having one day. But for them it felt so natural that thinking back on it brought comfort to Kristin. It was a casual and relaxing evening with friends, and they laughed with each other a lot. Their relationship grew quickly.

Emil stayed fit to largely keep up appearances with his job as he didn't particularly enjoy going to the gym. It was the one thing she felt he did that conflicted with his personality. His skin was tan, as usual, and his dark hair cut short. Stretched out on the lawn chair, he had a good ten inches on her.

"Did you get your dinner?"

"Yeah, just popped it in."

"How was work? I'm excited to hear about your big proposal!" He leaned forward with honest eagerness.

Her smile went from ear to ear, unable to hold her sense of pride for the accomplishment, "Mr. Wilmington said I had balls."

Emil's eyes widened, a little unsure what that meant, "Balls?"

"Yeah, he was impressed! Gutsy to make such a proposal before vacation. He told Ian to purchase."

"That's amazing."

"I know…"

Emil's genuine excitement for Kristin beamed through his smile and bright eyes.

"But Brad's being an ass."

"What?" His expression relaxed.

"Yeah, he cornered me on the way out to tell me about something he found in his cursory online research, which I already knew about anyway, and that he thought Mr. Wilmington should know."

"What an asshole."

"So I'll have to deal with that."

"What are you going to do?" He took a sip of his beer.

She looked down and shook her head, indicating she still needed to think it through, "Probably send material to Hawthorne in case there are conversations occurring while I'm away. Pay closer attention to email."

Emil nodded, "You're great at what you do, don't let it ruin your time with your parents."

Reaching for her glass, droplets of condensation

already forming around the outside, she noticed that moon again. It stared at her. Right at her.

Looking out from her small concrete porch, the awning overhead and straddled by the fences, it seemed that the moon had been placed there specifically to look down on her. Just like that giant eye she drove past.

Then a more ominous feeling washed over her, from her head to her toes making her shiver.

That glowing moon was a bowling ball, the fences the gutters, and she the last pin.

It was coming for her.

Aiming at her.

"Hey, babe?" Kristin turned to Emil keeping the bright object still in her view out of fear it would do something if she gave it the slightest opportunity.

"Yeah? You okay?"

"Yup, mind if we go in?"

"Of course."

They stood and Kristin scuttled quickly inside as Emil followed. Hurriedly she lowered the blinds to shut out the moon, then got her dinner from the microwave.

Emil grabbed another can of a local light beer from their frig and the couple sat at the mosaic-top small bistro table by the windows.

"You have a lot to do tonight to be ready for tomorrow?"

Kristin cut the chicken into small pieces. She liked to do that, cut everything on the plate first so she could put down the knife and just enjoy the meal. Emil taught her that, a way for her to be able to relax more and just enjoy the experience. "Just pack, should be quick."

"Figures the one vacation you actually take this year I can't go."

She reached across the table and placed one hand on his, "I know, babe. I wish you could come too."

Emil typically took time off when Kristin did, but that wasn't frequent. Her unused vacation time got paid out at the end of every year — given how busy she was at work, she didn't mind so much. She enjoyed what she did for a living, and the extra cash meant both more for her own investments and a little to her mortgage principle. Kristin planned well financially. When Emil asked her once if that meant she would retire early, she shook her head in confusion. Kristin started working at 13 at a small mom-and-pop country store stocking shelves and organizing the back room. She hadn't stopped since.

"It's okay, I understand. It's been a long time since I've spent a week with my parents, and you know my Dad, he never asks for me to visit. But he just sounded so excited about the eclipse I couldn't say 'no'. He went on and on about how 'Vermont is in the perfect position to see it', how I should go and watch it with them, and that an old friend of his had reached out to say we could go to their camp on the lake for it."

Kristin shook her head and shrugged, happy for the unusual but nice conversation she had had with her father, "He was so excited."

"Well, glad that Henry's including you in something he's excited about, that's cool. And I'll see you in a week." He pushed himself up a bit to stretch across the table and kiss her forehead.

She finished the supper Emil had prepared for her and put the dishes in the dishwasher.

The sun had set now and the temperature dropped a few degrees, offering Kristin a bit of a reprieve.

She went to the bedroom, just down the hall and

off the entrance by the stairs, where she pulled a medium-sized rolling black suitcase out from under their king-sized bed, and began to pack as Emil laid down to keep her company.

Their bedroom was a more traditional style. The walls a dark gray-green, the furniture a natural wood including an armoire, and a classic armchair with deep red velvet upholstery and a high back.

"What time's your flight?"

"Six."

"Ouch."

"Yeah, no sleeping in tomorrow. Oh, and I'll email you the itinerary so you have it."

"Thanks. Meeting up with any ex-boyfriends?" Emil looked away as he asked, half-joking, but feeling partially insecure as the two hadn't been apart for more than just a few days since meeting.

Kristin shot him only a quick glance without stopping the organizing of her clothes on the bed in preparation for packing it all together. "Oh stop. But no."

"Shelly?"

"Of course. Excited to see Shelly."

"She can be a handful."

Kristin stopped now and she and Emil made eye contact. Kristin understood her best friend and live-in boyfriend, both of whom she loved dearly, didn't exactly get along. After meeting the first time when Shelly visited a few years ago, they largely ignored each other. Shelly found Emil "weak", that was the term she used, and Emil thought Shelly brash, though he choose another word for her.

"Are you worried about something, Emil?"

He shrugged, "I just know her reputation. What

she's like."

"Well, I think your opinion of her is a bit exaggerated. She's…boisterous, outspoken, but it's not like she's a major partier or something."

Emil nodded, checking himself as he realized he was acting a bit immaturely, "Sorry, baby, guess I'm just going to miss you."

"Awww," Kristin tousled Emil's hair, "I'm going to miss you too."

She returned to her clothes, looking them over to determine if she had enough variety for what she may end up doing, while also not too much to lug through the airport.

Emil placed his hands behind his head on the pillow.

"You'll call me every day, right?"

"Of course!"

"And every night before you go to sleep?"

"Yes."

"I love you."

"Love you too, sweetums."

CHAPTER THREE
2021, Saturday June 19th

Kristin, in comfortable jeans and a t-shirt with her dark red purse slung over her shoulder and rolling her black bag behind her, stepped onto the escalator to go down to the tunnel that would take her to the connecting flight to Burlington.

She never saw Detroit beyond the airport and wondered if what people said about the city was true. The airport, for what it's worth, she rather liked, especially the tunnel between concourses with its shifting colors along the walls and rounded ceiling above. At the bottom, she took the few steps to the moving walkway and got on. Not far ahead was a man she recognized from the flight from Dallas. Something about him had caught her eye. The way he dressed and carried himself wasn't so odd, but for some reason made her immediately think him a Vermonter. He wore a short-sleeve plaid shirt, light-colored jeans, sneakers that were not entirely dirty but had also seen better days, and carried just a laptop bag. He was older than her, by 25 years or so with salt and pepper hair, and rather thin. He had that look of someone friendly, just minding his own business, but who would be kind were you to speak to him.

She wondered if he were heading to Vermont as well, and as she approached her gate she thought herself correct as he sat down in a row of empty seats by the large windows that looked out on the tarmac. With his back to the outside, he had a view of the seating area and Kristin caught his eyes for a brief moment, long enough for him to smile before he turned his body sideways to look out at the planes.

With only about 40 minutes to kill, Kristin browsed the news on her phone. She thought about opening up an ebook but hated jumping into something with limited time to dedicate so she stuck to the rather depressing political headlines.

As her group was called she patiently waited in line, noticing the man she had wondered about still sitting by the window, a boarding pass now in hand.

Not long later she was on the plane and found her seat at the back. She retracted her bag's handle and swiftly swung it up to the bin before sitting at the small oval window. As much as she hated having to ask the person next to her to move if she had to use the lavatory, she always booked a window seat as she loved to just stare out at the passing lands.

After a few minutes she could see the thin man making his way down the aisle, his eyes going from his ticket to the rows of numbers along the storage compartments. He found his spot, just next to Kristin, tucked his laptop bag under the seat in front of him, and sat.

He smiled at Kristin before buckling and she smiled

back.

"Business or pleasure?" He asked in a friendly tone.

"Pleasure."

"Home or visiting?"

"Hmm, well, sort of both. I grew up in the area but don't live there anymore. Just visiting family and friends."

"Oh good for you. I live in Vermont as well. Always have, love it there. Good for you for getting out though."

They sat in silence for a while. He retrieved a cell phone from his pocket and Kristin caught a glimpse of him turning on airplane mode before placing it back. She switched hers on too but kept it out for something to do during the flight.

The crew went about their pre-flight check, and in twenty more minutes they were at altitude.

For another few minutes or so they sat in silence, only interrupted by the steward, a young man who seemed out-of-place, offering them drinks or a snack, which they both declined.

The man next to her reached over with his right hand, "Jim".

Kristin shook his hand, "Kristin" and repeated *Jim Jiminey, Jim Jiminey, Jim Jiminey, Jim Jim Cheroo* to herself to remember his name.

"It's a good time to go to Vermont, you know."

"Yeah, I have to admit I'm looking forward to it."

He tilted his head and nodded to emphasize the point, "Yup, won't have to deal with the brutal cold, summers are beautiful."

"It's true, they are. Also excited for the eclipse."

"Oh yeah! The blood moon."

"Blood moon?"

"That's what some call it. Because the moon turns a

reddish color."

"Ah, I didn't know that."

"Should be quite the show," he said leaning just a bit closer to her.

"Hope so!"

"You know," Jim pulled his bag out from under the seat, unzipped the front pocket, and retrieved a long white box. He held it up between the two of them and carefully lifted the cover, revealing to Kristin a beautiful silver necklace.

The long chain glistened from the sun beaming through the small window. At its end it held a thick open metallic circle with strange markings along its face. They looked like runes, a series of simple lines and shapes.

At the center of the circle, attached by a thinner chain, a white sphere that, from the gray highlights, clearly was meant to represent the moon.

The piece appeared expensive. It looked heavy, and the pearl-like moon exotic.

"I purchased a number of these for my girls, they love fancy things. But, I actually got a few extras just in case. I'd like you to have one."

Kristin's eyebrows raised in pleasant surprise, "Oh, that's very kind, and generous, but I couldn't. I'm sure there are other women in your family that would love one."

"Well you may be right, but it would make me happy if you'd accept."

She looked at Jim skeptically. Was this just an innocent act of kindness? Or was there some ulterior motive behind the offer? Perhaps he was a pervert.

"Please," he said in a tone of vulnerability and as if reading her thoughts, "just a gift. No strings attached."

Kristin, against her better judgment, acquiesced. She

raised her hand to allow Jim to place the box on her palm, but Jim pulled it away as he raised the necklace from the soft padding it rested on.

"Here, let me put it on you."

Rotating in his seat to better face her, Jim unclasped the necklace and held each end in one hand. He nodded to Kristin for her to lean a bit forward.

She suddenly felt uneasy. Allowing Jim to give her, a stranger, a gift was one thing, but to have him actually place it on her felt too intimate. But she also felt trapped. To deny him, she feared, would make the entire trip incredibly awkward. Realizing she was about to give in, again, made her also suddenly feel ashamed that she wasn't protecting boundaries as a woman.

Her short smile, she feared, gave away her displeasure as she leaned forward, lowered her head a bit, and moved her hair aside.

Jim reached behind her to hook the jewelry, careful not to touch the young woman's skin.

As he did, Jim quietly whispered a poem only she could hear, "O moon! ambrosial moon! Arise on my desert of sorrow, That the Magical eyes of me swoon, With lust of rain to-morrow!"

"Thank you."

Kristin adjusted it so it hung center and shifted her hair back.

"Sorry if that was awkward. I just had a few extra and thought you might like one. You seem like a nice person."

Jim's acknowledgment of the odd situation helped her feel at ease again, and she now noticed his wedding band. She smiled genuinely, "Thank you again."

Kristin casually turned to the window in hopes of being able to pass the remainder of the flight in silence.

Though thousands of miles away, the moon appeared clear and large above the clouds. She wondered to herself if the moon knew, in any way an inanimate object might, that the dance between it, the Earth, and the Sun, was coming to a head. The Earth's shadow would block the rays that normally illuminated it, steeping it in a dark red.

She pushed the button to recline her seat, closed her eyes, and in time went to sleep.

* * *

Kristin opened her eyes to a dark plane.

She remembered an international flight to Germany she had been on in high school, a red eye, where much of the flight was this way. Like that trip a dozen or so years ago, all the window shades were drawn closed. The only illumination came from small and dim emergency lights along the outside edges of the middle aisle.

Some odd feeling came over Kristin, one she couldn't place. Something, she felt, was off.

That's when she noticed the strange silence.

She kept her head rested against the seat and held her breath to focus on any little thing she might hear.

The engine still roared, though dully, but there was an entire lack of conversation, motion, or anything else. It was like everyone slept silently. Not even a stewardess could be seen in the dark aisle.

Kristin shifted her head just a bit to peek at her neighbor, who had apparently also decided to nap as he sat reclined with his eyes closed. She smiled thankfully that she needn't entertain Jim.

She pushed the button on the arm of her seat again to sit upright and stretched to look above the seats in front of her. Rows of the heads of other passengers could just be made out along the lighter blues of the upholstery. But beyond a dozen or so rows was only darkness.

Sitting back down Kristin wondered why so many decided to sleep in what must have been a short afternoon flight, and why everyone had closed their shades. Certainly others, like her, had gotten up early and so were tired, but there must have been others whose original departure was Detroit and so could have even slept in.

In fact, she thought, why was her shade closed? She specifically remembered opening it when she took her seat and didn't shut it. Might Jim have?

Kristin looked to her right over Jim to the girl sitting in the aisle seat across from them. She squinted her eyes to capture more of the little light that emanated from the small strip on the floor.

She could just make out a bit of the young girl, who appeared maybe ten years old. Her body slumped forward in what looked like a painful position, her head hanging down almost touching the armrest. Her dark hair draped over her face, only allowing Kristin to see a part of her closed eye, some skin of cheek, and her open mouth. If asleep she was soundly so.

Just like the plane, Kristin felt something off with the girl.

Then a single drop of saliva, or water, Kristin wasn't sure which, dripped from the girl's mouth onto the cold metal armrest.

Kristin cringed a bit from the stranger's bodily fluid loose in the plane.

Then another drip, followed by a couple more.

"Gross," she said quietly as she watched.

Kristin pushed herself away, her back touching the closed window, as the water started slowly streaming from the girl. It ran from her mouth to the armrest and floor where she could see it starting to pool a bit on one of the lights.

The girl didn't move as the flow picked up speed, with the liquid now streaming off her upper and lower lips. Some water caught her hair, drawing the strands toward her face and causing the flow to constantly change direction.

"Oh god!" Kristin looked down to see the pool growing, actually reaching across the aisle to Jim's seat.

Instinctively she retracted her feet and clutched her knees.

She raised the curtain of her window to only reveal a black world outside. No light at all. No clouds or a world below. Just emptiness.

"Hey!" she yelled, not to anyone in particular, hoping someone would wake to see what was going on outside or with the poor girl. Was she alone? Did a parent sit next to her? Kristin couldn't tell through the darkness.

"Stewardess!" she yelled louder as she realized she just needed to hit the call button above her seat.

She raised her right arm as she looked up to push it, but before she did something far down the aisle, toward the front of the plane, caught her eye. In the blackness she couldn't give it shape or definition. She just saw… something…there. A hint of light reflecting off a couple of spots, like eyes.

The thing shifted slowly, the light dipping a bit and rising again, dipping and rising like it was slowly moving closer.

A suggestion of form took shape, but not clearly enough for identification. Whatever it was appeared massive, even with big round eyes so close to the ceiling of the plane she thought that it might have been crouching.

Kristin frantically and repeatedly pushed the call button, and unsure if it was supposed to respond with a signal of some kind she pushed it a few more times.

She noticed the sound now, the splashing sound of the water falling from the girl's mouth and the sloshing of it on the carpet where her feet were.

Kristin looked over to see the girl's hair wetter now and clumped along her face and head, which brought more chaos to the streams. But she hadn't moved. The girl just sat there, eyes closed, arms in her lap, now drenched in water.

A different noise came. Heavier. Deeper. Rhythmic.

She looked back up to see whatever the thing was at the head of the plane moving closer again, its obviously large feet pushing through the liquid as it stepped. Still seeped in darkness Kristin couldn't make it out. But she could see that it, with its large eyes, head, and shoulders, was looking right at her as it very slowly made its way to the back of the plane.

The water kept rising and now reached just inches below her seat.

Kristin unbuckled to provide more space to lift her body up if needed.

Worried the aircraft would fill with water and send them crashing she looked again to the girl, whose face still gazed downward.

Then the young girl raised her head, her gaze forward but her eyes remaining closed. Her hair still stuck to her cheeks, forehead, and neck, masking much of her features. And the water continued to flow from her open mouth.

"What the fuck!" Kristin began tapping Jim's left arm in a hurried plea to get him to wake.

"What?" she heard loudly as she woke, her eyes

opening to the bright plane and the sight of her own hand wrapped around Jim's arm.

She had been dreaming.

Embarrassed Kristin let go of the man and noticed that with her other arm she was holding her legs to her chest. She exhaled in surrender as she lowed them to the floor and dropped her head into her hands to hide her eyes.

"Bad dream?" Jim's voice not wavering from that kind stranger who first introduced himself.

Feeling blood rush to her face she didn't dare look up, "Yeah, I guess."

He laughed just a bit, "It happens. Hopefully it wasn't about the plane crashing."

"No."

She focused on her breathing and relaxed her face, hoping gravity would make quick work of her blush.

After what seemed a couple of minutes she looked up to see who sat across the aisle, but it wasn't the girl from her dream but instead some elderly woman with earbuds in and holding a small tablet.

Kristin turned back to the window to look out at the passing fields below. Nightmares were not something Kristin often experienced. In stressful times she would have dreams that she considered nightmares, but they weren't the stereotypical type of being chased by a crazed slasher or watching loved ones die. Instead, they took more metaphorical tones. She would feel overcome by a sense of some unseen force closing in all around her, or would be in an important situation with a lot on the line but feel totally unprepared.

This dream, she felt, was foreign. Was something other. It had power. It didn't feel like her mind working through some unresolved issue or processing a stressful change. It wasn't like imagery being presented to her in her sleep. It didn't feel like a story.

It felt more like a different time and place, but just as real as this moment at 35,000 feet. Kristin felt she had been brought somewhere else, teleported, and experienced something real.

My mind playing tricks on me, she concluded. Waking up early, the general stress of travel, her presentation, and sleeping on the plane. It all just added up to an odd, and to her a unique, occurrence.

She rested her head against the off-white plastic shell of the plane and somehow managed to fall back to sleep.

* * *

Kristin peacefully woke this time to the announcement that the plane was preparing for descent. She followed her first instinct to look around to ensure she wasn't back in the nightmare and was happy to see what could only be the real world.

She loved to fly but hated flying into Burlington, Vermont. Not because of the airport, whose small size made it quick and easy to navigate, and not even because of the generally cramped planes. But, for some unknown reason to her, there was always more turbulence. Maybe due to the lake. She didn't know.

Today was no exception. The plane bumped as they descended. She watched the landing through the window, trying to enjoy the view and pick out landmarks while being jostled around.

Jim still sat in silence and paid her no attention, which she was thankful for.

Sitting toward the back meant a long wait to stand and exit. This always tested her patience. Watching the passengers ahead could make her blood boil. Seeing them take their sweet time, not paying attention that they could actually move forward, the awkward standoffs between people while everyone else behind them waits for them to make a decision on who should go. Jim hadn't even unbuckled his seatbelt or pulled his bag out yet — a few more seconds of wasted time.

She thought of Jean-Paul Sartre, hell truly is other people.

Kristin took a big deep breath. Vacation should have her feeling relaxed, not anxious about getting off the plane. She had no meeting to race to, no clock to punch. But she still worried about what Brad might do. This is when Emil would help her be calm. She wished he had come with her.

When her time finally arrived, with Jim heading down the row without even a "goodbye", she moved quickly. One smooth motion from the seat to grab her luggage from the overhead and then down the aisle. *Take note passengers, this is how you do it.*

Kristin walked the short way to the terminal, then down the escalators and out to the front of the airport where she took an even deeper breath.

The weather was near perfect. Maybe 75 degrees, which actually felt a little chilly to her as she had become acclimated to the heat of Dallas, with a clear sky and no wind. The air smelled different too, fresh even though she stood just yards from a runway and by a short road lined with taxi cabs. She felt at home.

With no place for people to wait to pick up friends or family, her father said he'd park at the old deli and convenience store just across the street from the large parking garage at the front of the airport. Henry said he'd go in, buy her favorite sandwich, egg salad, her favorite drink, a spiked seltzer, and would pull the car in once she texted she was ready. Kristin politely declined, saying the short walk to the store would be welcomed after sitting for hours.

As she emerged from a walkway that cut through the garage she could see her father's Audi A4 waiting. Henry Fuller was a practical man, the Audi being the least practical thing he'd ever purchased. He both enjoyed the drive and regretted the expense, though you wouldn't hear him complain as he never did.

Kristin caught his eyes in the A4's side mirrors and smiled. Henry smiled back, widely. He exited the car.

"Kristin!" He flung his arms wide to give her a big hug.

She went in for the embrace, letting go of her luggage, and placing her cheek against his chest, "Dad!"

"So glad you came, Krissy!" After a gentle moment he let her go and grabbed her bag for the trunk.

Henry stood just over six feet tall, with thick salt-and-pepper hair. His doctor would say he would need to lose a few pounds, but just a few, and otherwise looked healthy. He wore a blue short-sleeve polo shirt and khakis.

He gave her a second hug, "Honey, it's so good to see you and I'm so excited to have you here for a week!" He pulled away to look at his daughter, "Mom would have come with me but she's prepping dinner for you."

"Oh, that's okay, I'm excited too!"

The two got into the car and started the short ride to Shelburne, a suburb of the state's largest city of Burlington. Kristin dug into the egg salad sandwich and black cherry spiked seltzer. She wasn't sure the flavor combination worked, but didn't care.

On the drive they caught up, first just niceties of how work is, and Emil. What Mom was up to.

"I'm starting to plan my retirement, which is both

exciting and a bit depressing," he said in a half-joking tone. Henry had been teaching business at the University of Vermont for decades and owned a lucrative consulting business on the side. He had built a proud reputation in the community as someone not only brilliant when it came to leading a company, but also as someone with a large heart as he volunteered for various organizations to help them achieve their goals. Every last hour spent on these things was a joy for him, none of it a chore.

"Mom and I were talking about you being in Dallas, and if you'd stay there long term. We're thinking about buying a second home, somewhere warm, and if you think you'll stay we'll start looking around."

Kristin had a sense that even though her parents lived modestly, somewhere they had a good stash of money from all of their years of hard work. But this was the first time she heard of the capacity to do something like buy a second home. As enterprising as her father was, Kristin's mother, Elizabeth, took a back seat to no one. As the head nurse at the medical center, she not only logged insane hours, but those hours often included nights and weekends. She connected so well with patients, and saved so many lives, that many of them became extended family. Like her father, she found her passion. And they occasionally combined forces when health-related organizations came calling for assistance.

"Oh, that is exciting! You'll have to give me some time to think about where I might be. I love my job, and the firm, but honestly Dallas is a little rough. It's a lot different culturally, and you've heard me complain about the summers."

"Yes, it does sound sweaty."

"But, we have other offices and Emil and I have talked

about potentially moving to one. With his job, he could likely just start anywhere. He would have to network to find clients, but it's a good field."

"Sounds good, Krissy, you let your Mom or me know."

"So what's the plan for the eclipse tomorrow?"

Henry lit up again. While his specialty was business he'd always been fascinated by cosmology, so his interest in the celestial event was no surprise to Kristin.

"Yes! An old friend of mine from college reached out about going to his cabin for it, he and his wife are having just a few people over. We'll head over sometime after dinner. The eclipse doesn't start until about midnight and lasts a few hours. He said we could always sleep there if we wanted but we certainly don't have to."

"Sounds like fun."

The 20-minute car ride was filled with laughter and good feelings. Kristin kept the window rolled down, appreciating the air.

Henry pulled the car into the long gravel driveway of the home, the same one Kristin grew up in as an only child. It turned through a row of trees to reveal the two-story house with a large covered front porch that held a few Adirondack chairs and a bench swing.

Immediately she saw her mother pop up from the swing and race down the few steps and stone walkway to just by the garage, where Henry brought the car to a stop. Elizabeth wore a blue summer dress, with a white apron draped around her that showed signs of her cooking efforts.

Kristin didn't wait for the engine to be turned off. She opened her door and equally excited embraced her mother, both jumping up and down slightly and screeching.

"Krissy baby! So happy to see you!" Her mother's

eyes shined from the forming tears.

"Mom!" She replied.

Elizabeth was a couple of years younger than her husband, but looked ten years his junior, surprising given the demands of her job. Emil would joke about Kristin's *good genes*, and how it initially made him nervous for Kristin to meet his father, who wasn't in tip-top shape.

Henry smiled at the sight of his two ladies so happy and popped the trunk to retrieve his daughter's bag.

The house's pale blue color, with white shingles, made it appear just a bit dated, but obviously well cared for as little wear-and-tear remained visible. It sat at the middle of a lawn that spanned just over an acre, with a few more acres of trees surrounding it. The nearest neighbor about a quarter mile down the road made it serene.

Kristin's father walked past the women, up the steps, and opened the screen door, placing his daughter's bag inside by the stairs up.

Elizabeth grabbed Kristin's arms and held her tightly, "You must be exhausted from travel. Do you want anything to eat now? Want to nap? Shower?"

"Let me get situated, bring my stuff up, then eat?"

"Okay," she smiled and gave her daughter a peck on the forehead before they turned to see Henry standing in the doorway holding it open for them.

"Come on, ladies."

They smiled and entered.

The downstairs hadn't changed much since the last time Kristin had been home. The living area to the right had a comfortable-looking cream-colored couch, leather recliner, and a television set in a nook under the stairs. The beige plush carpet made the space cozy. The open room lead to the dining area, with its hardwood floor and rustic table that comfortably seated six. The back wall had a large sliding glass door that provided access to a freshly stained deck.

To the left of the dining area, and largely behind the stairs at the entrance, the kitchen with its white cabinets and stainless steel appliances. And to the left of the stairs an office with a small antique desk that only held a closed laptop.

Kristin grabbed her luggage and climbed the stairs. At the top a half-bath greeted her with an open door. To the right and down the hall her parents' room, and through it the master bath.

To the left, where Kristin headed, two doors. On her left was a spare bedroom with a queen-sized bed, an empty dresser, and an old nightstand.

She went to the right and opened the door to find a time capsule that captured her middle school years.

The light-purple walls, and pink comforter on top of a twin bed that looked too damn small for an adult, clearly indicated it a girl's room, and Kristin stood a little ashamed that she never painted it a more neutral color as she started high school. She remembered begging her mom to paint it that purple when she was around eleven. Once in high school, she didn't spend much time at home, or in her room, so it just stayed this way. Between the bed and the window ahead, a small bureau held a photo of her at around sixteen with Shelly Arntz, her best friend, and their mutual friend Wendy whom they had lost touch with years ago. A dreamcatcher hung next to the window.

On the right wall a couple of posters of a young Justin Timberlake along with another window that provided a view of the backyard. Also there, a small desk that held an attached mirror, a probably empty now jewelry box, and a few old paperbacks she enjoyed when she was younger.

She thought a moment. Her plan had been to sleep in her old room as Emil hadn't come with her, but the old bed did not look inviting. So she turned in place and dropped her bag in the spare room next to the queen.

Kristin pulled her phone from her purse to quickly check her work email. At the airport she had sent all her research to Mrs. Hawthorne with a politically delicate explanation of why. She responded with only a wink, indicating she knew exactly what prompted it. No other messages warranted attention so she shut it off and went downstairs.

After dinner, a turkey that reminded her of Thanksgiving, the family spent much of the evening in the backyard around a small fire pit laughing, drinking, and reminiscing.

"So," Elizabeth had a few glasses of wine and her tone gave Kristin a warning of what was coming next, "are you and Emil doing well?"

"Yes, Mom," Kristin smiled and leaned toward her, egging her on.

"And…when's the big day?"

"Oh, well, jeez, Mother, I didn't expect that question!"

"Should I just go watch television?" Henry knew the routine between the two women and didn't mind it. He liked poking fun at them though.

"You stay dear, you can help me."

"You're not getting any help from me!" He crossed his legs and leaned back, expressing his desire to both stay out of it and watch the show.

"Well?" Elizabeth looked back to her daughter.

Kristin responded calmly, not willing to feel pressured, nor to get worked up over her mother's playful questioning,

"It'll happen when it happens."

"And babies?"

"Maybe."

"Maybe?"

"That's somewhere between 'yes' and 'no'."

"Let me put another log on the fire," Henry stood and placed a small cut of wood in the pit surrounded by stones and dirt.

The women laughed at him.

"Okay," Elizabeth conceded, "but WHEN it happens I need as much notice as possible. If there ever was a reason to retire, that's it."

"I'll call you as soon as I have news."

CHAPTER FOUR

2021, Sunday June 20th

Shelly Arntz grew up down the road from Kristin, and though a couple of years older, the two were very close. Growing up Kristin generally spent more time with older kids, since she often took accelerated classes with them and fit in well.

They met for lunch at a small American restaurant on the pedestrian-only Church Street in Burlington and sat outside to do some people-watching as they talked. The restaurant's location had been a bank decades ago, with a white marble facade and small windows. They sat under a black Guinness umbrella to shield them from the high sun.

Shelly was one of the few people Kristin made a point of staying in touch with regularly, so there wasn't much catching up to do.

She worked a draining office job, data-entry type. Though she graduated near the top of her class, she put all of her energy into her family shortly after college. She still very much seemed like the same person as a decade ago, and a part of that was due to her never talking about her job, completely separating it from her definition of herself.

Besides her slightly shorter hair now, about shoulder's length, and a few more pounds after having children, Shelly looked much the same to Kristin as she did in college.

"I'm jealous, Kris," only Shelly called her that, "living in a big city, no kids, making bank."

"Are you kidding!?" Kristin smiled genuinely, "You have freaking amazing and beautiful kids!"

Shelly took a sip of her drink, "Oh my god they are a pain in my ass."

They both laughed, completely in tune with each other as usual.

"They're terrors. Sometimes I think the only person they hate more than each other is me. They tolerate Joe only because he gives in to their ice cream demands."

Joe was Shelly's high school sweetheart, and a great person himself. They married shortly after college and started a family. The three of them spent a lot of time together through school and thought of each other as extended family.

"Sounds like you need to give them more ice cream."

"Fuck that, *I* need more ice cream! So, what are you doing the rest of the week, you know, after the eclipse?"

"No plans yet, so let me know when you have time. It would be great to see your family again, and do something else just the two of us."

"Hell yeah!" Shelly raised her glass to toast Kristin, "any chance to get away from those assholes!"

Shelly always made Kristin laugh. She knew how good a mother her friend really was, and how she cared for her children, but found it hilarious how she didn't put them on a pedestal like all the other mothers she knew.

"Are you going to wake little William and Beverly to see the eclipse?"

"No, they're too small. And, well, I'll probably be asleep by then anyway."

"It's supposed to be pretty cool."

"Maybe. I heard it'll be large, and red," she said it without emphasis to highlight how lame it all sounded to her.

"True, maybe not as exciting as it sounds."

"Your dad seems pretty pumped though."

Their meals arrived. A burger and fries for Shelly, and a chicken salad for Kristin.

"Very. I wonder if he really just wanted a reason for me to visit, so is just acting it out which is sweet. And Emil convinced me to just take a week off, not just to appease my father but to take a real break for once."

"That was nice of him," Shelly said the kind words with a hard swallow of both food and pride.

Between bites, Shelly motioned to a young girl walking up the street wearing skimpy clothes, fishnet stockings with pink boy shorts, and a small white tube top.

"Oh my."

"What I'd give to go back in time."

Kristin perked up a bit in surprise, "What?"

"Totally, wouldn't you?" She egged her friend on.

"Uh, no. No way. I much prefer where I am today. Besides, it's not like I'd pull off that outfit."

"Are you kidding? You totally could. Fuck, you could today! I've got the mommy rolls, you're still tiny."

"Mommy rolls! You're rocking your body!"

"Please. I own mirrors."

"Well, I think you're sexy. So does Joe."

Shelly smirked and shrugged, looking away from her friend and taking a big sip of her beer.

"What was that, Shell?"

She shook her head at first and focused on her burger.

"Is something up with you and Joe?"

Shelly exhaled loudly, "We're going through a rough patch."

"Oh no!"

"It's okay. It's just a hard time. I love him, he's amazing. He loves me. It's just hard. We've been together forever."

"Which is super cool."

"Yeah yeah yeah. It's nothing more than just…kind of…well, just seeing him all the time. And him seeing me. It's not just me."

"He'd take a bullet for you."

Shelly smiled. She did love that about Joe. "I'm sure Emil would for you too."

Kristin laughed and slapped the table, "He's a pacifist! He'd try to talk the guy down only to end up getting us both killed."

Shelly's smile shifted with one eyebrow raising as if to say *so you see it too*.

Kristin took a bite of her food, sitting for a moment in silent surprise, "You guys were meant for each other. You're rocks."

"I'm not saying we're done, Kris, just that it's a tough time. I'm sure it's just a silly phase. And it's not like we act like we hate each other. In fact, he said since you're in town he'd figure out the kids if I wanted to spend the week with you. He's still sweet as ever."

"Awww. That is nice."

"Totally. So, I guess I'm yours this week."

Shelly raised her half-empty glass and the two toasted again.

"I'm sure you'll want to spend time with your parents, and have some alone time too, but I'll check in with you every day. If you want to hang out, awesome. If not, don't worry about it, it's totally cool."

"Hey, I'm here. No alone time for me."

The women returned to their food and drinks, enjoying the warmth of the sun against the slight breeze that came up the hills from Lake Champlain.

"Here you go sir, I'll send your server over."

"Thank you."

The hostess left the table next to them and instinctively Kristin looked over. Jim, the kind man from the plane who gifted her the necklace, sat at the round table, a University of Vermont Catamounts baseball cap on, looking at the pub's menu.

Kristin quickly turned back to Shelly, her eyebrows raised a bit in surprise.

Shelly, in sync with her friend, tilted her head only slightly and gave that nuanced questioning look that friends do when they understand they have to be careful not to call attention or be overtly obvious.

"Jim?" Kristin turned to him getting his attention.

He looked up from the menu, shifting from expressionless to a quick smile. "Kristin!"

"Hi, how are you?"

"Well, enjoying the beautiful weather. How's the homecoming?"

"Nice. Catching up with my best friend. Jim, this is Shelly. Shelly, this is Jim. He's the one who gave me the beautiful moon necklace I showed you." As she said this, Kristin reached two fingers into her v-neck t-shirt and pulled the necklace out.

"Oh, so happy you have it on," Jim placed his hands one atop the other over the menu. "You keep it on too, it brings good luck."

"It's very pretty. The moon is so nicely done," Shelly shared her honest opinion.

"Yes, so beautiful," Kristin agreed.

"Well, glad you like it. Wish I had another on me for you, Shelly."

"Oh, that's okay. Sweet of you though."

Jim turned to Kristin, "I'll let you get back to your lunch, but keep that on for the event. Supposed to recharge the luck under the eclipse."

"Good to know," Kristin smiled.

* * *

The sun had set. The Fuller family dinner finished and the dishes put away.

They sat outside, this time on the back deck not wanting to start a fire only to leave for the gathering, and read under the patio lights. As a group they agreed not to go to the party until closer to the event, so as not to feel stuck there too long since Kristin didn't know anybody. The eclipse would make it fun and give everyone something in common to discuss, but they didn't need to drag it out either.

Elizabeth and Henry sat on the outdoor sofa, her legs stretched out over the lap of her husband, who selected to read Hawking's "A Brief History of Time" to mark the celestial occasion. She flipped through an old book she found about the solar system, not because she was overly interested, but because her husband was just so excited for the event. It was her way of showing him support.

Kristin, her phone resting on her crossed legs, shifted

from exchanging text messages with Emil to finally starting a novel, something she hadn't done in what felt like years.

Henry noted the moon hanging just at the tree line, "It's good we're going to the lake, doesn't look like we'll get much of a view from the house."

Kristin looked up and nodded in agreement.

Elizabeth checked her watch, "We should probably get ready. It's about an hour's drive."

Her husband gently slapped her thigh, "Yeah, you're right. Let's get this show on the road."

The family gathered their drink glasses and books and brought them inside. Henry locked the sliding glass door and flicked off the lights as Elizabeth went to the refrigerator to grab the containers of snacks, and a couple bottles of wine, which she then put in a canvas bag. The group quietly retrieved their coats in case it got chilly by the water and left the house.

They piled into the car, Henry driving his precious A4, his wife in the passenger seat, and Kristin behind him. Just like when she was a kid.

They headed south on Route 7 towards Shoreham, the road empty of other travelers. It was late, and with the trees so high and lined like a long towering wall close to the road, it didn't matter if there was a moon or not. The night was dark.

Kristin rested her head against the window, a bit tired from all the travel, her eyes locked outside at the edge of the high beams to watch the trees racing by. It had been a long couple of days.

She looked over at her mother who reached across the car to rub the back of her husband's neck.

Returning her attention to the night road the occasional break in the trees showed the lake to their right. The moon higher now, full and hovering in the dark sky just above the tree line.

They started a wide right turn and then, without warning, headlights came from the other direction...and into their lane. It happened in less than a second, with no time for Henry to react, swerve, or do anything but tense up.

There was no time to even scream.

Kristin didn't see the lights before the violent and abrupt stopping of the car, pushing her and everything else forward with a force she had never imagined.

After the initial impact, her body still rocking, she felt the back of the car slam as it returned to the ground.

Following this only a terrible ringing in her head as she settled back into the seat. Her vision gone for moments.

Slowly her senses returned, with sound first — a hissing of sorts, with a periodic sprinkling of glass or small bits of metal landing on asphalt.

Then came smell. A strong red wine, from the now likely broken bottles that her mother placed on the floor to her right. And a faint but pungent smell of gas.

Vision, from complete darkness to only slightly so. Outlines, shades, vague insinuations of structure and light. Blur.

Touch. Kristin's nerves came alive and hummed with electricity.

She touched her head and felt a warm and sticky substance. Blood, she thought, but not much of it. It hurt to move her left arm so she placed it back down.

After a moment some level of keen awareness came to her and she wiggled her toes to check for paralysis. Though painful, she had full access to her extremities. She feared moving too much, that she might further damage something.

Kristin checked her breathing next, it was steady. Even. The impact must have occurred so quickly, and without a moment of fear prior, that her heart rate didn't change.

Her vision then returned enough to witness the aftermath, and the horror made her wish she were blind again.

The collision with another car, as head-on as possible, caused the windshield to shatter, along with the side windows.

Between the front seats she could see her parents collapsed on one another, her mother on top. Neither moving, and Elizabeth's scalp partially torn from her skull, her shoulder clearly out of joint, and blood...so much blood.

The airbags hung like large deflated balloons from a mangled dashboard.

"Mom? Dad?" Her lungs strained for enough power to make her voice more than just a faint whisper.

"Oh, god."

With only a couple feet from her to her mother, she reached with her right arm and after pulling back some strands of hair, placed her fingers on Elizabeth's neck. She felt no pulse, nothing.

Using a single finger she gently poked at her father's back, "Dad?"

No response.

Kristin looked around the headrest in front of her, which leaned oddly forward from the bent seat.

She gasped at how close the other car actually was to her, the front ends of the vehicles must have crushed like tin cans. The parts she could see looked like crumpled tissue paper. It was impossible to tell from which vehicle, but at least a couple of headlights were still shining, casting strange sharp shadows, and the jagged tears through metal caused rays of the artificial light to streak upward through the night sky. Next to a few rings of the Audi insignia that jutted upwards rested the circular BMW emblem.

The other driver appeared half leaning out the side window, his eyes and mouth open with shards of glass sticking into his face.

A woman propped up against his side, her face down and out of sight. Her seat badly damaged lay against their dash.

And there she was.

Directly in front of Kristin, in the back passenger seat, sitting upright and looking back at her calmly, a girl of about nine.

Her skin was pale and without sign of harm. Her straight hair black and long past her shoulders. A white gown hung on her thin frame, which seemed odd for a car trip. Her eyes locked open, pupils dilated. She stared at Kristin, unblinking, unmoving, expressionless in the chaos.

One of the car horns started to blast, causing Kristin to startle. But the other girl didn't respond at all. She just kept looking at Kristin. Looking. As if the horrific accident wasn't what was wrong, but something else. Maybe something worse. She concluded the girl in shock.

Kristin still didn't move, giving her mind and body time to take some sort of subconscious inventory of itself. But she couldn't look away from that girl.

Finding the courage, she gently rubbed her chest, stomach, and then legs looking for any signs of severe damage. The movement did bring deep pain to her left shoulder, which, so far, seemed all that might be injured save the spot of blood at the back of her head.

Kristin noticed her new necklace, which had been beneath her shirt, now hung outside it. Obviously the violent crash had brought it out.

She had to gather herself.

She took a breath, slowly reached for the seatbelt release, and pushed the button. She became acutely aware of each little movement, paying attention to any pain she might feel, but nothing new emerged. Kristin pulled the door handle and thankfully it swung open, she wasn't trapped. As she got out the horn stopped. *Thank you*, she thought at the small gift that allowed her to think a bit more clearly. But then the shooting pain came to her left shoulder again. Kristin assumed the force of the impact sent her weight forward hard enough to cause the strap of her seatbelt to damage her collarbone. She held it momentarily with her right hand before deciding to try and put the pain aside, for now, while she focused on the critical moments ahead.

Kristin placed her feet on the ground. Not confident in her strength, she sat another moment and looked around.

She braced herself against the door and slowly stood. She took two thoughtful breaths.

Keeping her door open, she pulled herself closer to the driver's with her good arm.

"Mom? Dad?" she said more loudly.

Praying for a response Kristin cautiously reached in and rustled her father's shirt, where under his ribs should be. Though she couldn't see his head, lying somewhere under her mother, the damage to the car, the blood, the limbs at angles they were never meant to be, Kristin felt sadly sure he was dead.

After no response, she poked twice more.

"Dad?"

Nothing.

She needed to stay calm, find a way to get herself, and this other girl, help. She resolved to mourn later. First, Kristin thought, she needed to check on her.

Kristin took the few steps to the window to talk to the girl, whose eyes followed her.

Feeling light-headed, Kristin put her right hand on the frame to take some of the weight off her feet.

The girl sat silently, just looking up at her as if waiting.

Kristin's neck cracked slightly as she subconsciously tilted her head at the unexplainable sight. The young girl's seatbelt rested at her side, vertically — she was not strapped in. Then Kristin noticed her hair, how not even one strand appeared out of place. It was like the girl entered the car after the accident occurred.

Before Kristin could say anything the girl's eyes darted up toward something. She followed her gaze to see the beginning of the lunar eclipse, the birthing of the blood moon as an outer portion of it turned red.

Standing there, under the event that motivated her father to reach out and plan her vacation, she took a brief moment to witness the start of the eclipse.

After a silent *sigh* she turned back to the girl. She dropped her arm from the car and took a step back as the girl now sat there with a knowing smile on her face and her eyes locked on her.

"Are you okay?" Kristin asked, desperately wanting an answer.

But none came. The young girl just looked at her.

Kristin noticed she didn't have a seatbelt on at all. Perhaps she released it after the accident, there's no way she would have survived without it. Her body likely would have been launched forward and through the windshield, possibly even propelled into her own car.

Shock, she thought again. She would need to get them help.

Looking around the scene and up and down the road no one was coming. *We could be here hours*, she thought.

Kristin hurried as much as she could to where she had been sitting in the back of her father's car to grab her small purse, which she quickly found on the floor. Picking it up, its leather bottom dripping with what she hoped was the wine, she pulled her cell phone out. After unlocking it with her fingerprint the empty bars reflected no signal.

"Shit."

She would have to find another phone. With four other adults there, the odds were good.

Keeping one hand against the A4 she rounded the back, but then took a number of steps away, afraid of how she might find her mother.

From the side she could just see a bit of her mother's dark blouse, glistening a bit from the wet blood, wrapped around the woman's twisted shoulder.

The tears finally came. Kristin didn't want to see her mother like that but also knew she had to find a cell.

She would have stayed like that, crying, but for the odd sound she heard in the distance, far behind her parents' car. A slightly familiar *clickety clickety*. She looked over as she raised her right hand to wipe the tears from her eyes. In the shadows, and only slightly visible from the red tail lights and full moon, a massive moose crossed the road. Its antlers reaching out and up as if in worship.

Though she grew up in Vermont and made plenty of trips across New England, she had only seen a moose in-person once before. It seemed larger than the other she had witnessed and bigger still than those she had seen in photos. Its antlers seemed exaggerated, like the hands of some god. Its shoulders muscular, and body long.

The beast stopped. It moved its large head slowly, turning it to look at Kristin. Its eyes locked and unblinking. Steam escaping its nostrils even in the warm night.

It turned its head again, away from her and back toward the direction it had been going. It began walking again, each step steady, and disappeared into the woods.

Kristin looked back at the accident, an odd oasis of light surrounded by darkness under the red moon. The girl in the other car still watching her, her body unmoved. Though she still smiled, it now appeared more subdued.

She brought her attention back to her parents' car and rubbed her eyes again. Breathing in deeply she visualized taking in the necessary strength to touch her mother and father's bodies, followed by the anxiety escaping as she exhaled.

A few steps and she found herself at the window. Elizabeth's legs, covered by her jeans, both bent in ways indicating they were severely broken. One of her mother's shoes was missing.

Kristin looked up to the jean pockets, clearly empty, realizing her mother always kept her phone in the cup holder, which currently lay under the bodies of her parents.

She stood in contemplation. There were three others to check that might prove fruitful without having to touch anyone. Of course two of those were by that creepy girl, and the other was her father.

Realizing time was of the essence, Kristin reached in and pushed the unlock button for the door, then tried it. From the damage on the outside, it didn't surprise her when it didn't budge.

She checked the frame for any dangerous edges of

glass, knocked a couple carefully away, then leaned in. Dragging her body a bit further, brushing past her mother while keeping her eyes safely focused on the shifter, she reached under her parents.

The telltale round cavities of the cupholders held nothing. After the violent collision, only God knew where the phone may have gone. She quickly glanced around the floors before pushing herself out.

She put her mind on autopilot and set herself to the task of finding a phone without allowing emotions to get in the way.

Circling the back again she looked for any sign of the moose, then went to the driver's side where she reached in and patted her father's pockets. He never brought his phone with him to gatherings when he knew Elizabeth would have hers, Kristin knew that about him. He didn't want it, didn't want to be checking it or have the threat of interruption.

She only felt the square padding of his wallet.

Not bothering to acknowledge the girl, she went to the front passenger seat of the BMW. Glancing in she should see a small blinking light coming from the floor by the woman's bare and mangled feet.

Carefully she leaned in and with a fingertip dragged it close enough to grab.

Standing again and holding it up she saw the outline of a typical iPhone, but turning it around revealed a shattered screen.

"Shit."

She pushed the circular button at the bottom, but nothing happened. With no response from the power button at the side either she tossed it back inside.

Kristin felt the girl's eyes on her as she crossed to the

driver's side.

The man, his black hair darker than the shadows through the trees, had his left arm hanging out the window.

Still focused Kristin looked around the floor but seeing nothing checked his pockets.

Empty.

She stood and glanced at the windshield, and saw another black brick phone. It looked like some kind of Android version.

Reaching in, Kristin carefully grabbed it, avoiding the landscape of glass shards along the frame.

Pulling it toward her she immediately saw the spiderweb of cracks and a portion of the metal frame bent and open.

Completely busted.

No working cell phone.

Fuck she thought.

The trees surrounding her, the road, and the crumpled steel all shifted colors. She looked up to see the moon almost completely red now. It changed how the lights from the car appeared on the asphalt and victims' skin. As she looked around it oddly even changed the change the shadows. Everything had a tint, an unflattering one.

With no way to communicate, she had to think about what to do next. Surely someone would come by, but there's no telling when. She decided to pop the trunk of the Audi to get the emergency kit her ever-practical and prepared father kept. She would put out the flares and emergency triangle to warn oncoming traffic.

She made her way to the driver's door and was able to reach the trunk release easily. She went around to the back where she lifted the lid, pulled out the small case, and with some pain managed to shut the trunk again.

Her eyes naturally looked straight ahead as she closed it, and she should have seen that girl. Kristin should have been able to see her clearly in the back seat, probably still staring at her.

But she was gone.

Kristin looked around quickly, turning in place to check behind her, then back around.

Terror rose in her. Filled her belly then made its way up her throat to her head.

That's when she saw the girl, standing behind the BMW, far enough back to almost be in darkness. The red tail lights and moonlight barely washing her white gown and the skin of her arms and legs.

Horrified Kristin jumped back and dropped the kit, her quick movement sending pain searing from her toes up.

The girl was looking right at her. Staring. Though in virtual darkness, Kristin could tell exactly where she was looking. She felt uncomfortable, threatened by that child.

Kristin took more steps back, off the road, and over the shoulder to the tree line hoping that the girl would no longer be able to see her. She wanted distance between them. Kristin kept her eyes locked on her, fearful of losing track of the thing. Then she also noticed the eerie silence. No sounds of nature. Nothing.

The girl took a step back herself, into the complete darkness and out of sight. Gone.

"Oh god," Kristin looked around, desperate for help. "Please…someone…"

She took further steps into the wooded area, guiding herself by touching trees as she passed. She knew if she kept going that way she'd eventually find the lake, but that was no solace. And she didn't want to end up too far from the road in case someone were to drive by.

A snapping sound, like someone stepping on a small fallen branch, from her left broke the silence. It's possible that girl ducked into the woods after retreating into the night, Kristin thought. She kept her eyes in that direction, but couldn't see anything as the leaves and branches blocked the moon.

She heard the snapping again and screamed as she moved further into the woods, away from the road. With the fear taking her over and preventing good decision-making, Kristin could do nothing but back away. She lost all sense of control.

The snapping came again, this time closer, like the source was inches from her.

Kristin lashed out, throwing her fists at the sound and striking only air in a feeble punch before turning to run as fast as she could. She held out her hands to feel for trees and branches. She tripped over something, a log or rock, she wasn't sure. She felt damp grass, dirt, and leaves slide across her arms and face as she hit the ground. Her left shoulder raged at her.

She stood as quickly as she could, forcing herself up, nearly tripping over herself again doing so, and ran a few more yards before stopping to look back.

She took a deep breath to try and gain some control as her heart pounded in her chest.

The car door. She realized she didn't notice if the door the girl sat by had opened or not. It must have, she thought. But she didn't hear it, that she knew.

She found herself surrounded by darkness, but from the direction she came she could see the white and red car lights between trees, and now in the darkness noticed the moon hanging from around her neck had turned a deep red. She thought perhaps it was from the brake lights in the distance, but it seemed different. Darker.

She waited, listening closely and hearing nothing. Whatever it was, be it that girl or just some random animal, seemed gone. Gone, or she wondered, just biding its time. Waiting for her to take another step before pouncing. Before taking her.

Then came a distinct shift of light and color. What were slivers of reds and whites just ahead, became accompanied by a pulsing blue and white, from the north, just behind her father's A4.

She recognized it immediately, the strobe from a police vehicle.

Kristin broke into the fastest run she could muster, picking her feet up higher than normal with each step in hopes of not tripping again.

With each stride her shoulder hurt, but she paid no attention, all of her focus on those brilliant blue flashes.

As she got close she could make out the car, a green state trooper sedan, and the officer, a tall man about her age with a bit of a belly, walking to the scene speaking something into the radio strapped to the top of his shoulder.

Kristin emerged from the woods, frantic, startling the trooper who instinctively moved his hand to his holster. She approached him quickly, desperately, reaching out for him.

"Ma'am?"

He caught Kristin under her arms as she collapsed and lost consciousness.

PART TWO

CHAPTER FIVE

2021, Monday June 21st

The drawn shades kept the hospital room dim. The only light coming from the EKG's green display, a small lamp at the bedside, and the crack under the heavy and closed door. The machine's rhythmic beeping kept Shelly company. The darkness comforted her and made her feel like the outside world no longer existed. The entirety of the universe's energy collected itself in this room to help her friend.

She sat on a chair that looked like it came right from the 70s, with drab wooden arms with an olive green cushion at the back and bottom. She had dragged it over to Kristin's bedside when she arrived early in the morning, close enough to reach her if she were to wake.

Shelly heard the news from her mother, who heard from Kristin's aunt Ruth. She stopped preparing for work, left a voicemail for her boss, then put up her hair and went to the hospital not yet even knowing what floor to find her friend on.

Ruth, Elizabeth Fuller's younger sister, greeted Shelly in tears in the hospital room when she first arrived. After an hour or so, Ruth left to take care of some things with her children, leaving Shelly alone.

She then turned off the lights and stationed herself close to Kristin.

The hospital room had a single bed, with more equipment than she had ever seen, and a curtain draped by the side to allow for privacy as needed. In the light, when she arrived, she saw the thoughtful design of the room. The pale blue walls evoked calmness, and the windows overlooked the Fleming Museum.

She checked her phone, *10:35 a.m.*, no new voicemails but two new text messages. One from her husband, Joe, with the sweet "let me know if you need anything, I can bring you some lunch if u'd like". The other from Emil. Shelly had talked to him at least three times, and the empathy she had overcame the less-than-stellar opinion she had of him as a man. She told him everything she knew and reassured him she would not leave and that the moment anything happened she'd call him.

"Working on flights still. News?"

She quickly typed back, "nothing. Still sleeping. Suppose that's good."

Shelly tucked the phone back into her purse and placed it on the floor next to her.

As she looked at Kristin, peacefully asleep in the bed with her head inclined about 30 degrees, she remembered her thoughts when she first walked into the room after preparing for the absolute worst — a brutally injured friend. But Kristin appeared unscathed save for the wrap around her left shoulder. Strands of her hair went in all sorts of directions, and her light makeup had seen better days, but she actually looked healthy.

The nurse popped in every half-hour or so to check vitals and remind Shelly to alert them when Kristin woke — she had been unconscious since being found by the officer.

Kristin let out a small groan and turned her head just slightly.

Shelly remained in her seat but reached out and placed a hand on her friend's.

Kristin groaned again, then opened one eye and slowly the other.

Kristin went to raise her left arm, then let it fall back down after a wince of pain.

"Hey, Honey," Shelly said to her friend softly. She decided to give Kristin a few minutes before calling in the nurse.

"Shell…" Kristin's voice sounded like someone who hadn't spoken for years, barely able to find itself, dry and raspy.

"Hey."

Kristin scanned the room, "Oh my god."

"How do you feel? Do you want some pain meds?" Shelly stood and grabbed the device hooked into Kristin's I.V., holding the big round button protruding from it up to her friend. "The nurse said this delivers some pain medicine."

Kristin shook her head, "No."

"You sure?"

"My shoulder hurts," she partially reached for her left shoulder before placing her right hand back down on the bed.

"Yeah, they said you bruised it bad, but you're very

lucky. Nothing broken."

"Lucky…" Kristin said as she looked up to the ceiling, clenching her jaw in an attempt to fight off sadness as the realization that she just lost her parents came sparking back.

"I'm so sorry, Kris."

Shelly gave her friend time to grieve. Held her hand softly and touched her right shoulder gently.

"Emil and I have been talking. He's getting here as soon as he can. Finding the soonest flights has been a little tough for him, so doesn't look like he'll arrive until tomorrow. He wants me to call and obviously wants to talk to you if you're up for it. He was pretty upset, had to tell him over and over that you seemed okay, just sleeping."

Kristin smiled. "Thank you for calling him…and being here." Her voice found its way close to normalcy, though with that groggy signature.

"Of course. Aunt Ruth was here too, but had to leave."

"Oh."

"Now, I'm going to get the nurse. They should check you over."

"Yeah," she nodded in resignation, not really wanting to talk to anyone else.

Shelly flipped the small metal switch on the side of the long fluorescent light attached to the wall just above the bed, figuring the nurse or doctor would need it. She then left the room to track one down.

Kristin squinted, her eyes still accustomed to the darkness.

The bulb flickered a bit, and Kristin looked up at the fixture. Behind the opaque plastic covering she could make out the shape of the fluorescent tube. She watched it darken at its center and extreme edges as if it were dying, forming two individual and elongated entities. The dark portions expanded, causing the lights to continue to shrink until they took the shape of two perfect circles.

She watched as those then grew brighter, like headlights barring down on her.

"Kristin?"

As she heard the unfamiliar voice the bulb returned to its normal shape, and she looked up to see Shelly entering with a nurse who, Kristin thought, probably knew her mother.

The name tag pressed to her blue scrubs read *Anne*. She had very short, dark, and stylized hair along with a colorful sleeve tattoo on her left arm.

Kristin expected to be poked and prodded, but Anne only checked her vitals on the machines connected to her before asking questions.

"Good morning, do you know where you are?"

Kristin nodded, "The hospital."

"Do you know why you're here?" She gently placed her hand on Kristin's left in support.

"Yes, a car accident."

The nurse paused, giving Kristin a moment as she teared up, looked away, and tensed her muscles in emotional pain.

"You remember your name?"

"Kristin Fuller," she composed herself. Kristin never liked showing that kind of emotion to people and focused on the nurse to keep them at bay.

Anne rubbed Kristin's lower leg to try and help soothe her as she turned her attention to Shelly, "Virtually a miracle."

"She's a tough cookie."

"Would you like something for pain?" Anne turned her

attention back to her patient.

"Just ibuprofen."

"You sure?"

"Yeah."

"Okay."

Just as Anne was about to leave the room, Kristin stopped her with a question, "How's the little girl?"

Anne turned and looked confused, "What little girl?"

"She was in the other car, young. Like ten years old. She got out and walked around."

Kristin could see Anne's eyes searching for an answer. "I'm sorry, you're the only survivor. I'm not aware of anyone else. No little girl."

Shelly sat again, and not one to remain quiet, tried to get more answers, "Are you saying there wasn't a girl found?"

The nurse took another moment, her eyes this time locked on Shelly, then she nodded knowingly, "I'll call the detective in charge. He'll likely want to ask some questions."

"Thank you," Shelly responded as the nurse left the room. She turned to her friend, pulling her cell from her purse, "Why don't you call Emil now? He's worried sick."

"Yeah okay."

Shelly stood again and handed the phone to Kristin, who dialed her boyfriend. He answered on the first ring.

"Hello!"

"Hi baby," her voice cracked and tears formed in her eyes again, which she silently admonished herself for.

Shelly took position by the large window, drew it open to view the hill section of Burlington, trying to both give her friend space to talk to her boyfriend and also be close enough for anything she might need.

"Oh, Jesus, sweetie," Emil punctuated his words with exhales, clearly both relieved to hear her and anxious at the same time, "it is so good to hear your voice. I love you so much. I am so sorry."

"Thanks," she replied solemnly.

"I've got flights and I'll be there tomorrow. Can you tell me how you feel? Maybe that's a dumb question."

"My whole body is sore, not bad though, like after a workout. But my left shoulder is bad."

"I wish I was there for you."

"I know. Shelly has been amazing. She's been keeping me updated."

"Yeah, she's a good friend," Kristin smiled at the woman standing at the window that she has known for years and that Emil had finally given some credit to.

"Once I get there I'll take care of everything, okay? You don't think about anything. I'll take care of the services, all the arrangements. If you want, that is."

She hadn't thought about any of that yet. Kristin's words had to fight through her emotions' grip on her jaw muscles, "Thank you."

After a few more minutes of mostly Emil talking, they hung up. Shelly told her to nap, that she had been awake long enough. Kristin couldn't argue, she felt like she could sleep for days.

Anne returned with the painkillers just before Kristin drifted off.

Only about another hour passed, with Kristin fast asleep and Shelly paging through outdated magazines and playing some mindless game on her phone, before a man in an old suit entered the room. He appeared in his late 50s, a bit overweight, and wore a tight haircut. He had that air about him like decades ago he was an attractive and athletic individual, but time and carbohydrates caught up with him.

He introduced himself to Shelly, "Hi, I'm Detective Franks."

"Hi, Shelly Arntz, a friend," she stood and shook his hand.

He motioned with his head toward the patient, "How's she doing?"

"Surprisingly well physically. Handling the rest the best anyone can."

"Yeah, I can't imagine. So, what's this I hear about a girl?"

Shelly shrugged slightly, "I don't know. Kristin just asked the nurse about her, I think just curious if she was okay. Sounds like she was in the accident but was walking around after."

"Hmm," he said looking at Shelly, "I'm going to see if I can wake her, already checked with the nurses to make sure it's fine, and see if she has anything additional."

"Sure," Shelly stood on the opposite side of the bed from the detective, and again took her friend's hand, ready to end the questions if she felt it was becoming too much.

"Kristin?" Franks leaned into her a bit, and spoke softly, "Kristin, can you wake up?"

Her eyes opened and turned to the man.

"Good afternoon, Kristin, I'm Detective Franks. Can I ask you a few questions?"

Kristin shimmied up the bed a bit and checked that she was fully covered, "Yeah."

"Your friend says you saw a girl at the accident, walking around. Is that right?"

"Yes," her voice not as raspy as it had been, "She was in the other car, the BMW. She got out, I saw her."

"Did you see where she went?"

"I think into the woods, on the lake side of the road."

"Okay that's good, thank you," he spoke softly, "What did she look like?"

"Long dark hair. Maybe nine or ten years old. She wore a white nightgown."

"Did she say anything?"

"No."

"Hmm," he said again, looking down in thought before returning to Kristin, "You sure she came out of the BMW?"

"Positive."

"One more question then, and I'm so sorry about your loss, but how were your parents leading up to the accident? Did they seem normal? In good spirits? Maybe anything off?"

Kristin pressed her head against the thin pillow, literally taken aback by the question, "They were fine, why?"

Franks gave one of those smiles that covered a thought, "No reason."

He stepped a bit back as he pulled his card from a back pocket, and reached it out to Shelly, "If she remembers anything, please have her call me."

"Of course," Shelly pocketed the small piece of paper.

He turned again to Kristin, "Thank you for your time, and my condolences."

With a nod to each of them, he left the room.

"What do you think he meant by that? By my parents before the accident?"

She shrugged her shoulders and shook her head, dismissing it altogether, "You know cops. Half the questions they ask are stupid but they have to ask them."

"Yeah, I guess."

Kristin's eyes locked onto the white sheet covering her, it acting as a blank canvas for her mind to paint on.

The question consumed her. Why would he ask about her parents? They were normal and happy since she arrived, she was sure of that. But what if they were not? What would that mean? Why might that be important to Franks?

If they were depressed, perhaps he might interpret that as a suggestion they caused the accident — as a suicide tactic. But that couldn't be the case, they not only were not depressed, but their daughter was in the car. *They wouldn't ever do that*, she thought. The vision of the accident came to her in all its horror, the darkness of the trees, the red tail lights, the blood splatter and pooling.

This had nothing to do with her parents, but his question disturbed Kristin nonetheless.

She turned away from that bedsheet, that in her mind now burned red with her parents' blood, "I want to go home."

Shelly looked at her friend, unsure if she meant the question rhetorically.

"I want to go home."

She could see Kristin's shield over her pain, her direct gaze now telling her in no uncertain terms that they needed to leave the hospital immediately.

"Dallas?"

Kristin shook her head.

"Shelburne?"

"Yes. Get me out of here."

* * *

Shelly pulled her two-year-old silver minivan into the Fuller's driveway around seven that evening, the porch light still on from a day ago, and parked. The sky reflected a deep blue with still an hour or so of daylight left. Kristin held the garbage bag in her lap which contained her clothes and purse. Not wanting to spend another minute there, she still wore the paper-thin baby blue pants and top the hospital provided. The warm evening made the garments comfortable enough.

It took convincing for the two friends to get out of the hospital, and the doctors' tried their delay tactics, like tracking down paperwork for hours, but with Shelly's stubborn persistence they prevailed.

Kristin leaned over the divide between the front seats and tightly embraced her friend, "Thank you so much for taking care of me today. You're the best."

Shelly, careful not to squeeze her bruised friend, gave Kristin a little peck on the cheek, "I honestly feel like shit leaving you here. It just doesn't feel right, Kris. Like I said, you can stay with us, it would be fun and no bother at all. Or I could stay here, just be here if you need something… anything."

Kristin sat back in the passenger seat and put one hand on the door handle, "Yeah, I appreciate that, but this really is what I need. I'm going to go to bed soon, hopefully sleep. Why don't you come by after work tomorrow if you can?"

Her friend smirked, one of those small smiles that was more disappointment than anything, "I don't think I'll be going in. They'll have to do without Shellster. I'll call you and come by. I'll bring food. Lots of it."

"You are the best."

"Do you need anything for tonight?"

"No, I'll be fine."

The women hugged once again before Kristin got out, and Shelly watched her friend walk to the front door of the nice home to ensure she made it inside. Once the door closed behind her, Shelly turned the van around in the driveway to slowly make her way out.

Inside, Kristin dropped the bag on the wooden rocking chair just by the front door and exhaled loudly. She stood a moment looking around, wondering exactly what she should do now. Try to sleep? Watch some TV? Look at old family photos? Find the electricity bill to make sure she had time to pay it? Track down a last will? Cry?

It was too much. She could barely think and pain raged through her shoulder. The doctor, whose name she could not remember, gave her a prescription for more powerful pain medication after sharing his generic concerns about her being discharged so quickly.

Kristin decided to go to bed and climbed the stairs to the second floor where she turned right to the master bedroom, passed through to the master bath where she knew some ibuprofen would be, and popped five into her mouth, drinking straight from the faucet to wash them down.

Returning to the master bedroom, the shades were drawn giving the room a dampened yellow tint. Her parents' bed, where they had slept for the last 35 years or so, placed between two far windows. A bureau rested to her left along an outside wall and a small television on her right next to the door to the hall. A closet also to the right sat closed.

On the bureau she saw the teddy bear, Buttons, she had attempted to make for them when she was about 20 years younger. The thing didn't look very good back then, but time treated it well as her parents always kept it in that safe spot. It had seemingly random tufts of short brown hair on its head, more than a few threads poking out from seems, and black button eyes.

Kristin crossed the room to the hallway, where she passed the stairs, half-bath, and spare bedroom. She entered her old room, the closed shades against the purple walls making it darker than her parents' room. Feeling an odd comfort from the space she took the two steps to the twin bed and collapsed. Within seconds she fell asleep, still in the clothes the hospital gave her.

When she woke later she had no idea the time, but the room now sat in complete darkness.

She shifted her body with care to sit as the pain had come back with force. After a moment to allow the streak of sharp agony to subside she slowly stood. Unsure of her footing, Kristin took a few deliberate steps to the window that looked out to the backyard. With her healthy right arm, she reached for the cord and pulled open the blinds. Outside she could see the moon, virtually full, hanging over the trees.

Kristin pressed her tongue to the roof of her mouth. Its dryness made it feel completely foreign. She needed water...and painkillers.

After a step towards the door, she stopped and placed one hand on the wall, needing a second to check herself as she became slightly light-headed. She didn't want to fall and hurt her shoulder further. She gently shook her head a bit before starting again and leaving the room to go to the half-bath just a few feet down the hall. She flipped on the light that hung just above the small mirror ahead.

Immediately she could see her reflection and startled as she didn't look herself. In fact, she looked like shit. Her dark eyes almost matched the bruising that she could see peeking out from the hospital's top. Her left shoulder hurt like hell, and Kristin didn't dare remove the garb to see just how bad it looked.

She took the small plastic cup from the corner of the pedestal sink, filled it with water, and sipped. Allowing the water to sit in her mouth before swallowing, the sensation of her tongue coming back to life made her feel better and she repeated that a couple more times before checking the medicine cabinet for painkillers. Empty.

She groaned as she closed it, not wanting to move any more than she had to for some more meds, and cursed herself for not just grabbing the bottle earlier. With each step down the hall to her parents' room she winced and wondered if taking the more powerful drugs may have been the best idea. But she had a fear of becoming one of those people dependent on them and felt she could manage just fine with the over-the-counter stuff. Now she second-guessed that decision.

The master bedroom sat dark as well. Kristin felt her way from the door to the bathroom where she turned on the light. She popped five more capsules and swallowed with water. Keeping the bottle with her as she retraced her steps, she re-entered the master bedroom.

The light from the bathroom leaked in, and she saw Buttons sitting there, the lone watchman over the room. The house felt different without her parents in it. So quiet, dark, lifeless. She could hear the low hum of the central air's fan, but no other sound.

Kristin turned the light back off, and with her eyes not yet adjusted, felt her way back down the hall to her childhood bedroom where she placed the ibuprofen on the desk and lay back down.

A part of her felt like she should be too sad or afraid to sleep, but from the travel, accident, and whatever drugs the doctors may have given her at the hospital, dreamless sleep took her willingly.

CHAPTER SIX

2021, Tuesday June 22nd

When Kristin woke the next morning the sun shone into the room from low in the sky and from around the shades, shining off the white desk and onto her face. The bright light made her feel good and warm, and helped fend off the sharp edge of sadness.

The clock read 8 a.m., and up from the plush beige carpet where it rested, the LED on her cell phone blinked green repeatedly.

Kristin, lying on her stomach, stretched her right arm out, but the device sat just out of reach. She shimmied over like a seal, cupped the phone, and swiped the screen on with her thumb.

The black notification bar at the top indicated three new voicemails. She hit the voicemail icon, turned on the speaker, and hit play on the first, which has been left just after 5 a.m.

"Hey, Honey, I hope you're sleeping well," Emil's

voice sounded both tired and ridden with guilt for not being with her. "It's early here but I'm heading to the airport. Can't sleep anyway and paranoid about lines in security. Just calling to say 'hi', let you know how much I love you, and that I'll see you today. Love you so much. Wish I was there. K, bye."

The computer-generated voice came on to give instructions on how to save or delete the message, not being able to make a decision she just skipped to the next message which had been left only 45 minutes ago.

"Hey, me again. Just calling to see if you're up. No pressure to answer, do what you need to do. Call if you want. Love you."

She skipped again, to the last message, five minutes old.

"Kristin, this is Doris Hawthorne," like Emil's her voice had that low tone and slowness we associate with compassion and sympathy. "I spoke to Emil yesterday, he told me what happened and I let the board know as well. We are all thinking about you. You are our bright star, and we want you back only when you feel ready. Your career isn't on pause, it's just here waiting for you when you're ready. You should know Mr. Wilmington is excited about what you presented last week, he talked about it with all of his friends and I think they're buying stock as well. Please, if you need anything call me. I mean it. We're taking care of everything, don't worry about a thing, not even sleazy Brad — I'll just say that he has been taken care of. Even if you want to work from Vermont for a while, or need an extended break, whatever it might be, just let me know and I'll take care of the rest. Okay, well, we're thinking about you. Bye."

Kristin closed the voicemail app and felt appreciative

of both Emil and Mrs. Hawthorne. Work had been on her mind, but her mentor set her at ease. She could focus on herself and not worry — and Emil would assuredly help her with that.

She stood, with gentle care, and went to the spare room where she had slept the first night in the house and where she had left her luggage. She grabbed a t-shirt and sweatpants and brought them, along with the pain meds, to the master bathroom.

There she quickly took a few more pills before standing in front of the mirror for a moment, just staring at herself. She still looked a mess, of course, but she accepted that. What she feared was just how bad the bruising would be. She could still see some of the dark purples by the base of her neck.

Kristin exhaled before clenching her jaw in preparation for the pain as she bent forward and raised her arms to slide off the hospital's thin blue top.

The pain struck at her with multiple knives at various angles, and as she straightened back up she felt a bit of relief. She didn't know what to have expected, and certainly the bruising looked painful, with streaks of dark hues along her collarbone, shoulder, and across her left breast. But she also felt that it seemed not nearly as bad as it likely should have been.

Not daring to touch it, she carefully put her gray t-shirt with *Vermont* in green text on before swapping the cheap pants for her soft and comfortable pajama bottoms.

Taking each step thoughtfully she went down the stairs and rounded the corner to the left. She stopped as she saw the hospital bag waiting for her on the rocking chair.

Kristin opened it and peeked inside, seeing her clothes and purse. And there, poking up between, the moon necklace.

She dragged the purse out and placed it on the floor,
then pulled the necklace and kept it clutched in her left
hand as she used her right to pick up the bag and place it
on the stairs for her to bring back to her room the next time
she went up.

The moon didn't look so menacing anymore as it
appeared its usual white and grays. Kristin looked at it in
her open palm as she went to the kitchen. She looked at it
some more. A part of her wanted to toss it as it reminded
her of the rare event on the night of her parents' death.
But, she admitted to herself, she also found it beautiful.
Alluring. Seductive even.

Favoring her right arm she raised it up and back around
her neck, tucking it under her shirt.

A moment later she found herself staring at the
contents of the refrigerator mindlessly. Eggs, cheese,
veggies, ham…all the makings of the omelet she craved,
but she didn't want to go through the actual effort of
making it. It made her feel stupid, like that's how
dependent she was on Emil. Logically she knew that
wasn't the case, that her hard work paid for their lifestyle,
but that didn't stop her feelings.

Begrudgingly she took out the ingredients and started
the process of making her breakfast.

As she cracked the eggs onto the small frying pain the
sight of the splintered shell brought the vision of crumbled
metal and shards of glass flashing before her, and she held
her eyes tight a moment to push them away.

She wished for a sibling, a brother or sister that had
grown up in the same house to talk to. Kristin wanted to
share memories of life in the house with her parents with
someone who was there. Reminisce about holidays,

spontaneous moments, or her parents' habit of saying they had "a project to work on" when they went up to bed together. Someone to look at and see her mother's or father's eyes, chin, or hear in their voice.

At the same time, she felt thankful that her grandparents had all passed — they didn't have to live to see their children die. Kristin wasn't so sure she could both grieve for herself and show empathy to someone who lost a child.

She turned her attention back to the morning, which she always loved in this house. The sun peeked through the trees, and the house sat quiet except for the ticking of the large clock in the reading room. This morning, however, all of that was lost on her. She didn't feel the same joy.

At about nine her phone buzzed, alerting her to a text message from Emil letting her know that he was in line to board the first flight. She responded with a quick "okay" followed by a kiss.

Kristin slid the omelet onto a plate and picked up the kitchen a bit. The room was maybe the most outdated in the house, but oddly tastefully so — like it was just retro enough to be cool. Her parents had good taste, and so generally the designs of the rooms were timeless.

She filled a glass with water and took her breakfast to the front porch where she sat and slowly ate.

Thankfully, due to the trees and long driveway, no neighbors could see her. She didn't want people seeing her here, being tempted to come to give their condolences, or just staring at her in pity from their windows. She dreaded the coming times of having to hear people say how sorry they were, how tragic the whole thing was. She understood everyone needed to mourn, that coming together to remember was healthy, but also wished she could just let it pass in solitude.

Kristin heard the telling noise, the heavy sound of a car against the rocks, that someone had pulled into her parents' driveway, just around the corner from a row of trees. Seconds later she could see Shelly's van approaching, kicking up a little dust behind it.

Kristin watched the van come to a stop by the garage, and her friend get out as the rear gate automatically opened. She reached in and grabbed a large covered glass container and held it up to show Kristin, "Lasagna to fatten you up."

Kristin smiled. Nothing changed Shelly, at least it seemed that way.

She put her empty plate on the small tiled table at her side and took the few steps down to the walkway, where she met Shelly and looked into the back of the vehicle.

"Lasagna for tonight. I also have donuts and bagels for breakfast for us, and already cooked chicken and a big salad. Plus some snacks."

"You're amazing, Shell. Thank you. I did eat breakfast though."

"That's cool. There's always room for breakfast cake."

"Breakfast cake?"

"Donuts you dork," Shelly said as she handed Kristin the light bag of pastries. "You good carrying that?"

"Yeah."

Shelly brought the lasagna inside, Kristin following, and found a spot for it in the refrigerator after moving some items around. She then made another trip for the salad and a few reusable grocery bags. Kristin placed the donuts down and leaned on the counter, watching her friend put all the food away in silence.

"So," Shelly's attention now squarely on Kristin, "how are you doing this morning?"

Kristin shrugged, afraid speaking would start the waterworks.

Shelly nodded then pulled the day's newspaper from one of the bags and held it up, "Today's paper. Do you want me to just toss it? There is a small article on the accident."

Kristin had to think for a moment. She acknowledged her desire to avoid it all, but also knew she couldn't.

"I'd like to read it."

"Okay," Shelly slid the rolled-up daily across the counter to her. "Let's take it outside with these donuts." She grabbed the small paper bag from a local bakery and led Kristin outside where they sat together on the swing.

She only flipped through a few pages before coming to the short article.

"You sure you want to read it, Kris? It's okay not to."

"Yeah, I'm sure."

"You still like the jelly donuts?"

"Yeah," Kristin responded softly, her attention turning to the article, as Shelly wrapped one in a napkin and placed it on her friend's lap.

"Awesome, I get the chocolate!"

Kristin read the article three times, thinking maybe she had missed something.

CHARLOTTE - At about 10:34pm on Sunday, June 20th, Vermont State Trooper Parker came across a fatal accident on Lakeview Road involving two vehicles. The head-on collision killed four and sent one person to the Emergency room, who was released the next day. No names have been released. If you have any

*information pertaining to the accident, you are asked
to call the Vermont State Police or Detective Franks at
802-555-8463.*

Kristin closed the paper and placed it at her side,
looking off into the distance as she thought.

No mention of that girl. They may be still looking for
her, but wouldn't the paper communicate that? Wouldn't
they tell readers that a kid was missing and then ask that
any information specific to her possible whereabouts be
sent to the police? Shouldn't they ask for help in searching
since she's obviously injured? Shouldn't they provide a
description? Could it be they don't believe her?

Shelly noticed her friend staring off, lost somewhere.
"You alright, hon?"

Kristin snapped her head back to Shelly, who had just
taken a large bite of a glazed chocolate donut. "Yeah, I'm
fine."

"What's up?" Shelly's voice was a bit muffled from the
pastry.

Kristin looked at the paper and back at her friend,
shaking her head just slightly to not be seen as concerned
as she actually was, "Nothing really. Just…remember the
girl I told you about? The one in the accident?"

"Yeah, of course. I was there when that detective
talked to you."

"Well, there's no mention of her. I just thought…
thought that they would ask people for help finding her."

"It's still early, it just all happened. That's the first
report, I'm sure they'll follow up."

"Right." Kristin turned her attention to the jelly donut,
"You're the best, Shell."

"I know, kid."

Kristin took a bite, "This is amazing. I can't remember the last time I had one." Her depressed tone didn't match her words.

Shelly looked her thin friend up and down, "Yeah, you don't look like you've been eating donuts. You look great."

"Aww, thanks, Shell. Emil makes it easy, he does the cooking and it's always healthy. And when it's not blazing hot out I bike in to get exercise."

"You don't go to the gym?"

"No time. So biking for my commute is super helpful. Two birds with one stone, you know?"

"You work a lot?"

"So much. Too much." Kristin wiped away a dab of red jelly from the corner of her mouth, "The job's demanding, and there's millions I'm responsible for. But I've impressed the partners, and they pay me generously."

"But how much do you work?"

"Oh, probably 60 to 70 hours a week or so."

Shelly shook her head, "Kris, that's awful. You're going to work yourself to death." Hearing her choice of words Shelly cringed inside, "I mean, do you have time to even enjoy your life?"

"Not right now, but if I keep progressing I'll eventually have more say in where my time goes. Maybe one day have more time to travel the world with Emil."

"I don't hear kids in that equation."

Kristin had to turn her gaze from Shelly. As much as she wanted a child, she just didn't see how one would fit, "Well, we'll see."

"It's okay if you don't want any. God knows I've brought enough little shits into the world for both of us."

They laughed a bit, with Kristin's turning into tears.

"Sorry, Shell," she managed between sobs.

Shelly turned towards her friend and took her hand, "It's totally fine, Kris. You cry if you want to cry. I'm just here for you. I called out of work all week, and Jim said he'd take care of the kids as much as needed. I thought we'd try to enjoy some food, talk through your feelings, and help out with whatever comes next. But whatever you need."

By the afternoon Kristin had started to feel a little better, she wondered if it was some calm before an emotional storm. She still didn't want to go anywhere and avoided her phone except for updates from Emil, who appeared due to arrive at 10 p.m. The other messages she ignored.

Shortly after 1 p.m. Kristin, feeling exhausted, went upstairs to nap. Shelly checked in with her husband who was at work and then set out to do a little cleaning even though the house already looked pretty spotless. She did the downstairs bathroom anyway, figuring there would be company in the coming days.

When she woke, Kristin forced herself to check her voicemail. There were two calls from Emil, both left at various times when she was asleep, three from coworkers, all of whom they were close to and so probably heard the news from Emil, more than a few from relatives checking in and offering condolences, and the last from an attorney representing her parents' last will. That message she saved, and wrote down his name and phone number to call later.

Kristin went downstairs to find Shelly sitting on the living room sofa watching a science fiction movie starring Justin Timberlake. Kristin sat at the other end, stretched her feet out, tucking her oddly cold toes under her friend's thighs. They used to sit like that in high school, Shelly

virtually insisting on it as she always commented on Kris'
"corpse toes."

"He's hotter than he was when we were in school,"
Shelly motioned to the television, "But, how are you, Kris?"

"I'm…you know. Like numb. It's just all so much."

"Yeah, I'm so sorry."

Shelly rubbed Kristin's legs.

"How's your shoulder?"

Kristin rotated her left arm some and winced only a bit,
"It's honestly not even that bad, all things considered, but I
don't dare touch it. Looks like hell though. Sometimes I
forget about it."

"I guess that's good."

Shelly waited another moment, "Look, it's okay if you
don't want to know, but I did see an update to the news
about the accident."

"No, I want to know."

"Okay," she turned the volume down a bit, "They
released the names of the couple, they're Peter and Lila
Hubberton. There was no mention of anyone else in that
car."

Kristin nodded quietly.

"I'm sure we can get more info."

"Emil's good at Googling, maybe he can find
something."

Shelly didn't know what to think. Was there a girl in
the accident? Could it have been some hallucination during
the incident due to the impact? Or some dream she had
after the fact that she confused with reality? She thought
she'd approach the situation assuming Kristin's experience
happened since Kristin was always the most level-headed
and realistic person she knew. But her friend noticed the
doubt on her face.

"It's okay," Kristin shrugged.

"What?"

"You didn't see her. You weren't there. All you have is what you've heard, so I get it. You think maybe she wasn't real."

"No, Kris…"

"Shell," she interrupted, "seriously, it's fine. I don't even know. But…but I think it was real."

"Good enough for me."

Shelly reached to gently take Kristin's right hand, "You know if you want help with anything I'm happy to. Emil said he'd take care of all the services stuff, but if there's anything else, please ask."

"Thanks, Shell."

"Nothing's a burden or embarrassing."

Kristin gave a slight chuckle, "Please, after ninth grade you think I could feel embarrassed around you?"

The afternoon slowly drifted by with the women bouncing from watching old movies to sipping drinks on the porch. Even though the refrigerator was now stacked with food, they ordered Chinese and had it delivered, Kristin refusing to let Shelly pay.

Emil arrived at 10 p.m., the headlights of his rental Subaru illuminating the front porch where the girls sat on the bench swing.

He opened the driver's door and ran up the walkway, not wanting to wait another moment to hug his girlfriend and see her for himself.

Kristin met him halfway, the tears forming as new again. Though Shelly was her longest-known and best friend, Emil was the one she really needed. She needed to feel his warm skin, see his face. Rest in his calm eyes.

They embraced, Emil holding her gently, feeling her

between his arms and against his chest. Her hair soft against his neck.

"Kristin," he moved his right hand to the back of her head, "I am so sorry."

Shelly started gathering the food boxes and empty cider cans to bring inside.

"I'm glad you're here," Kristin leaned back and gave Emil a quick kiss.

"Of course. Let me get my bag."

He returned to the car, shutting the front door and retrieving a duffel bag from the back.

Kristin waited for him, taking his hand as he approached and leading them inside where Shelly was cleaning up in the kitchen.

"Hey, Shelly," Emil nonchalantly waved.

She took a few steps towards him, "Hey Emil."

The two had met a few times, and this small greeting was probably the most they had spoken since they first met.

With Emil now there for support, Shelly only stayed a couple more minutes before returning home to her family.

When her friend left the couple sat on the couch where Kristin's emotions got the best of her. The sobbing came on with force, the tears running quickly.

She didn't realize this release somehow waited for Emil, but it made sense to her and she welcomed it nonetheless. Emil held her mostly in silence and into the night.

* * *

It took some time for Kristin to settle down. She caught her breath and dried her eyes on her t-shirt. They sat in the living room, with only the light on in the adjacent kitchen, and the television off. The silence deepened the somber mood and gave the house that feeling of missing its true occupants.

Emil felt for Kristin. He knew that while she lived so far from home, she loved her parents dearly. She would often send letters to them from Texas, even though she spoke to them regularly, and would include printed photos she had not yet shared with them on social media.

"Why don't you go upstairs, get ready for bed. I'll close up down here."

Kristin nodded and Emil watched her climb the stairs to the second level.

He stood and walked to the kitchen, and then through the small doorway to the mudroom. He checked the door, locked, and the window, closed and locked, before turning back to the kitchen.

He flicked the lights off and stopped in his tracks, turning to the window over the kitchen sink which normally offered a view of the patio and backyard, but now was just darkness. Emil could have sworn someone's face had been in that window. He hadn't been looking right at it, it would have been in his peripheral vision, but something was there. Something, or someone, caught his eye.

He thought a moment. Being in a rural part of Vermont, what felt like the safest place on Earth, it seemed most likely either an animal somehow got on the porch and up to the window, or just a trick of light.

To the right of the window, past the cupboard and clock on the wall, the sliding glass door to the back patio rested open. He took the few steps over the wood flooring, across the combined kitchen and dining area, and slid open the screen door. He took a step outside as he flicked on the outside light.

Save for the typical outdoor bistro set, a patio sofa and

lounge chair, and a gas grill, the patio was empty. Twenty feet or so in front of him were the steps down to the lawn.

Emil looked around, but the light didn't offer much help as the woods surrounded the yard and prevented the illumination from penetrating further in.

Not entirely satisfied, Emil went back inside, closing and locking the door behind him.

He also locked the front door, and shut off the kitchen light, before heading up the stairs.

At the top, he walked straight, into the small bathroom to freshen up. He grabbed his small toiletry bag from the sink, unzipped it, and pulled out his toothbrush. He found the tube of toothpaste in the only drawer and began brushing. Emil watched himself in the mirror, the shadow from the doorway making a part of the hall behind him visible, while the remainder rested in darkness.

He figured Kristin was already in bed, which seemed a good thing.

Kristin sat on the bed in the spare room, where the two would sleep since it had the larger mattress. She needed a moment alone to catch her breath.

She noticed the ibuprofen on the small bedside table and realized she didn't have water, so decided to return downstairs for a glass. She stood and quietly rounded the corner out of the bedroom to the stairs, not catching Emil's attention.

The moon gave enough illumination to not warrant turning on the lights, so Kristin walked through the living room to the kitchen, where she took a glass from the cupboard. She brought it to the refrigerator to get filtered water from the dispenser in the door. As she waited, the water coming out slowly as usual, her thoughts drifted to nothing. She stared off at the floor patiently.

Then, very quickly, a shadow raced over the hardwood as if something large had run across the back deck, causing her to drop her glass.

"Shit," Kristin bent down to pick up the luckily intact cup, and she placed it on the kitchen island before going to the window over the sink to look outside.

Whatever blocked out the moonlight must have been large. It didn't make any sound, so she thought it could have been a large bird, maybe a hawk, flying by.

The high moon cast shadows of tree limbs at the edge of the wooded area. It reminded her a bit of a couple nights prior, being on the road just feet from the tree line, feeling trapped and scared. She remembered running into the woods like it were the only escape when she saw that creepy girl. Now, from the safety of her childhood home, she wouldn't dare run in there at night.

Then she saw the movement.

Something…white. Glowing just a bit from the moonlight, just past the first row of trees, dancing between shadows and slowly moving from her left to her right.

Formless, and probably 30 yards from the window, Kristin couldn't make it out.

She squinted and leaned closer to the glass pane, stretching over the sink causing some pain to creep up her hurt shoulder.

Then it stopped, and from the shifting of the shadows, seemed to turn a bit, like whatever it was was now looking back at her.

Kristen stretched further, pushing her hands against the sink, and grunting a bit from the pressure on her bruised flesh.

She jumped back, screaming, quickly and forcefully shoving herself against the island behind her.

"Ahh!"

The young girl from the accident stood at the edge of her lawn. Kristin could see her plain as day.

Her white arms shone under the moonlight, as did the cleaner parts of her nightgown. Her hair was darkness, darker than the shadows within the woods. And her face... her face looked at her expressionless, but with this hint of a terrifying amalgamation of impatience, desire, and need.

"Oh my god."

Kristin turned and ran up the stairs to find Emil standing at the top, his toothbrush hanging from his mouth, his eyes wide.

He mumbled and gurgled through the paste, shocked by Kristin's frantic stomping up the stairs and her now white complexion, "What's going on?"

She stumbled over her words trying to get them out as quickly as possible, "Girl outside. That accident girl. Saw her. I saw that girl from the accident outside!"

Emil's brow scrunched in. He thought he had seen someone at the window minutes earlier. It all sounded so crazy, though. Like fiction. Kristin had told him about the accident, of course, but she never mentioned the girl again — but Shelly kept him informed as she worried that Kristin may have hallucinated the encounter.

He turned back to the bathroom, spit out the toothpaste, and quickly wiped his face. "Okay, I'll go look."

"No, don't!" She blocked him from the stairs.

Emil's confusion had him take a step back, "What? What do you mean, why?"

She could only shake her head, her fear gripping her body.

"It's okay, honey. I'm just going to step onto the deck and look around. If I see anything then we'll call the cops."

"Promise, don't go into the woods."

"I promise."

She let him pass and he walked down the stairs, rounded the corner through the living room, into the kitchen, and opened the sliding door.

He took a single step out and looked from left to right and back again before taking the few more steps to the edge of the deck.

Emil stood in silence, aware that Kristin had followed him down but stood just inside.

He turned to his girlfriend and shook his head.

"She was there, I saw her." Kristin folded her arms, entirely conscious that she may be perceived as making the whole thing up.

"I know," he went back into the house, shut the door behind him, and held her.

Kristin felt uncomfortable by the window but still peeked around Emil's shoulder to look outside. She should feel safe in Emil's arms, but she didn't. She felt watched. Like something in the trees waited for her.

"Can we just go upstairs?"

CHAPTER SEVEN
2021, Wednesday June 23rd

Neither Kristin nor Emil generally slept late, and this morning was no different. About 7 a.m. she woke to him gently rubbing her back. She opened her eyes to see the morning's light creeping between the blinds and the window frame.

Emil must have seen her eyes as he immediately spoke, though quietly. "Would you like some breakfast?"

She nodded without saying a word and curled her body, bringing her knees up to her chest, and turning away from Emil.

"Downstairs or in bed?"

"Downstairs."

Kristin felt the mattress shift as he stood and heard him walk out of the bedroom, calling out "Ten minutes" as he left.

After coffee, eggs, and toast, Kristin called the attorney back to make arrangements to meet the following week.

"Straight forward," he said, "Won't take much more than an hour since everything is left to you. Just a lot of papers to sign."

She also made a few courtesy calls to the few cousins, aunts, and uncles that had left messages for her. None she spoke to very long, just thanked them for their concern, told them she was doing well, and that the services would likely be Friday.

Emil then secluded himself in the front office room to make calls to the funeral home, florist, and cemetery, and do some searches online to make sure he didn't forget anything. She didn't worry much about that, Emil's decision-making was always good and she trusted him. His handling of the services, she thought, was perhaps his greatest gift to her.

Just before noon, Shelly arrived with burgers and fries from a favorite local shop. After joking about Emil the nutritionist not approving of the lunch choice, they sat down to eat on the back patio. Emil, of course, refused to eat the bun and turned the burger into a salad with some spinach they had in the frig.

"So, before Emil has to go to the funeral home, would you two do me a favor?" Kristin knew her friends couldn't say *no* given the circumstances, and she shamelessly took advantage.

"Of course, Kris," Shelly responded confidently as Emil nodded with affirmation and a mouthful of salad.

"I want to go to the site of the accident."

Her friends paused a moment, not expecting the request nor really understanding why Kristin would want to visit the place her parents died, especially so soon after the event.

"You sure, babe?" Emil asked as he choked down his food.

"I'm sure," she said with a pointedness that didn't invite argument. "I know we need to go through photos for you to bring to the funeral home today, so won't take but a couple hours tops."

They didn't talk much after. Emil and Shelly not daring to ask or challenge Kristin on her request, and also feeling a bit uneasy about visiting the location of the morbid event themselves.

At 1 p.m. they got into the Subaru, Kristin demanding the keys and driving, with Emil in the front and Shelly just behind.

They made the trip in mostly silence, a solemn drive on an otherwise beautiful day.

"Here."

Kristin slowed the wagon and pulled it off the side of the road, her shoulder aching from turning the wheel, onto the thin gravel strip just before the small recession to the wooded area. She switched off the ignition before checking the side mirror for any vehicles and exited.

She took a few steps toward the sharp right-hand corner ahead, passing over the four skid marks.

To her right a glittering of white and red light caught her eye, stopping her from walking further.

Kristin turned and walked to the side, bending down to pick up a piece of etched red glass that she assumed came from one of the vehicle's taillights. All around were other small bits of the shattered material.

She hadn't noticed her friends had left the Subaru and made their way to her.

"Kristin, you sure about this?" Emil asked just feet behind her.

"Let her be, Emil." Shelly stood further back, the pose of someone standing watch over something to protect.

"I just don't think this is the best idea, you know, the wounds are still fresh."

"It's what she wants, just support it."

Emil turned back to Shelly and outstretched his arm toward Kristin kneeling to his left. "I'm a little concerned."

Shelly tried her best to respond softly, "Shut the fuck up, Emil."

He frowned and turned from her, looking down to his girlfriend who flipped a small shard of glass in her fingers.

Kristin stood, keeping that sharp artifact in her hand. Not knowing what to do with it, she decided to just hold it for a while, to make the decision on whether to throw it out or not later.

"Look…" Kristin pointed to the rubber streaks in the road as she walked back to them.

"They're not in the middle of the road, all four are clearly in the right lane. He braked. Dad braked."

"How do you know those are from your parents' car?" Shelly asked not to contest her friend's statement, but to get her to share more of her insights.

She stopped just short of them, "They're in the right lane. Clearly, the other car must have been as well since it was head-on. Even if these marks were from the BMW, they're still in the right lane. Meaning, they were driving in the wrong lane regardless."

"Right." Emil sounded like he was saying it with some sort of authority, and that pissed Shelly off even more. She crossed her arms and tried her best to ignore him.

Kristin pointed down the street, to the blind corner, "That's where I saw her."

"The girl?" after a quick glance behind them for any

traffic, Shelly dropped her guard and walked closer to her friend.

"Yeah, well…" Kristin pointed down, "first I saw her around here. She was in the car, that's when I talked to her."

"You spoke?" Emil asked, his curiosity awoken.

She nodded, "Yeah, well…*I* did. She didn't say anything, but I figured she was in shock. Hell, I know I was."

Kristin first took some further steps down the road, "Then she suddenly was out of the car and standing down there," she turned to the side of the road and stared blankly out at the thick woods. "Then she was in the woods. She followed me. Stalked me."

"Kristin?" Emil's concern now grew, to think a young girl stalked Kristin through the woods after such a horrific accident seemed absurd. He immediately regretted his tone, admonishing himself silently, and made a mental note to allow Kristin to believe whatever she wanted to.

Shelly decided to only respond by showing support to her friend. She went to her side and took her hand.

"It's like she's out there. Watching." Kristin said softly.

Emil followed suit, standing to Kristin's left, "Do you want to walk around the woods a bit?"

Kristin knew immediately how she felt about the offer, she didn't need to think about it. Didn't need to weigh the pros and cons, consider the parked car, or fathom any sort of plan. But she let the question hang in the air just a bit.

"No. No need. I know she's there."

She then turned away from her friends, releasing Shelly's hand, and got back behind the wheel. She felt she got what she needed, enough affirmation that Henry didn't drift across the median to satisfy her.

Shelly claimed the front this time, causing a short pause in Emil and he huffed to himself and surrendered to the rear seat, behind Shelly so he could better see Kristin.

Kristin triggered the ignition and checked for cars before turning the wheel to head back the way they came. As she did, the sharp pinch of the small piece of glass clutched between her hand and the wheel reminded her she had not yet decided what to do with the thing. She figured she'd tuck it into a pocket now, and then away into her luggage once back.

"One more stop."

Emil mouthed *what* before checking himself, "Where to?"

"Dad's office, at UVM. Just have to see…if there's anything."

"Detective Franks?"

"Yeah."

"Who?" Emil felt suddenly out of the loop.

Shelly spoke up, taking the burden off Kristin. "After the accident, a detective came to speak to Kris. I think her saying there was a young girl is what got him to go up there. But…anyway, as cops do he asked how her parents were before the accident. You know, like if there was any depression, odd behavior, that sort of thing."

"Oh."

Kristin continued up Route 7, passed the road they should have turned down to return to the Fuller's, and through the busy part of the small town. They approached the hill section of Burlington with old, large, Victorian homes, many of which had been quite unfortunately turned into apartment buildings to support the college's housing needs.

They then pulled into a virtually empty parking lot by

the library, and Kristin parked. "It'll be quick and easy, students aren't here yet."

Shelly and Emil followed Kristin across the green, heading for the rear of a large red stone building that looked like it had been built in the 19th century.

A decade or so prior Shelly had visited Henry's office with Kristin, she forgot for what exactly, probably to pick up something, but still couldn't remember exactly where it was.

They circled to the front and entered through the large main double doors, and ascended the granite stairs on the right to the third floor, not seeing a soul as they went.

"Here." Kristin stopped at a relatively flimsy-looking brown and old door halfway down the hall. The large window offered a view of the room behind. A single wooden desk with an antique lamp sat in front of the window at the back, a bookcase along each wall, and a weathered leather chair tucked into a back corner.

Kristin reached for the knob and attempted a twist, but it wouldn't budge. "Shit."

"Think there's someone that will let us in?" Emil looked each way wondering if there might be a receptionist of some kind with access to keys.

"Fuck that."

Emil watched, initially not comprehending Shelly's movements as she tucked her arms into her t-shirt and shifted her body like Houdini escaping a straight jacket. After only a few seconds her arms emerged again, her right hand holding her bra.

"Let's fucking do this," she said as she looked at her friend.

Shelly placed the slightly padded portion of the cup of her bra against the bottom right corner of the window and then gave it a solid and quick jab.

The delicate glass shattered where she struck, impressively quietly, into the room.

She dusted off the cup then reached inside, turned the knob, and opened the door as she looked to Kristin, "Never burn your bra."

"Uh," Emil felt uncomfortable with the sudden realization he was an accomplice in a breaking and entering. "What about that?" He asked as he pointed to the obvious hole, nervous that anyone that happened to walk by would notice and call the police.

Shelly, twisted her lips in thought as she looked around.

"Here," she crossed the hall, her black bra in hand, to a pink sheet of paper taped to the opposite wall advertising a summer barbecue that passed a month ago. She removed it, careful to keep the masking tape intact, and returned to the glass where she covered the hole tightly.

She gave Emil a *problem-solved* smile and followed Kristin in, where she, through some womanly magic, tucked her arms back into her shirt and placed the bra back on.

The window fix didn't make Emil feel much better, and he did his best to hide his anxiety over it as he took his place in the small office — closing the door behind him. "What are we looking for?"

"Just anything," Kristin said as she scanned the top of her father's desk, and Emil checked the bookcase closest to him.

The desk looked decades old and handcrafted, with two drawers on the right.

She picked up the framed family photo that sat toward the left. "The fair."

Shelly and Emil appeared at her side to look at it.

Elizabeth knelt down next to a young Kristin, a lighted Ferris wheel behind them.

Kristin remembered that day well. The late summer Champlain Valley Fair, a tradition for her family, along with virtually everyone else in the state. She didn't much care for the rides, though did love all the lights at night — which is why she always asked her parents to go late. She really wanted the fair food, the cotton candy and funnel cakes, and to play the games for giant stuffed animals or real live goldfish.

"You should take that, it's cute." Emil felt he threw caution to the wind as he suggested what might, or might not be, theft.

"Yeah," Shelly agreed.

"I will." Kristin placed it down and focused her attention on the drawers. She pulled the bottom one to find a few file folders laying flat, which she quickly rifled through, and noting nothing of significance she shut it and opened the top.

There only a pile of papers that all appeared to be either graded exams or old syllabi.

"Nothing." She slid it shut and turned to the bookcase at her left as Emil and Shelly looked around the room.

"I'm not seeing anything, Kris," Shelly threw up her arms a bit. "But that's a good thing, right? Your parents were happy."

With her hands now on her hips as she looked around, Kristin quietly nodded.

"Just regular business stuff," Emil shared as he dragged a finger across the spines of books.

"Yeah...yeah, regular stuff. No surprises."

"I get it, you had to look. To know for yourself." Shelly reached over and rubbed Kristin's right arm.

Kristin picked the photo of her and her mother back up and headed for the door. "Let's go."

Emil closed the door behind them as he followed, checking to ensure that no broken glass remained visible from the outside.

They descended the stairs and crossed the doors to the outside without incident.

The University's green sat largely vacant, save for three students with backpacks in place who either took summer classes or were a part of the academic medical center that abutted UVM.

Kristin navigated through the meandering campus roads to head back to Shelburne, "Thanks, guys, I really appreciate you both supporting me through that. I know it was weird."

"Of course, honey." Emil reached over and gently squeezed her right hand that rested on her leg.

"Any opportunity to be lady MacGyver I'm there."

Kristin smiled and looked up at the rearview mirror to see her friend, "I can't fucking believe you used your bra to break in!"

"Tits are like a superpower. I learned that in middle school."

"What would your superhero name be then?" Kristin asked jokingly.

"Hmm, maybe Wonder Tits."

"Juggernaut." Emil offered.

The group had a laugh at the absurd solution Shelly had found.

Back at her parents, Kristin placed the photo from her father's office on a small end table in the living room and then went to the closet in the spare bedroom for the album of photos dedicated to her growing up. She wanted to put the little road trip behind her, and focus on finding photos for Emil to use for the funeral. Kristin decided she'd sit with her small support team and flip through the album — perhaps it would make her feel close to her parents one more time.

Kristin sat on the living room couch, between Emil and Shelly, with the book on her lap, the television off, and room quiet.

She started on the first page and worked her way through, showing photos of her as a newborn being held by her mother, her father leaning into the picture. There were the typical shots of bath time, playing with stuffed animals, with people she hadn't seen for years, and with others she didn't even recognize. There was her holding up the teddy bear, Buttons, that she had just finished making, and another covered in cake icing at her 8th birthday party after her friend Abby had mushed it on her. A number of photos were taken by a body of water, not surprising given the proximity to Lake Champlain.

The album ended around the time she went to high school.

Along the way they selected four photos to enlarge and place by the front of the church. One of the day her parents brought her home from the hospital, a nice one taken by the lake with her and her father fishing, one of her and her mother playing dress up, and the last a shot from Henry and Elizabeth's wedding that they found in another album.

Emil took the photos with him. He'd have them scanned and enlarged at a local office supply chain store after his visit to the Farely Funeral Home.

The women took the opportunity to have a couple drinks on the front porch. The day being warm, they made vodka seltzers with lemon. Kristin couldn't remember ever drinking so frequently. She set aside the urge to judge herself for it.

They sat quietly at first, having reminisced already when they had lunch together. They watched birds come to the feeder just off the center of the lawn and listened to the local radio station that streamed from Shelly's cell phone. Its small speakers making the music tinny and without bass.

"Mind if I go get today's paper from the mailbox?"

Kristin nodded in approval.

Shelly put her drink down and walked the length of the driveway, passing out of sight, to the blue box by the road dedicated to the Burlington Free Press. She was gone a bit longer than Kristin had expected to just retrieve it, but she figured her friend wanted to ensure nothing in it was related to the accident and so might cause her undue stress.

Shelly appeared again, and crossed the yard, not bothering with the walkway.

She returned to her seat and held up the paper, confirming what Kristin had been thinking, "The obituary for the Hubbertons is in it. Do you want to read it?"

"Do you mind reading it to me?"

"Yeah, sure." Shelly flipped to the back, "It's a pretty short one. *Peter and Lila (Joquenne) Hubberton, both 55, died in an unfortunate accident on Sunday, June 20th, 2021. Peter, the son of William and Annabelle Hubberton of Monkton, a 1987 graduate of the University of Vermont, ran a successful dentistry practice in Burlington for the last 22 years. Lila, the daughter of Ike and Doris Joquenne of Rutland, a 1987 graduate of Goddard College, was a partner at a local marketing agency. Both Peter and Lila were known for their generosity, particularly with locally-run charities focused on children's health. Peter is survived by his mother, and his sister Betsy. Lila is survived by her parents, and her three brothers, Carl, John, and Roland."*

Shelly folded the paper and took a few seconds to look up at her friend, not wanting to press a point that didn't need to be. Kristin did her the favor of saying out loud what they both were thinking.

"No kids."

Shelly just shook her head, briefly so as not to emphasize it.

Kristin turned her attention to the large front yard and the surrounding trees, as if something were there worth focusing on. She looked down quickly, then to her glass, which she snatched up and took a big sip from.

"Well, maybe I'm fucking brain damaged."

"You were just in an accident, a really bad one both physically and emotionally. Who knows what happened, or why you saw what you saw. Just don't be hard on yourself about it." She reached over, placing her hand on her friend's forearm that rested on the Adirondack chair.

Shelly let a moment pass before sharing the rest, "There is one more thing it said."

"What's that?"

"The funeral for Peter and Lila is tomorrow, at the Unitarian Church."

Kristin had to take a moment to process why Shelly had held that bit of information to share, when she understood she looked at her friend questioningly, "You think I should go?"

Shelly held Kris' arm a little more firmly as

reassurance, "It might be good. I'm sure some part of you, I know you, you're a very empathetic person, feels for them too. It could help you heal. And…and I'll go with you."

Kristin's eyes darted around, looking for some sort of answer. "I don't know."

"Hey, it's up to you, Kris. But it would be easy, I would make sure it was as easy as possible for you. We wouldn't talk to anyone, just walk in at the last minute and sit in the very back. Listen to the services, and then be the first ones to leave. No one will even know we're there."

Kristin wasn't sure why, but she found herself nodding. "Yeah, okay."

"K. It's settled then. You can decide if you want Emil to come."

Having Emil there, she thought, would add more stress. Though he brought her peace she thought three people would bring more unwanted attention to their presence than just two.

* * *

"Please, come in."

The Farely Funeral Home sat in the hill section of Burlington, in an old Victorian home. At some point they had purchased the lot behind them, demolished whatever had been there, and turned it into parking. It had been in Burlington for ages and meticulously maintained. Emil felt as though he were traveling back in time as he entered.

Wood accents along each threshold to large adjacent rooms greeted him, along with an ornate wooden banister on the stairs leading up.

The man closing the heavy door behind him introduced himself, "Charles Farely." He smiled a smile that that only comes from funeral attendants. To Emil they always seemed knowing, like the universe held no mysteries.

Charles stood about 5'10", and maybe in his mid-forties. He seemed fit enough to pass as in his thirties and with black hair, likely dyed. His suit pressed and spotless.

"Emil Gifford, nice to meet you."

"Likewise."

The man motioned up the stairs just to their left, "Our office is up."

To Emil's surprise the stairs didn't creek at all. They felt and sounded solid under his feet. Along the wall hung small framed photos, probably of the Farely family as they all were taken around the home.

"Straight ahead."

At the top, Emil saw the open door to a room, brightly lit by both a window and a couple of floor-standing lamps. He could also see a large, and very heavy-looking, old desk with a small laptop and planning book on it.

He entered.

The extra large room, he thought, must be the result of breaking down the wall to what was an adjacent room to his right as it all seemed far too big for houses of the time. In that extended area were arranged six caskets, two vertical rows of three in what must be custom display cases. Each was open to present the white plush interiors.

Charles entered behind him, "Please, sit."

Emil sat on the right of the two chairs at the front of the desk as Charles circled it, sat, and opened the laptop.

He turned to Emil, his attention purposeful and focused on him, "First, I'm very sorry for Kristin and your loss. It's very sad, very sudden. I'm sure it has been difficult."

"Yes, thank you. Kristin's still a little in shock."

"Of course, and it's incredibly thoughtful of you to handle the arrangements. I'm sure she appreciates it."

"Thanks."

He opened his planner, turned a page, and went from the paper to the screen and back.

"Did you bring the information we discussed over the phone?"

"Oh, yes." Emil dug his phone from his pocket, unlocked it, and opened the notes app. "I've got the birth dates, death dates, socials…"

"Great, if it's easy for you you can certainly email what you're looking at." Charles slid a business card from a holder at the side of the desk and passed it to Emil like he had done this a thousand times before.

"Sure, that's fine."

"Fantastic. Now a few questions to help us prepare. I apologize upfront, as some we've discussed already, however, I want to ensure everything is correct."

"K."

"Kristin has decided to forgo a traditional memorial service or wake?"

Emil allowed himself to show some disappointment in the decision. It was Kristin's to make, no doubt, but he couldn't help but feel for others in the family who might want time to get together to share stories and reminisce. He told himself that in a few weeks he'd approach the subject with her, and suggest a trip back to Vermont to bring the family together with her. "That's right. We're just doing the funeral at Saint Mark's."

"Alright, and we've begun the embalming process, and will need you to select a casket."

Charles stood and motioned to the selection, "We do have a catalog that you can browse with a greater variety, but these will give you a sense of various options."

Emil followed the man and stared at the caskets. They

all looked virtually the same to him with just variations in color and seemingly minor details. The bottom two were clearly wooden, though, while the others appeared metal.

Charles pointed at the top caskets, "To give you a sense of our organization, the top are the most expensive on display at about four thousand each. The middle are two-thousand, and the bottom about one."

Emil nodded. He had no idea what a common or fair cost would actually be, but also knew he wouldn't be haggling.

"The top left is all bronze, fully locking…"

Emil interrupted the man, "What's your most popular?"

He nodded knowingly, "Here," he tapped the right middle casket. It had a deep silver finish and some tastefully ornate features. "It's stainless steel, full rubber gasket, locking, with a full swing bar handle. Tasteful. Not extravagant."

"Okay, let's do that one."

"Two?"

"What's that?"

"Two of them. For Mr. and Mrs. Fuller?"

"Oh, sorry, yes."

Charles led them back to the office area where the men returned to their respective seats. He took a note in his pad.

Emil looked down at the Oriental rug under his feet, asking his question without making eye contact. "Can I ask you something, Charles?"

"Of course."

"That other couple, the Hubbertons, are you coincidentally handling them as well?"

"It just so happens we are."

"Is it just them? The couple? I mean, was there

someone else brought in with them? A little girl perhaps?"

"No, just the couple. I'm unaware of any child."

Emil nodded only slightly.

"And, the Fullers, they're here right? I mean, in this building."

"Their bodies, yes."

An uncomfortable feeling crept slowly through Emil's body. He awkwardly shifted his body in his seat with his hands pushed against the seat cushion, making it apparent to Charles that Emil had more on his mind. "I know this will sound like a strange question, but was there anything odd about the Hubbertons' bodies?"

Charles didn't blink, his professionalism true, "Odd?"

Emil took a deep breath in before speaking, "Yeah, just anything unusual, maybe unexpected in some way."

"I'm afraid I'm not the one working the Hubbertons, that would be my brother. I haven't seen them, though likely wouldn't be able to say so if I had. Now," Charles redirected the conversation, "let's continue with the Fullers."

Emil's thoughts drowned out Charles' words. He wondered if he could ask to see the Fullers, to have a moment with them alone to say a sort of goodbye, and use that as an opportunity to check out the Hubbertons. Granted, he may not know what to look for, but perhaps something would stand out about them, or their belongings which he assumed would be in the same room.

That would put him in a precarious position. If found he'd at the very least be asked to leave. Possibly they'd even refuse to continue serving the Fullers, which would rightfully anger Kristin. Worst case, the Farely's would call the police, and perhaps charges would be pressed against him around trespassing or something to do with disturbing bodies.

He couldn't risk it, not for an unknown result. Not without a better understanding of what to look for or what he might actually find.

Resigned to complete the task of organizing the services, he left the thoughts behind.

* * *

Shelly left shortly before dinner, joking how if she didn't help out a little with the kids she'd end up a single mother. Emil and Kristin ate one of Shelly's prepared meals, fought through a comedy involving some kid and adult magically swapping bodies, then watched the day turn to night on the front porch.

They sat quietly for a while, each checking messages and sending quick replies on their phones.

"I wonder if my parents did this after dinner, sit on the porch."

Emil looked up from his phone, "I bet they did. It's so peaceful."

With the overhang, they couldn't see much of the night sky, but the moon must have still been large given the relative brightness of the yard.

"Do you think they would have sat out back on the deck though? I bet on nights with no moon they could really see the stars."

"Hmm, good question."

Kristin suddenly felt frantic, her anxiety hitting her quickly, "Did you lock the doors?"

Emil wasn't sure he had, but he felt admitting that might make Kristin feel worse, "Yes, of course. I'll double-check."

He went inside, first to the side door in the mudroom. Locked.

Then to the sliding door. Closed but unlocked.

He looked out into the backyard as he twisted the lock shut quietly. He couldn't see anything and wondered again if this thing with the young girl in the accident was something in Kristin's mind that she might struggle with for a long time. Emil loved her, and if that were the case would certainly help her through it. The thought, though, of Kristin feeling haunted by some imaginary specter made him feel even more sorry for her. They say time heals all wounds, but if she felt regularly spooked then time would do nothing but reopen them.

Emil returned to the front porch, "Yeah, locked up."

"K, good. Thank you."

They sat a while longer, talking about the funeral plans, and the fact that Kristin didn't want a wake — she realized that was selfish, but they were her parents, no one else's. And she figured someone in the family would open their homes to whoever wanted to gather after the funeral.

They joked lightly about moving to Vermont, taking over the house, and maybe opening up a general store in some small town.

The night grew darker, and Kristin more tired.

"I'm going to go to bed, babe. Feel free to stay up if you want," Kristin stood and brought her empty glass with her inside.

Emil followed, locking the front door behind him.

Kristin went upstairs and into the small bathroom to get ready for bed. She placed her phone down on the toilet seat before starting with washing her face.

Emil took a few minutes to put the dishes in the dishwasher before heading up as well. He went into Kristin's old room, where he had placed his bag, to gather things for the night before heading to the spare bedroom.

Kristin patted her face dry before taking her toothbrush from the plastic cup on the sink. Before she had the chance to collect the toothpaste, the power went out — all lights went off without a flicker. With the shade of the small bathroom window drawn, she found herself in complete darkness.

"Shit."

The idea that perhaps the electricity bill was past due came to her mind, but she quickly dismissed it as there hadn't been any warning, typically messaged via a red envelope in the mail. There would have to be another cause, perhaps the entire street out from some squirrel getting into a transformer which happened from time to time.

About to turn to feel her way down the hall, the lights shot back on. Kristin saw herself in the mirror.

"Oh thank God."

Relieved she grabbed the toothpaste, only for the lights to flicker and go out again.

"Fuck."

She started to feel frightened, not liking the darkness and the sense of being both alone and vulnerable.

She yelled, "Emil!"

The light over the small round mirror came to life again.

Kristin screamed in terror as she saw in the mirror, standing just behind and to her left, the girl from the accident. Her eyes dark and vacant, expressionless with her mouth closed and lax, her black straight hair down the back and sides of her head.

Then the lights went out again, and Kristin turned to her right to race passed her and down the hall to the spare room. She moved so quickly that her left leg slipped down one of the stairs, sending her to the ground. The adrenaline pumping all sense of pain away, she bounced back up as if nothing had happened, still moving forward, and dashed into the bedroom where she slammed the door shut behind her.

"Kristin, what's going on?" Emil's voice came from somewhere in the dark room. She couldn't see where with the blinds closed.

Her heart raced. Kristin's voice stuttered through heavy breaths, "She's here. That girl, she…she was in the bathroom. I saw…saw her."

Emil forced himself to stay calm. He reasoned quickly, a strength he developed over time. Either this was a hallucination of Kristin's, in which case there was no real danger, or that girl really was in the house, in which case… well, in which case *what the fuck was happening*? Playing it safe meant treating the situation as the worst-case scenario.

"Okay, hold on." Kristin heard the bed creak as Emil stood from it.

He felt the wall until he found the first window and he raised the blind, sending moonlight into a portion of the room. With that, he easily found the other window and raised it as well.

He turned to find Kristin at the door, standing and pressing her back against it to hold it shut.

She pointed to the small dresser just a few feet from her, "Move that here. There's no lock on the door. Have to barricade."

Emil did as she asked, shimmying the furniture over and softly lowering it to its side in front of the door as she moved out of the way.

Kristin stood at the center of the room, her attention focused, "Where's your phone?"

"What?" Emil looked at her, his back now to the door.

"Your phone, where is it?"

"It's in your old room."

"What?" She sounded shocked.

Emil threw his arm toward the wall to his left, the other side of it being the room she grew up in. "I put it down and grabbed some stuff to bring in here."

"God damn it, Emil! We need a phone!" Kristin was panicking now as she paced a small section of the floor.

"For what?"

She stopped, "For what? To call the fucking cops!"

Emil slowly nodded, realizing to play along with whatever was going on also meant playing it out, and the logical next step for any intruder would be to call the authorities.

"Well, where's your phone?"

"In the bathroom," she said clearly pissed.

"Is there a phone in the room?"

She shook her head, "My parents got rid of their landline years ago."

Emil thought. Being on the second floor, with the front porch just out the window, meant an easy descent. Certainly doable if needed, but the house wasn't burning down. An odd little girl didn't seem to justify abandoning ship.

He went to Kristin and put his hands in hers, leading her to the bed where they sat. "Look, we're safe in here. And I'm not going to let anyone hurt you, let's just wait. If enough time goes by with nothing, I'll go out there and check the house. You would just need to stay in here, hold the door shut and wait for me. Okay?"

"You said the doors were locked." Kristin's anger sounded in her tone. All she wanted from Emil was to lock the doors. She knew he wasn't the hero type, not the big strong man who'd take on attackers, but the least he could do was lock the fucking doors.

Before he could answer they both heard the noises.

First a singular and soft bump somewhere in the hall, like flesh tapping a wall. At any other time they might think it the house shifting a bit as the temperature changed. Emil thought that might be the case — with their senses on high alert, anything might be taken as proof positive.

But then came the unmistakable.

Footsteps, starting off somewhere further, like down the hall, the bathroom perhaps. They grew louder before stopping altogether, at what sounded like the door to their room.

Only seconds passed, but to Kristin and Emil it seemed an eternity as neither dared speak, move, or even breathe.

Then the footsteps again, this time receding, and then the telltale sound of them slowly descending the stairs.

Kristin thought she heard what sounded like the deck's sliding door open and close, but no windows in the room offered a view of the back.

The electricity sparked back to life.

Kristin dropped her head to her hands as she fell to the floor sobbing and shaking.

Emil, in a virtual daze at experiencing what Kristin had been communicating all along, dropped to sit next to her. He wrapped his arms around her and held her tight.

It's all real, he thought to himself. *This girl was in the accident, but nobody believes Kristin. She's...after her. Or haunting her. It's insane.*

"Well figure this out. Together."

CHAPTER EIGHT
2021, Thursday June 24th

Neither slept well.

After checking the house together, double-checking the locks, including those on the windows, and grabbing their cell phones and charging cables, they returned to the bedroom.

Emil, without saying a word, put the dresser back in front of the door. He couldn't say what Kristin saw, but he *knew* what he heard.

Afraid to not have an easy view of the bedroom door, they both lay on their backs and held hands under the blanket. Each only fell asleep after losing all their energy to fight off the exhaustion.

At 5:30 a.m. Kristin's happy-toned alarm went off. She groaned as she reached to the floor and dragged the device toward her. She turned it off and rolled over to Emil, wincing from the pain of her shoulder before putting one arm on his chest. His eyes slowly opened to meet her's and he pulled one arm out from the covers for a hug.

They rose from bed and Emil returned the dresser to its rightful spot along the wall. "Kept you safe," he said half-jokingly — fully aware what kept them safe from whatever that was was his lack of bravery to just confront the girl.

Kristin laughed a little as she gathered clothes for the long day, "Knight in shining armor?"

Emil shrugged, "Never been so afraid of a little girl."

"Let's not talk about it." Without much thought, Kristin opened the door to the hallway and found it empty. As plain and unexciting as it should have been.

"I'll check the house," Emil said as he left the room first.

"I'm going to take a shower," Kristin followed behind.

Emil started the steps down and called out behind, "Want anything from the kitchen?"

"No thanks, honey." Kristin's voice sounded tired.

She entered her parents' room and went to the far wall to the right first where she opened the two shades to get some natural light into the room.

It's funny how human eyesight works — we are strong at pattern matching, so when something breaks a pattern our eyes just lock on. And Kristin's did. As she turned from the windows her eyes immediately went to the bureau where that misshapen teddy bear, Buttons, typically rested. Now, though, just an empty space. The other items, small perfume bottles, an open jewelry box, and a decorative cross from their trip to Ireland, sat undisturbed. But no Buttons.

Kristin looked around the room quickly, then checked each side of the piece of furniture. Nothing.

She thought about the last time she came into her

parents' room and saw the bear. She noted it to herself and saw it on the bureau. She wondered if she had moved it. Did she pick it up? Did she move it? Did she even touch it?

No. She was positive she didn't touch it.

That meant either Emil did, which he had no reason to, or…or that girl took it.

"Emil?" Kristin called out loudly, "Emil!" she called again louder.

She heard his steps approaching then climbing the stairs quickly, and she could see him look toward her old room before turning to the master. He appeared at the door, shaking his head with his eyes wide in worry, "What? What's wrong?"

Kristin pointed to the spot where the bear had been, as if Emil would even know what she meant.

"There? It's gone."

"What? What's gone?"

"Buttons."

"What's 'Buttons'?"

She dropped her arm to her side, exasperated and now clear that Emil had no idea what she was talking about, and so obviously didn't move it. "A stuffed animal I made for my parents," her defeated tone caused Emil to enter and stand closer to her. "It was here, it was here before. She took it."

He looked at the top of the dresser and could see where something had obviously been as a thin layer of dust surrounded a spot that lacked any at all.

"Okay," he reached out and took Kristin's hand, "we're going to figure this out."

Kristin didn't say a word, just let him go as she went to the bathroom to get ready for the day. It's not that she didn't believe him, or at least that he'd help her, but that it all seemed so impossible. What were they going to do? Somehow track down this unknown girl, someone who authorities say wasn't even in the accident, who doesn't even exist? Were they going to set up a trap? Confront this nightmare?

Bullshit.

Bullshit, she knew it. She didn't know where to begin, and Emil, as wonderful as he was and as much as she loved him, was no Marvel's Avenger.

Shelly arrived at 8 a.m., dressed in black for the services.

Kristin, already dressed in the most appropriate clothes she brought (a slim black skirt and a blue blouse she had in case they went to a nice restaurant) waited in the driveway.

Emil didn't go with them but planned on leaving the house to wrap up some things for the Fuller's services, not feeling like staying in the place alone after the experience of the previous night.

Kristin exhaled loudly and brushed her skirt with her hands as if it held something to actually brush off.

"You look tired, you okay?" Shelly asked as they drove up Route 7.

"Didn't sleep great." Kristin didn't feel like getting into the details of their evening. Not that she didn't want her friend to know, in fact Emil's hearing footsteps reinforced what she had been experiencing. She just didn't have the energy and decided to approach the subject later.

For the rest of the drive the two remained mostly silent, though the sun and warm day made the short trip pleasurable.

The light traffic, being after rush hour, made the drive easy and they arrived at the iconic church at the top of

Burlington's Church Street early.

Shelly parked toward the lot entrance and checked her watch. "Fifteen minutes. Let's wait until two minutes of, then we'll go in. Be right on time, sit in the back. Sound good?"

"Yeah." Kristin fidgeted with her hands. She thought about the couple, who were her parents' age, and the terrible scene. She thought about her own family, torn apart in that accident, and their services to happen tomorrow. A not insignificant part of her wanted to just take Emil and return to Dallas. Go back to work like nothing happened. Leave the house to become a slowly deteriorating memorial. Skip the sympathy and mourning process entirely.

"K, let's go." Shelly turned the car off and opened the door, the day's heat entering the previously air-conditioned cabin.

They walked hand-in-hand, Shelly a half-step ahead, and Kristin's gaze downward not wanting to catch anyone's eye or risk anyone actually knowing she was in that accident. Would they blame her? She knew pointing blame to be a natural reaction, and even part of the healing process, but she certainly didn't want to cause a stir.

It went as planned as they took the few steps up to the door, nodded to the attendants, and signed the guest book, Kristin deciding to use her real name, that sat on a table in the foyer.

After signing they turned to the large doors that led into the chapel. An usher at each door opened one to allow them in.

Kristin took a couple of steps in before stopping at two large photo prints of the deceased, the doors shutting behind her and Shelly.

They stood at the back of a virtually packed church with rows of natural wood pews and tall white pillars that led up to the arched ceiling.

Shelly looked to her friend at her right, standing by the photos of Peter and Lila. Peter's was an obvious shot from his work, likely for an advertisement, as he appeared posed with his light blue face mask hanging from his neck and his pearly whites showing.

Lila's photo showed her at what may have been a party. She sat at a long table, with only the shoulders of the people on either side of her in the picture. She held a drink up to the camera, a happy smile on her face and an empty but dirty plate in front of her.

Shelly grabbed Kristin's arm gently, and stepped closer, "What is it?"

"Oh, nothing. Just wanted to see them." Kristin turned and Shelly led them to the closest pew, the seats at the very last row. With only one other person in the pew, an older gentleman possibly there discretely as well, they felt anonymous enough.

At the front were the caskets, just about a foot apart.

The attendees were naturally quiet and many wiped at their tears.

The Reverend, or priest, Kristin wasn't sure exactly his title, took the podium and spoke a bit about loss. About how new beginnings are what happen at times like this. That Peter and Lila were still with us.

Then he introduced Betsy Hubberton, a woman who appeared about 60. Her mostly gray hair up in a bun, her heavy body struggling up the two small steps. She didn't dress in dark clothes like everyone else, but instead had a white skirt and blue jacket over a light blue blouse. Kristin felt the choice odd for the woman's large frame, but she appeared classy and natural.

The woman pulled a notecard from her jacket and placed it on the podium. She spoke with a soft and soothing voice. A natural confidence. She spoke like someone who would be your favorite teacher.

"Being an older sister to Peter is a highlight of my life. Watching him grow, mature, and become someone to be proud of was a thrill. As his sister, I gave him a fair share of grief, and he certainly returned it with interest."

The audience chuckled.

"But we were close throughout life, and that didn't change when he met Lila, who I came to love as a sister of my own. I remember when Peter introduced me to her, he was a Junior at UVM and had met her while hiking. To say he beamed is an understatement. I feared she might break his heart to a point of no return he was so happy. But they stayed strong together too, loved each other…were inseparable."

She shifted and cleared her throat, "To say they were meant for each other doesn't do them justice. And as odd as it sounds, I'm glad neither of them had to experience life again without the other. Happy times outnumbered the sad, for sure, but when that sadness did come they held each other for support."

Betsy leaned back a bit to compose herself, and when she returned to the microphone Kristine could see the smile on her face was one of true appreciation for the couple, "After they married I never worried about them. They really were forever. And when the unthinkable happened, when Kacey died on that damn beach…"

Shelly quickly turned her head and asked softly of Kristin, "Kacey?"

Betsy continued, "I saw the two circle each other like

true heroes. When Lila felt down, Peter picked her up. And when Peter was down, Lila lifted him. They say the death of a child is something that can break marriages, and Kacey's drowning certainly hurt them beyond words, but their love was one that many of us don't experience in life."

She continued, but Shelly and Kristin now eyeballed each other. Hungry for more information it became difficult to sit in silence.

Peter and Lila had a daughter, Kacey, who drowned. There was a daughter. But…but that couldn't be the girl who was at the accident and now terrorizing Kristin. Right? She'd be older…and dead.

The friends looked at each other, communicating their thoughts and confusion without words.

At the very least they needed to know more before jumping to conclusions or excluding any possibility.

"Somehow Peter and Lila found happiness again after the tragedy. I'm sure through hard work and love. And they started a charity to help others. They kept photos of Kacey up, and her room intact. I always had the sense that they kept her a part of their lives."

She paused again and took a deep breath, "When I heard the news my heart sank of course. But then I thought about the three of them back together."

Betsy tucked the notecard back into her jacket pocket, "I'll leave you with something a friend of our family shared with us a number of years ago. He said, 'Masters learn to live in the moment. The great ones can make a moment last a lifetime.'"

With that, she shifted her weight from one leg to the other to turn, braced herself with the short metal railing along the steps, and took each slowly as she returned to her seat.

The official called for communion service and the women used that as their cue to leave. Kristin felt terribly rude for exiting before the procession of family, but also thought very few people would have seen them escape that way since they sat so far back.

Once outside they hustled down the concrete steps and virtually ran to the car in the parking lot at the side.

Shelly started the van and backed out of the spot without even looking. Both felt like they were making a getaway. She turned left onto Pearl Street and pushed it to the red light at the intersection with a Chinese restaurant, deli, and a nondescript office building at the corners. She tapped the steering wheel anxiously.

"You really saw a girl?"

"Yes. I saw her, Shell. She was there. I didn't tell you about last night because I was so tired, but I saw her again, and she was in the house. In the bathroom with me! I think Emil didn't believe me, but we holed up in the spare bedroom and he heard her footsteps, Shell. He actually heard her walking around the house and then leaving."

"Holy shit."

The light turned green and Shelly got her large vehicle up to speed as quickly as she could.

"Yeah. I thought maybe I was just seeing things. Like maybe she was some reflection of me. She looks like she's younger than me by 20 or so years. Maybe my mind was working through some sense of loss, bringing me back to a time when I lived closer to my parents."

"Right, that kind of makes sense."

"It does, but fuck it. It's bullshit because she was real. She was there. I'm not entertaining another thought about it. I'm not crazy. It's not some brain damage. And now…

now to learn, well, the Hubbertons had a daughter. Who else could it have been?"

They came to another light and Shelly quickly turned right, heading south to return to the Fuller's house.

"Maybe someone they were babysitting."

"Then why is no one looking for her? Why isn't there a missing person's? Why didn't that detective ever reach out?"

Shelly had to think about that. If what Kristin told her was true, then that girl was in the accident. She left the scene as no one else was reported injured. And no body was found. No one is missing. So there was one other possibility.

"Maybe whoever it is found their way home. Right? No one is missing, they walked home."

"Okay, then what?"

"Then…then her parents or friends or whatever would either check her out, cleaned her up because she says she's okay, or take her to the hospital."

They go through a series of stop signs before reaching Route 7 again to take them back to Kristin's old home.

"Neither of which is very satisfactory an explanation," Kristin's logic skills kicked in. She felt back in her office in Dallas, using what she felt was her greatest strength, her mind. "Whomever she went to wouldn't just accept that she was fine, it was a horrific impact and they would bring her to a hospital. Unless…well unless they were hiding something. Otherwise, she goes to the hospital. The doctors would ask her what happened, she'd tell them and they'd connect the accident to me. It would then be in the paper."

"Unless she had a concussion. Maybe she didn't remember anything, couldn't tell them what happened."

"Maybe. Possible. But they wouldn't just let it go. They'd look into it, they'd backtrack. Ask her friends and family where she was that day, what she was doing. They'd figure out she was with the Hubbertons."

"Right."

"Nothing else makes any real sense."

"But, Kris, you have to admit it still doesn't make any sense," both women talked excitedly, feeling like they were solving a mystery. "You're just accepting that this dead girl, Kacey, who died who knows when, was somehow in that car and nobody but her parents knew."

Kristin nodded. That was very clearly an issue for her theory, but for some reason it felt true.

Shelly brought the car to a stop at a red light, the traffic a bit heavier from the lunch crowd. "Did that woman say how old Kacey was when she died?"

"I don't think so. The way she said it made me think she was young, like in elementary school. But maybe that's just my imagination visualizing her story."

"Yeah, plus she said she drowned, on a beach I think. That doesn't sound like an adult. What was that woman's name?"

"Betsy." When she saw Betsy take the podium with her blue top, she immediately started calling her *Betsy Blue* in her head. "Betsy Hubberton."

"She seemed like a nice lady."

"Yeah, she did."

The light turned green and after a few seconds of waiting for the cars in front of her to move, Shelly let off the brake and accelerated. "Maybe she'd talk to us."

Kristin took a moment to think. What would she learn? What could she learn? Maybe she was asking herself the wrong questions. Maybe she had no idea what she could learn. Maybe the right question was *what's next?* Talking to Betsy seemed a natural step.

"Maybe. But I think I should go alone."

Shelly agreed with the strategy, even though she wanted to remain involved. "Right."

"With just me she may feel more understanding, sympathetic. With both of us she might feel outnumbered, like defensive."

"Yeah."

"I can't wait to tell Emil."

The two remained fairly quiet after their plan had formed. As they entered Shelburne they started listing things to do. Google Kacey Hubberton, and Betsy. Look for obituaries, Facebook and Twitter profiles. Check all the blogging platforms. If they had to, they could start hitting up the city and town offices for birth or death certificates. They weren't even sure if that was something that would be shared with strangers, but she would try if necessary.

They reached the house and Kristin went straight upstairs for her laptop, while Shelly made two very stiff, very tall, drinks.

As they settled at the dining room table to start their research, with pen and paper at the ready, Emil emerged with his rental car.

He entered the house with a couple bags of groceries, even though they probably didn't need anything, to an excited Kristin and Shelly. They eagerly had him sit at the table as they explained what they learned from Betsy. Shelly also gently grilled him about the previous night, Emil confirming that without a shadow of a doubt, someone was in the house when the power went out.

Emil slid the laptop over to himself. Kristin always complimented him on his Googling skills.

"Okay, let's start with 'Kacey Hubberton'," Kristin demanded.

He performed the search, and thankfully no one famous came up. If they had, then the challenge would be excluding all of those results as they would dominate the search. They would then need to narrow down to places, like *Vermont*, or other ways like *obituary*, and *death*.

"Easy." The ease actually surprised him. Apparently, *Hubberton* wasn't that common a name, and after excluding *Hubberdton*, which Google wanted to include as it seemed more common, Kacey's obituary came up first.

He read it aloud, "*Middlebury, VT - On August 6th, 2010, Kacey Hubberton passed unexpectedly at the age of 9. Loved by so many for her unbridled enthusiasm, and ruthless good nature, she will be sorely missed. Kacey had many friends from school, activities like soccer and dance, and from the small neighborhood. Kacey will be remembered by her cousins Gabriel, Jacob, Peggy, and Alice. Her parents, Peter and Lila, will never forget her spirit and sweet nature, and she will never leave their hearts.*"

Kristin became more anxious, "Okay, now click *Back* and see what else there is."

"Wait, first…" Emil opened a new tab in the browser and did a search for *august 6 2010 drowning Vermont*. Again the first result gave him what he wanted — an article about a drowning at a private beach, but at the time of publishing the name had not been released nor a body even discovered. The article detailed a young girl, at her parents' camp, swimming out a little too far. Her parents called out to her, but she got caught in something under the water. She went down, and sadly never came up again.

She died at nine, that was about ten years ago. "The

girl I saw could have been nine or ten."

Shelly and Emil looked at Kristin, believing but uncertain as it all seemed so impossible.

Kristin tapped the laptop, "Can you track down a photo of her?"

Emil went back to his original search of just her name and clicked over to the image results. There, a couple photos in, seemed a match. A thumbnail of a photo of a dozen or so kids.

He clicked on it and it took them to a page about a local soccer club, the 2010 Champlain Valley Cougars. The photo's caption listed each child in order from the back row forward.

There, just right of center and in the front row, sat Kacey Hubberton. The photo's small size made detail difficult, so Emil zoomed in a bit.

Kristin leaned closer, as did Shelly, for a better look at the now pixelated photo.

"That could be her." Kristin looked at Emil and Shelly, "I mean, it's not the best photo in the world. But yeah, that's her."

Emil exhaled loudly, pursing his lips in astonishment.

"You have to talk to Betsy." Shelly almost said it to herself.

"I'm going to call her. Tomorrow after the funeral."

* * *

For the remainder of the day they planned for the next, laying out clothes, Kristin wearing the same as she did for the Hubbertons' service. She also checked in with Mrs. Hawthorne. She apologized for the lack of communication beyond the initial email stating why she would be out, but noted things had been difficult in Vermont. Hawthorne wouldn't accept her apology and told her to take the time she needed.

Again Shelly left before dinner, with Emil and Kristin still working on the meals she had previously brought.

With more cloud cover, the night was darker than they had seen all week.

Kristin and Emil cuddled on the couch and watched whatever sitcoms happened to be on the first channel they turned to.

They sat in silence, but neither one paid much attention to the shows as their thoughts drifted.

Kristin's mind weaved through the past few days, looking for a thread of logic that might explain what she experienced. She broke down the events and ran through them obsessively. First, the decision to return to Vermont for the blood moon, or perhaps first was her father inviting her. What sounded like hooves in the garage of her work. The dream on the plane. The accident on the way to her father's friend's house. That girl who survived and seemed to want to get to her. The odd moose at the accident. Going to her parents' house, Button's disappearance. Learning about Kacey then seeing her outside, then actually getting in.

Whatever thread there might be eluded Kristin. She loved riddles and the process of solving them. She had little tricks she used to help, like challenging the natural assumptions one makes when reading one. Kristin tried with the events, but it didn't get her feeling any closer to what seemed like truth. Nothing made any sense to her.

Emil thought more about the next day's services. He selected the caskets and flowers, printed and delivered the photos, Kristin helped pick out the clothes for her parents, and he went with the standard readings. He notified everyone, with assistance from Kristin's aunt Ruth, and also let them know there wouldn't be any reception after. Emil handled it all with care. He worried, though, that he might have forgotten something, and only hoped that the day would be as easy for Kristin as it could be.

The most difficult part was delicately approaching Kristin about delivering the eulogy. "I wouldn't want you to regret not speaking later in life, but the decision is yours." She agreed but hated the thought. He offered to help her write it, but Kristin said she would "wing it." That was Kristin's way with certain things. She had more wisdom than her years at times and understood that sometimes what mattered was your approach — that you spoke authentically. She would consider the points she would want to make and decided she would leave finding a way to deliver them until she made her way to the podium.

"Do you think Shelly will bring her kids tomorrow?"

"Yeah," Kristin answered quietly but quickly.

"Really? Huh, she doesn't talk like they would behave well."

"Oh, that's just Shelly being Shelly. She's an amazing mother and raised those kids well. She just likes to joke. She'll sometimes say something that isn't true if she thinks she'll get a laugh out of you."

"Ah."

"Do you think everyone's mad at me for not having a reception?"

Emil thought that there could be some hurt feelings, but didn't want to admit it to her, "Well, that's your call. Don't worry about them."

"Yeah, but they might think I'm being unkind. Maybe someone is planning on one without me. You know, for the other family members."

It had crossed his mind, but he saw that now as not

only possible, but probable. "Yeah, maybe. They might want to get together to just talk about them. I understand that. But that doesn't mean you have to go if you don't want to."

"It would be awkward if they invited me and I didn't go."

"I'm sure they'd understand how difficult it is for you."

Kristin shifted her weight and placed her head on Emil's shoulder, "I just don't want all these people coming up to me saying how sorry they are. Is that odd?"

"No. It's the same reason you don't like your own birthday parties."

"Huh?"

"You just don't like the attention on you like that."

Kristin corrected him, "I don't like undeserved attention on me."

"Okay, that could be it."

It kind of ticked her off that Emil said "could", but she decided she was being sensitive and let it go.

"I'm going up to bed, will you come?" Kristin didn't want to be alone.

"Of course."

Kristin headed straight up and Emil double-checked the locks and turned off all the lights before following.

Without saying a word, both Emil and Kristin stayed close while upstairs, not wanting a repeat of the previous night. They brushed their teeth together and generally followed each other from room to room.

This time Emil didn't block the door, confident that the house was sealed tight, and he held Kristin until they fell asleep.

Emil woke at some point during the dark night and gently stretched his legs out. At home they had a king-size bed, and it wasn't entirely uncommon for them to not disturb each other's sleep. In the queen, however, he felt like he sensed where Kristin lie along with each of her movements.

Which is why something felt a little off when he woke.

He lifted his head a bit and looked over to the other side of the bed, simultaneously reaching with his right arm.

Empty.

Kristin wasn't in bed.

He sat up and looked around the room.

With the blinds down, the only light came from the digital clock on the nightstand.

2:39.

"Kristin?" He said softly.

No response.

"Kris?" Just a bit louder, but nothing.

She's probably just in the bathroom, the thought, but he felt the need to check to be sure.

Emil lifted the single sheet and swung his legs around. He stood and with a few steps was at the closed door. He gripped the knob and turned it, intentionally loudly wanting to announce his movement as not to scare Kristin.

The hallway sat dark, but he could see the outline of the open door to the bathroom. He thought it possible she was using the toilet in the dark, "Kristin?"

Nothing.

He approached the room anyway and flicked on the light.

Empty.

He kept that light on as he returned to the hall, going to the end to her parents' room.

Emil reached in and flipped the switch.

The empty room showed no telling sign of his

girlfriend. He ignored the master bathroom as he figured she would just use the one in the hall.

He quickly descended the stairs, turning on all the lights as he went as he entered the first level of the home.

"Kristin?" He called out more loudly but again received nothing in response.

He noticed the sliding glass door open, the deck and yard beyond in darkness.

Emil rushed to it and forced the screen door open without care. He ran to the edge and looked out, but without the back light on the area surrounding the house was draped in night.

He quickly returned to the house, racing inside to flick the deck light on. He turned back and took a big step to rush out, but stopped as fast as he could, stumbling a bit.

"Oh God," the horror caught in his throat.

On the back lawn, just forty feet or so from the deck stairs, near the dormant fire pit, stood Kristin. Wearing only a long gray nightshirt the skin of her arms and legs shined in the light. Her blond hair down and frazzled. The moon of her new necklace glistened, a lone beacon in the night.

Just inches in front of her stood a massive moose. It towered over her small frame. Its antlers stretched out from the sides of its head and reached upward imposingly. The large creature's antlers were molting, with sheaths of bloody flesh hanging from them like skin in the aftermath of a long and terrible battle.

The beast just stood there looking down at Kristin with steam rising from its nostrils.

Emil wanted to yell out but feared enraging the thing, and so called with just a whisper, "Kristin!"

She didn't budge.

"Kristin."

No response.

What now?

With Kristin unresponsive it meant either going for her, which would mean getting close to that giant creature that could stomp him to death, or somehow getting it to go away.

"Shoo! Go away!" Emil waved his arms toward the woods as if directing a plane on a tarmac.

With the beast not moving its attention from Kristin, Emil thought about getting some food from the kitchen to throw into the trees, but for the life of him couldn't think of what food specifically would be very enticing. After all, the thing would be more likely to actually eat the leaves off those same trees than anything likely in the kitchen.

"Go! Shoo!" He tried again.

This time the animal twisted its head toward Emil, the swaying of the shredded flesh causing some to shift and tear further downward.

Emil took a step back, though he could jump inside the house in two quick steps and slide the door shut before the moose could make it to the deck, he still felt unsafe.

The moose stepped around, slowly turning its body, and made its way to the wooded area.

"Jesus."

Emil, keeping his eyes on the massive animal retreating, cautiously took the few steps down and started his way to Kristin, his arms out to grab her quickly if needed.

"Kristin," he said again as he approached, but still only received silence in return.

He got close enough to grab her right arm, which he held tightly.

Holding her strong he took a step back and Kristin

followed, her weight moving with him seemingly as a physical response to prevent a fall but also not a deliberate attempt to walk with him.

Keeping his body facing the creature, who now crossed the treeline, he took faster steps, virtually dragging Kristin along.

He reached the stairs, wrapped his arms around his girlfriend, and lifted her, taking them quickly.

They reached the top and he carried her inside. He caught a glimpse of Kristin staring glassy-eyed when he placed her in a dining chair before turning to slide the glass door shut.

Through the door he could see the woods, the moose disappeared to somewhere beyond — but never saw the girl in the woods watching them silently, unmoving.

"Jesus Christ," he said loudly to himself in complete fear.

He locked the door but kept the light on, afraid of not being able to see what might be coming.

Emil turned to Kristin, dropping to his knees and placing his hands on her upper arms, "Kristin?" he said loudly.

Life returned to her eyes, "Emil?"

"What are you doing?" his voice just shy of frantic.

"What do you mean?"

"Why were you outside?"

Kristin's confusion grew, "I wasn't. Why am I downstairs?"

Emil felt her cold legs. He wondered how long she would have had to of been outside to get so cold. He also wondered if summer nights in Vermont typically were this frigid.

"You were just outside, I brought you in. Do you

remember?"

"What, no!" Kristin rubbed her head.

"You don't remember the moose?"

"Moose?" She genuinely sounded surprised.

"What do you remember last?"

She shook her head at first, her eyes looking around for some answer, "I got up from bed to go to the bathroom. I didn't turn on the light because I didn't want to wake you. Something…something out the window…I looked out, but I couldn't see anything. Something was there though, I could feel it."

Kristin looked at Emil with an expression of part helplessness part fright. She clutched the necklace. "Something was outside and I went to it."

"The moose, Kristin."

"I didn't see a moose. There was a moose? I was outside?" She instinctively rubbed her aching left shoulder.

"You stood right in front of it, it could have stomped you. You could have died."

Tears began forming in her eyes, "Oh my God, Emil. What's happening?"

CHAPTER NINE
2021, Friday June 25th

Kristin woke to the sound of light rain hitting the metal roof, just a few minutes before her alarm was to sound. She looked over to Emil, who slept soundly next to her, close enough to feel his body heat.

She dreaded the day ahead. The loss of her parents, particularly losing them the way she did, the senseless accident, and seeing them in the car lifeless were all hard enough. Then the thought of having to talk to her relatives, the friends of her parents, look at their long faces as they stare back at her for some sign that she's okay.

Those thoughts made her feel like a bitch. Everyone who knew Henry and Elizabeth felt sorrow and needed to come together to mourn. She told herself to *suck it up*.

She preemptively dismissed her alarm and gently woke Emil by rubbing his back and kissing him on the forehead, "Time to get ready, Love."

She let him wake as she stood and collected some

clothes.

Off the door handle hung two cooking pots tied together at the handles with string, a makeshift alarm that Kristin, or anyone, was turning the door handle. After Kristin's frightening adventure outside, Emil placed these on the door so he'd wake if it happened again and he could calmly get Kristin back to bed.

Trying to not make too much noise given the early hour, Kristin carefully removed the pans and placed them in the hall.

Tired from the night Emil stood slowly and gathered his clothes. He checked in with Kristin before heading to the full bath downstairs.

Steam puffed out from around the shower, Kristin always liking them hot, "How'd you end up sleeping, honey?"

"Hey, took a while to fall asleep. I'm scared."

"Yeah right. You feeling up for today?"

"Have to. Just have to get through it."

He drew the curtain back a bit and peeked in at Kristin, making a kissing expression as he looked at her body. Though wet and as sexy as he always found her, his eyes went to the purple bruise. Today a little more yellow showing, it still looked very painful. "Love you. Remember that you can tell me if you need anything at all, and I'll make sure it happens. You want to leave, stay, invite people over, whatever."

"You're sweet." Kristin leaned forward to give him a little kiss before returning to lathering her hair, "It'll be tough, but I'll be fine."

The couple got ready without interruption.

They arrived at the small church an hour ahead of schedule. The old building had seen better days. Its white paint chipping away, and the wooden sign at the front weathered from severe Vermont winters. A not atypical small Vermont town place of worship.

Emil pulled the rental around the back of the building, to the small dirt parking lot, and parked by the short ramp up to the back door.

"You okay?"

Kristin gave one of those little smiles that Emil knew meant she wasn't but would fake it anyway. "Yeah, fine."

Inside they met the pastor and reviewed the order of events, before taking their seats at the front right pew.

Not long later Nancy, her father's sister, and Ruth, her mother's sister, arrived together at the main entrance.

Both dressed appropriately in black, and Ruth's gray hair up and disheveled like seemingly all Vermont artists, they greeted Kristin with warm hugs and tears before sitting at the front left.

Shelly arrived with Joe and their children just minutes later, Joe taking the kids and sitting at the very back. Emil and Kristin gave a friendly wave to the family.

Kristin's friend made her way down the aisle and sat next to her, close enough that their bodies touched.

From then on Kristin didn't turn around to see the people enter and take their seats, not wanting to have to greet everyone or be seen. But from the faint whispers, shuffling of feet, and creaking pews she could sense the room had quickly filled.

Even so, she was surprised to see just how many people there were when she walked up to the podium and looked out. She saw plenty of family and friends she knew. But many people she had never seen before. Kristin assumed some of the younger ones were students of her father's, and others likely patients her mother got close to.

Co-workers too, she supposed.

She forced a small smile before starting, with no note cards to refer to, "Thanks everyone for coming. And thank you Emil for making all the arrangements, the flowers are gorgeous. And thank you Shelly for all of your support the last few days," she fought off a sudden urge to cry, "you've both been so incredible I don't know what I would have done without you."

Kristin adjusted her stance and shifted the microphone down a bit if for no other reason but to give herself a moment to collect herself. Her plan had been to have the skeleton of what she wanted to say all laid out, but she never put any time into it. *Why not?* She now found herself wondering. A feeling of disappointment crept up, and she hoped her parents wouldn't feel the same. She wasn't a lazy person, but for some reason she just couldn't bring herself to put the time into thinking about what to say. She felt terrible.

Perhaps, she thought, she'd share the standard talk tracks of *my parents were very loving*, but cliche was not her style.

Fuck it, Kristin said to herself, *just start somewhere.* She took a deep breath.

"One of my first jobs, besides baby or cat sitting, was at a clothing shop in the mall. I was really excited because I liked the products that they sold, so it seemed like it would be fun. But, well, I was also terrified for some reason — probably because this was the first position where I interacted with the public. I thought I might mess something up, or something would go wrong and I'd have a long line of customers all staring at me, pissed, as I struggled with the register or something."

"My parents were no help leading up to my first day.

They drove me to the place to get the application, but beyond that were no support. No meaningful encouragement. No 'you'll be great, Kris, don't worry!'. Nothing really."

"So my first day they drop me off but went in to get breakfast at the IHOP, which was so unlike them. They didn't eat like that. But it was also weird because I loved pancakes, and they knew that! It was like they wanted to rub in that I was working and they were having fun."

"But, why I ever doubted them I don't know."

Kristin looked down for a brief moment before returning to her speech.

"Not too long after I clocked in and got through training on products, the register, and all the regular things, I was walking around the store, just picking up random items that were on the wrong rack, they came in. When I saw them I got so embarrassed. Why were they in MY store? Are they going to make a scene? Typical teenage bullshit reaction, right?"

A couple chuckles echoed.

"They came up to me and just said, 'Could you help us pick out some clothes for our daughter?'"

She began to tear now.

"I was relieved and started showing them some of the nice clothes, playing along, thinking they'd look and then just leave. They asked questions, which was good practice for me, and when they had a few jeans and cute tops they said they were ready to check out."

Kristin could see Emil smile at her, approvingly, and she smiled back.

"So, I brought them to the register, my first customers, and rang them up. I folded the clothes nicely, packed them in a couple bags, and that was that. They left, never said anything to the effect that they were my parents."

"I got a ride home from a friend, Shelly of course because she was older, could drive, and we were inseparable. When I got home the clothes they had purchased were laid out on my bed. They didn't say a word to me about it. And the receipt for the purchases was on the refrigerator with this goofy little drawing of a smiling face my dad used to draw. He was the worst artist."

More laughter.

"But those faces were cute in some odd way."

Kristin paused for a moment. "That's my parents. There was never any fanfare. They didn't go around singing my praises, didn't tell me how amazing I was constantly, didn't cheer the loudest, or at all, at soccer games. But they always found some way to let me know they were proud, loved me, and were there for me."

"Looking back now I appreciate how they raised me. Whatever success I might have today is because I did it. Not because they baby-stepped me through everything. But, with each step that I took, somehow they made sure I felt rewarded for doing it."

The faces in the crowd all looked at her smiling now. She figured this was why getting together to grieve was important. The room felt less somber, more appreciative.

But she also felt like she wasn't done. That there was something remaining that had to be said.

"Look, I don't know what happened that night."

The faces changed. Smiles gone.

"I don't know what went wrong, why it happened. And I may never know."

She looked toward Emil, whose expression now showed worry.

She paused again, suddenly lost in what she wanted to

say.

What was she trying to say? Where was she going with this? Was this even an audience for whatever it was?

Kristin began to panic, and in her heightened state it came to her, and she spoke it out loud. She realized that this feeling sprouted deep in her gut days ago, and grew. Now, ready in its developed form it sprung out from her in front of everyone.

"But I do know it was no accident."

She turned from the podium, took the few steps down, and returned to her spot between Emil and Shelly.

Fuck was the word that came to her as she sat. Everyone must think her crazy. In denial. Pointing blame. Pressing for some meaning in an otherwise meaningless event. She knew those thoughts were crossing everyone's mind, very possibly even those sitting right next to her.

Kristin also knew saying it aloud had been a mistake. But she also felt it true.

Emil took her hand and she gripped it tight, thankful.

The pastor took over, making no reference to Kristin's eulogy. He managed through communion and the closing, with the procession out led by Kristin, Emil, Shelly, and the couple's sisters.

Outside they waited. Hugged, talked, and shared a few stories with others.

After what felt like hours, they retreated, with Elizabeth's sister Ruth offering her house for people to go to for snacks and drinks. Kristin politely declined, saying she still had a lot to do and had to start planning for her return to Dallas.

The group of friends, along with Joe and their two children, made their way to the parking lot.

Joe gave Kristin a hug before turning to his wife, "I'm

going to bring the kids home. Are you coming?"

Shelly looked to her friend, "Mind if I stick around and get a ride later?"

"Of course."

"I can give you a ride whenever," Emil kindly offered.

"Thanks," she smiled and then turned to Joe, giving him a quick kiss on the cheek. "I'll see you later. Thank you."

Shelly knelt down to her kids, each properly dressed for the occasion and well-behaved, "Mommy will see you later, okay? You be good for Daddy."

"By mommy," Beverly hugged her mother.

As Shelly stood Joe leaned in for the kiss. "Your purse is in the car, I'll stop and hand it to you."

"Oh, thank you."

Joe turned to Kristin, "My condolences, Kristin. Your parents were really cool people."

Like Shelly, Kristin had known Joe for over a decade, and spending some years of high school and college together he had the opportunity to meet the Fullers on a few occasions. His kind words made Kristin tear up, which she of course stubbornly fought off. "Thank you, Joe. You're extremely sweet to lend me Shelly for the week and take care of the kids."

"Of course."

With his kids in tow, Joe crossed the parking lot to their van, got them situated in their seats, and handed his wife her purse before pulling to the front of the church out of sight.

Emil, Shelly, and Kristin hovered around the Subaru. Used to what heat does to cars in Dallas, he unlocked it and cracked the door open as they stood and talked.

With Joe gone, Kristin leaned in close to Shelly. "Haven't told you about last night yet." Her tone demonstrated the anxiety and fear around the unspoken event.

Shelly cocked her head in curiosity.

"Probably better if Emil told it," she turned to her boyfriend.

Shelly listened intently to Emil's recounting of the terrifying encounter with the molting moose, and Kristin a breath away from it.

"You're shitting me," she said turning to Kristin.

"Something fucked up is going on, Shell.

They stood in silence a moment, Shelly's mind adding the information to her understanding of occurrences.

"You did great in there, honey." Emil changed the subject, knowing some solution wasn't so close as to need to obsess about it now.

"They think I'm crazy," Kristin virtually whispered as she motioned with her head toward the front of the church. She may have been convinced the first portion of her talk had been fine but felt her compulsive conclusion made her appear weak and delusional.

"Not true," Shelly jumped to defense, happy to have something other than the moose to turn her attention to. "You said what a lot of people are thinking."

"How so?"

"Well, it's what is hard to share, to say to someone so close to the victims."

"What's that?" Kristin was genuinely curious.

"That the accident was weird, Kris. I didn't tell you, but there was another article and I heard some people talking before going into the church."

Kristin shook her head, "I don't care, what'd they say?"

"The obvious, what you…what we already know. Your

father was driving, and he was clearly on the right side of the road, but it was a head-on collision." Shelly took her friend's hand, "I'm sorry if this is hard to hear, I can stop."

"No, please, I want to hear."

"Everyone there knew that the other driver, Peter, was in your lane. And not by a little bit."

Kristin nodded. Emil placed a gentle hand on Kristin's back. While she appreciated their attention and care, she also didn't like a suddenly rising feeling in her that she was somehow being babied.

Shelly continued, "He was driving in the wrong lane on a two-lane road. They released the toxicology, he was stone sober."

Kristin released Shelly's hand and shimmied to give Emil the hint to stop touching her back. She thought to herself a moment.

Since her short visit to the accident scene she had been focused on the girl. Now hearing some affirmation, some agreement from her closest friends that the crash wasn't an accident, gave her a bit of energy. She needed to learn more about the other victims. Needed to do the job that Detective Franks should be doing.

Detective Franks...

"You have Franks' card, Shell?"

"Yeah, it's in my purse. Why?"

"We're paying him a visit."

Emil shifted his weight from one foot to another, appearing uncomfortable, "You sure that's a good idea?"

"Jesus, Emil." Shelly immediately regretted her words, "It'll be cool, just ask some questions."

Shelly unzipped the main compartment of her purse and retrieved the card, handing it to Kristin.

"Can I use your phone?" Kristin asked Emil, figuring it

easier than going through her own purse which still sat in the Subaru.

"Yeah, of course." He reached into his right pants pocket for it, unlocked with his fingerprint, and handed it to his girlfriend.

Kristin opened the dialer and tapped the numbers for Franks. After a couple rings the vaguely familiar voice answered.

"Franks."

"Hi, Detective. This is Kristin Fuller, I was in the accident you were investigating."

Franks' tone didn't indicate any surprise or even much empathy, "Yes, how can I help you?"

After only a few seconds, with Shelly and Emil watching her closely, Kristin hung up. "Let's go."

"To?"

"The Williston barracks. It's not far."

"Let's do it." Shelly opened the back door of the Subaru and took a seat, eager herself for answers.

Kristin got in as well, in the front passenger, leaving Emil standing alone outside.

He nodded to himself and quietly got behind the wheel.

As promised, the drive wasn't that long and took him through various beautiful roads with horse farms and well-cared-for homes that overlooked the lake on one side and mountains on the other. Besides the directions of when and where to turn, the trip was also largely quiet.

At the green building with the Vermont State Flag flying, Emil parked and the three exited the vehicle.

After only a couple steps they noticed the detective walking towards them from the entrance.

He reached out his hand to shake Kristin's, and she obliged.

Franks looked the group up and down, from their attire correctly ascertaining that they had either just come from services or were on their way.

"Should we go in, sit down?" Shelly asked Kristin, uninterested in Franks' thoughts on the matter.

"No, it's fine."

"You have some questions?" The detective wore a clean white button shirt and brown slacks, his badge hanging around his neck.

"Have you learned anything new about the accident?"

He shrugged, "Nothing that hasn't been released. The case is closed at this point, it was an accident."

"Doesn't it seem odd for a car to be completely in the wrong lane?"

Shelly was proud of her friend for asking such direct questions and stood close by her side. She noticed Emil close as well with his attention directed at Franks.

"Sure, odd. But odd doesn't mean it's not an accident."

Kristin thought a moment, and while she couldn't disagree she did feel it evidence of another explanation.

"Okay, well what about the girl?"

"The young girl you asked about earlier? That you saw at the accident?"

"Yes."

"I have no evidence of any girl being in the accident. No body, no one missing. Nothing."

"Did you talk to Officer Parker? He was there."

"I did, he didn't see a young girl."

Emil chimed in, frustrated for Kristin, "So Kristin seeing a girl is not evidence *of* a girl?"

"I'm afraid not," the detective answered Emil then turned back to Kristin, "I'm not saying what you saw wasn't very real for you…"

"But," Kristin interjected, "not necessarily objectively real."

"That's correct."

"This is bullshit," Shelly said, this time directed squarely at Franks.

"I understand the desire for some other explanation, accidents are difficult that way. We want more meaning, or *a* meaning as an accident just doesn't feel like it offers one at all."

Shelly continued pressing, "What about their daughter?"

Franks put his hands in his pocket, and turned his shoulders to Shelly to impress upon her his authority, "You mean the daughter who died years ago?"

Shelly realized how ridiculous that would sound to the officer and felt slightly embarrassed.

Kristin, seeing her friend struggle for words, took over. "Well, I'd appreciate another look."

"I'd need some reason. We don't open closed cases without an indication we got something wrong."

Kristin nodded, "Fine, appreciate your time."

She turned from Franks and returned to the car, Emil quickly following with Shelly lagging a bit behind.

"That's it?" Shelly asked her friend as she caught up.

"What would you have me say?"

Shelly raised her arms a bit in both frustration and admitted ignorance, "I don't know, something."

"What are they to do, Shelly? It just looks like an accident to them." Shelly knew Emil was right, but her anger was getting the best of her.

Shelly shook her head and got back into the rear passenger seat, crossing her arms and remaining silent.

The others took their respective seats as well, and Emil

turned onto the busy Route 2A toward the highway to return to Shelburne.

Kristin thought as she enjoyed the warm rushing air from the open window. She had to keep opening doors, asking questions, investigating. As long as a stone remained unturned she had work to do.

Once at her parents' house, she pulled open the kitchen drawer under the microwave.

Emil grabbed a small bag of almonds and poured them into a bowl to share as a snack before they had lunch, stopping as he saw Kristin flipping through the Yellow Pages book, "What are you doing?"

She didn't respond at first, just kept turning the pages, and dragged one finger down a column of names, "There she is. Hubberton, Betsy."

Shelly turned her attention to Kristin as well, "Are you going to call her?"

Kristin grabbed her cell from the counter, "Damn right."

"Be careful, hun," Shelly took a step closer, wanting to hear the conversation, "you don't want her to think you're threatening."

Emil and Shelly both listened, not moving or doing anything to make noise.

Kristin spun around and leaned against the counter, her eyes going from her friend to her lover as she waited for someone to pick up at the other end.

"Hi, I'm looking for Betsy Hubberton."

Emil tried to ignore his growing hunger and the noises his stomach made.

"Oh, good. My name is Kristin Fuller, do you happen to have a minute?" She spoke softly, somberly, "I'm sorry if this is a bad time, and honestly I'm sorry for reaching out like this, but I felt the need to talk to you. I was in the other car, in the accident, the one where you lost your brother."

There was a moment of silence from Kristin. Her small audience watched her intently.

"Yes, I'm sorry for your loss too. I know it's hard, and thank you for even talking to me. Anyway, if you don't mind, I'd love to just meet and talk. It's such an unfortunate event, so sad, that I'd like to just get to know Peter and Lila better. I'm hoping it'll help me heal, and maybe you too."

Another moment passed before Kristin straightened her back upright, "Great, does tomorrow work?"

PART THREE

CHAPTER TEN

2007, Tuesday April 3rd

The car had been off for a good ten minutes as Peter Hubberton sat there, alone. He stopped on the dirt road in order to gather his thoughts. Getting the news was hard enough, but then delivering it to his daughter defined gut-wrenching. *Gut-wrenching.*

His mind relived the experience.

Sitting in that small, windowless, conference room with Lila and Kacey, and the two specialists, caused actual physical pain in his stomach. One he had never experienced before. He now knew the term held real meaning and wasn't just something people said in hard times.

The family sat along one side of the conference table with Dr. Cuevas next to them, and his assistant Dr. Bradley, a younger oncologist, at the end.

Dr. Cuevas looked to be about 70 but acted nowhere near ready for retirement. He clearly gave up styling what little gray hair he had left, so it waved and curled in all sorts of directions in constant need of combing. His tanned skin made his hair more stark. He seemed always at the hospital and would call early mornings and late evenings to share news or for a kind check-in. Supposedly the best in Vermont, Peter felt lucky to have him supporting his daughter.

His assistant, the much younger and mousy-looking Dr. Bradley, didn't say much but when she did Peter took mental notes to look up the words she used later. Even with his medical background, she often confused him. Dr. Cuevas recognized this as we would sometimes translate.

An empty whiteboard across from them kept catching Peter's eye. He hated its emptiness, like it mocked his daughter's future. He wanted to stand up violently, the chair being flown back behind him loudly, stomp to the board, and frantically scribble on it. *Something* needed to be there. *Anything*.

Dr. Cuevas nodded to Lila as they all settled into the moment to play out the purpose of the gathering.

"Honey," Lila put a hand on Kacey's knee, the just six-year-old girl sitting between her parents, "the doctor got the results back."

Lila cleared her throat and paused, putting her strength into not collapsing into tears in front of her little girl, "You have what's called Hodgkin Disease. It's a type of cancer, and that's what's causing those swellings in your neck and armpits."

"Okay," Kacey looked at her mother with big eyes, searching for assurance that everything would be fine.

"Luckily," Lila continued and turned her gaze to Peter for reinforcements, "it was caught pretty early, and this type of disease is very curable — meaning the doctors will make you better."

"That's right," Peter leaned forward so Kacey could see him without turning away from her mother, "since your special doctors got this so early we will just do some treatments. They won't be fun, but you'll be okay."

"Thank you," Dr. Cuevas, his slight Spanish accent and gentle tone reassuring to the parents, "and Kacey, both Dr. Bradley and I have treated little girls just like you. And now they're all grown up and happy."

"What will I have to do?" Kacey asked her mother.

"Well," she turned to the specialist, "maybe Dr. Cuevas can help answer that."

"Of course," he placed an arm on the table to appear more relaxed, like it all was no big deal. Just another day at work. "Well, there are some drugs to take that fight off the cancer. We'll also consider what's called radiation therapy, that's where we hit the bad cells with radiation to kill them."

He shifted back in his chair a bit and adjusted his tone to an exaggerated grumbly old man, "This can make you feel icky, but it makes the cancer feel even worse."

"We'll leverage Conformal radiation therapy. A procedure where we utilize three-dimensional scans of the tumors, from our computed tomography scans, to shape the beams and avoid healthy tissue." Dr. Bradley spoke to the adults in the room, but Peter still felt like a child.

Lila, realizing the big words might scare her daughter, tapped her hand on her knee to get her attention, "Those are scientist terms for 'they're going to kick the cancer's butt'." She followed it with a big smile.

They all waited patiently for some reaction from Kacey, the young girl with a brave but confused face.

"Okay. I want to kick the cancer's butt."

Lila brought her hand up and she and her daughter high-fived. Peter placed one arm around his daughter in a supportive hug.

"Then it's settled," Dr. Cuevas sat up straight, "we're going to kick butt — your doctors do that for you, you don't worry. You just focus on being fun Kacey, do things you enjoy and don't worry about the rest."

Dr. Cuevas directed his partner to take Kacey out to their children's play area, and the other three walked to his small office down the hall.

"It is early, that's true," he said with his usual calm tone, "but it also appears aggressive with Kacey. Her tumors have grown in a short period of time, so we'll start the treatments soon but may need to get more aggressive if we don't see improvement."

"What would that mean? More aggressive?" Lila, a worrywart by nature, needed to know what the scenario meant.

"Surgery. Higher dose chemotherapy."

"Higher dose? That sounds bad."

"There can be side effects, like fertility challenges, damage to other organs, bone and muscle development issues."

Fertility issues.

That knotting of Peter's gut returned. He wanted his baby to not only live, but experience all that life had to offer. A memory came to him, from when Kacey was just days old. He held her while sitting on the couch by their big bay windows. He heard Lila in the kitchen, bottling breast milk or something, and Kacey slept soundly.

He watched Kacey, her skin a reddish pink and wrinkled, a tuft of hair, eyes closed. And for whatever reason, she woke up and just looked at him. And she reached out with that little hand to his that rested on her stomach, and wrapped her tiny fingers around his index finger. Kacey looked at him just another moment before falling back to sleep clutching him tightly.

He decided then, back when he held her as an infant, he'd do all he could for her.

Peter felt his promise coming to collect at that moment he sat silently in his car.

With the road too narrow to pull over he worried about someone coming along, but so few traveled it that no one did.

He thought maybe if he stopped he'd get some sort of sign, one that would make the decision ahead for him. But like life, he needed to make it.

Peter inhaled as if taking in energy and then reached for the key, starting the ignition.

He pushed the accelerator gently and the car began climbing the hill again. Trees on either side made it darker than the day was, a sunny early April.

Ahead he saw the clearing for Arthur Ross' house and he slowed as he turned into the driveway.

Arthur welcomed him warmly as usual, and the two sat making small talk in the living room before Peter mustered up the courage for the reason he came.

"Arthur, I have to ask you something."

"I know, Peter. It's fine."

Peter looked at his friend quizzically. Perhaps he should not have been surprised Arthur knew why he was there, but he was nonetheless.

"And I don't blame you. I can't imagine the pain you and Lila must be feeling, the fear."

Peter wiped a tear away that had quickly formed in his left eye. What he heard from Arthur was horrifically true, but he still didn't want to cry in front of his friend.

"Do you think you can help?"

"Sure," Arthur crossed his legs much like Peter remembered Arthur Ross Senior doing.

The two families, the Ross and Hubbertons, had been connected for decades, if not longer. Peter's father, the head of a local bank at the time, worked closely with Arthur Senior who presided over a small religious community — for some religion Peter didn't know much about. Bertrand, Peter's father, attributed his success to Arthur Senior — something Peter didn't fully understand.

But what he did know was that whatever this thing was he didn't understand, it was powerful. And the Ross family grasped it just fine.

"I just want her better. Nothing more."

"Of course."

"And I'll pay anything."

"There's no money involved. Your family has been good to ours."

"Thank you."

"It won't be easy," Arthur warned.

"It won't be easy regardless."

"The process, Peter. It comes with…difficulties."

"That's okay. I'm willing to do anything."

"And you just might have to."

"Where do we start?"

"I'll need to meet with Kacey first, will that be okay?"

"Yeah, sure."

"Just a talk, nothing special, perhaps over dinner. I'll need to see her space, where she sleeps."

"Fine."

"There may be other things that come up that I will require. I don't know what those are yet, but know that I will be asking."

Peter shook his head, making mental notes of everything.

"I will also need to know everything about those close to you. And I mean everything."

"Why?" This he found odd.

"Don't worry about that. I will also need your patient files."

"What?"

Arthur uncrossed his legs and leaned forward, his hands clasped in front of him. "This is not something where you'll be asking me for justification. I told you to be prepared and you said you'd do anything."

"Yes...but," Peter sought the words that might help, but none came that did a better job than the straight truth, "but I would be breaking very strict health-related laws by sharing."

"I imagine so."

He quickly gave in, "Okay, I'll get those to you."

Arthur relaxed back and smiled, "Excellent. Now, Peter, you just continue doing what you're doing. Get Kacey the best modern medicine can provide for treatments, and I'll do what I do. Share with Lila what you'd prefer, but know, too, that sometimes less is more."

That's how they left it, returning to the idle chit-chat mixed with reminiscing about various gatherings of their families.

When Peter finally left it was dark, past nine. He fought the urge to drive to his office to start downloading patient records. As much as he didn't want to out of fear of consequences to his profession as a doctor of dentistry, he settled on doing it. But being so late he felt the need to get home and planned on getting to his office early the next morning.

He thought about what to tell Lila and Arthur's recommendation. "Less is more," he said. Peter decided he'd only share that Arthur would be getting to know Kacey better to support his prayers, and when opportunities came he would determine how much more to divulge based on the situation. He knew Lila would sacrifice everything for Kacey, like him, but she also leaned on the conservative side and certainly didn't have the background with…with…well, the Ross family like he did.

What he did need to do, was find a way to get Arthur the information he needed without raising suspicions. And, somehow, allow Arthur to see her room. An odd request, for sure, and he fought off the creepy factor, but wouldn't further question Arthur.

Peter turned his BMW slowly but sharply to the right, passed the antique street lamp he had installed, and into his stone driveway. He pulled the car passed the large yellow Victorian home with dark blue trim to his recently built detached garage. He had spared no expense to match the style of his home.

As he approached the large door opened and he led his car in.

About eight years ago he opened his practice in Middlebury, and a year later moved into their home just north of the town. He did well, but not well enough to afford their home — a three-story Victorian with a modernized interior. *The privilege of being a Hubberton*, he would tell himself, *is being privileged*.

Peter's father made a significant amount of money leading a local bank, which had sold to a much larger financial entity just over a dozen years ago and shortly before his father passed. But, his father's father also did very well as the owner of a popular ski resort and various other properties and businesses around the state.

It seemed virtually all the Hubbertons owned something. And not just something, but something recognizable. Something everyone in Vermont not only knew but loved. This made his decision to attend dental school a difficult one. He felt a sense of shame as he told his father, and the look on that always stoic man's face didn't help young Peter.

"Are you sure?" was all he said in response.

Peter knew well enough what that meant coming from Bertrand. What he did not mean was, *Have you really thought about what would make you the happiest in life, and will dentistry do that? It's a noble profession, and I will support you 100% if that's your decision.*

Nope, Peter clearly and accurately understood his father's meaning as *Dentistry? Really? With a name like Hubberton you could be Governor, Senator, hell even President...but you want to put your hands in people's mouths instead*?

Peter stuck to his guns while ignoring his father's unspoken disappointment — which grew deeper as his sister made the difficult decision to essentially cut ties completely with their parents.

But, he still inherited millions. It allowed him to pay cash for his million-dollar home, and for the building that became his practice.

The ease it brought to his life did make having any animosity toward his father impossible.

Peter entered his home from the back sunroom, which opened to the large kitchen. Not getting home until 10 p.m. meant Kacey was long asleep.

"How was Arthur?" his wife asked as he sat on one of

the high stools along the island that faced the stove and brass hood set against a wall of white subway tile.

Lila placed a glass of water in front of him and then leaned back against the cold stove, her arms crossed.

"He's good, and sends his love and was very sorry to hear about Kacey."

Lila just nodded. Condolences were nice, but they really did nothing for her.

"He said he's happy to help any way he can and volunteered to make us dinners a few nights a week as she goes through treatment."

"That is nice," the effort meant more to Lila and she suddenly became thankful for the friendship between her husband and that man she always found strange.

Lila never thought to ask much about the connections between the Hubbertons and the Rosses, but she knew Bertrand and Arthur Senior were close and through story-telling at family events also knew that their families went further back. She even thought she heard about some cousins marrying.

"What's today?" she asked as she turned her gaze to the windows out to the dark backyard, thinking somewhere out there she'd find her answer.

"Tuesday."

Lila's voice sounded tired and faint, "The days go by so slowly now."

Peter stood and rounded the Vermont marble-top island and embraced his wife. The couple stood in silence for a moment, appreciating each other and fearful for their daughter.

"Thursday is the CVC surgery," she said like he didn't know.

"Yeah. Let's fill her up on cake tomorrow."

CHAPTER ELEVEN
2007, Wednesday April 4th

The sun only started peeking over the horizon behind
one of the old stone buildings of Middlebury College when
Peter pulled his 2004 BMW 325i into the multi-story
renovated home that was his practice across the street. He
went to the back of the building and parked in the spot
furthest away from the door out of respect for his patients
and employees.

As he put it in park he glanced up at the rearview
mirror out of habit and saw the stuffed Kermit the Frog
buckled into the back passenger seat. Seeing Kacey's
favorite travel companion set his mind at ease and he
released his tight grip on the wheel.

All morning he thought about taking his clients' private
information, illegal and morally wrong, and weighed that
against the odd chance Arthur could save his daughter's
life. It was no contest, but still didn't sit right with him nor
make any sense. The breach of trust would have him

disgraced and out of business. So, the entire drive in, and completely unaware he was doing it, he choked the steering wheel. But Kermit reminded him why he found himself at the practice at 5:30 in the morning, hours before anyone would arrive.

He would need a couple of hours with the computers, only because he wasn't terribly familiar with the system. It would take him time to figure out how to download it all, assuming it was even possible, to a couple of USB sticks he carried in his pocket.

The BMW beeped as he locked it and he walked up the small driveway to the front entrance. A loud metallic clanking from a garbage truck around a corner somewhere startled Peter, and he brought that image of Kermit back to his mind to settle his nerves.

Closing the door behind him he didn't bother with the lights, instead rounding the reception area and pushing the start button on the few years old desktop computer that sat tucked under the lip of the desk.

He could hear the machine boot and the hard drive whir.

As the monitor displayed its start progress Peter thought about turning on the coffee machine, but decided against it as it might give his staff a sense of how early he came in and he wanted to avoid the questions.

Within a couple of minutes, he saw the classic tiling of applications against the blue background. He double-clicked the one he knew Patrice used for patient management, and after another moment he saw the relatively familiar interface.

He clicked "File" at the top left, and in the resulting drop-down saw the *Export* option. Clicking it brought up a small window with another series of options including

Scheduler, *Billing*, *Accounting*, and *Patients*.

He clicked *Patients*.

Another box appeared, this one with a big warning icon, a white exclamation point in a red yield sign.

Not wanting to read it he only glanced it over, seeing the abbreviation HIPAA he knew exactly what it was for — warning him about exporting private patient data and the legalities.

He tapped the *OK* button and the window changed to ask him the file type he'd like the data exported as. Only recognizing *csv* he selected it, believing he could use Excel later to open it.

Clicking the *Continue* button resulted in the file explorer opening to determine a location on the computer to save it.

He smiled at how easy this had all proved to be and dug for the two USB sticks, flipping them over each other in his hand as he looked at them. The blue one he knew was empty, so he tried that one first, inserting it into the front slot of the computer.

He selected the new drive that appeared as a destination option and clicked *Save*.

After what seemed like minutes of no activity on the screen, Peter began to worry. Patrice sometimes complained about how finicky the system was, and though she never asked about upgrades, he sat in that chair kicking himself for not having the latest state-of-the-art hardware and software.

Then, the progress bar appeared with a sliver of blue under the *1%* indicator.

It ticked up at a reasonably fast enough pace.

He became less nervous as he watched it climb, and with a good two hours before his staff arrived thought about the now long day ahead.

Fine, he thought, *at least I won't have to worry about this*.

As the software did its thing, Peter went to the room just behind the reception area where he kept the practice's equipment.

He arranged a half-dozen metal trays along the counter where he draped the same paper they used for patient bibs, and then placed the sterilized standard utensils he and the hygienists will need for the day. Though typically completed by his lead hygienist, he figured he was here and would be productive. He then went from exam room to exam room, in each wiping down surfaces and placing headrest covers.

Once the four rooms were prepared he went to the very rear of the building, a small area he had nicely put together for staff. Large windows looked out the back, over the small parking lot and into a large grassy plot that included the town's baseball field — most often used by the middle school.

Two couches faced each other, a small coffee table between, and along the wall, to the left of the door he had entered, a counter with the coffee machine, cups, napkins, sugar, and a sink. Next to it a refrigerator held cream, bottled water, and a selection of cheeses, yogurt, seltzer, and other snacks, all as a courtesy to his employees.

He stretched out on the couch with his feet hanging over the arm and his head on the pillow, staring out the windows.

The morning's light illuminated half the baseball diamond, evaporating the spell of rain from the night before.

Peter didn't realize just how tired his body was, and so drifted to sleep after only meaning to close his eyes for a moment.

* * *

"Peter?"

He shot up to a seated position, placing his feet squarely on the ground.

"Patrice, hi, sorry. I guess I dozed off."

"Is everything okay?"

Patrice, in her blue blouse and soft white sweater to combat the air-conditioning, stood a few feet away. Old enough to be his mother, she looked at him with genuine concern, her hands cupped in front of her.

She had short hair, a light brown color that she probably dyed. Short, maybe 5'3", and with a round face. She wore comfortable white sneakers, which Peter always found curious. The kind you might expect a nurse to wear, but Patrice generally sat all day.

She was his first employee, and incredibly loyal and caring to his family. She regularly brought pies or other baked goods, and always overfeed everyone around the holidays.

"Yes, I guess I dozed off." He thought about providing some excuse, perhaps he had just woken up early that morning and decided to get a jump start on the day, but then got tired and lay down. He chose against giving any excuse at all.

She took two small steps forward and opened her hands, like she was prepared to receive communion. In them, the blue USB stick rested like a victim requiring a guilty party. "I found this in the computer. And a message on the screen about patient data export."

"Oh, yes," Peter took care to stand slowly, to show no reason for alarm or concern, and gently took the device from her. He held it up quickly for her to see, hoping the gesture would convince her it was nothing to worry about, before slipping it into his pocket. "Thank you. Was it complete?"

"Yes."

He turned to the coffee machine to make a pot, realizing that his receptionist generally opened the office and his other staff would soon arrive.

Patrice turned her body to follow him, "Do you mind if I ask why you were exporting patient information?"

He looked at her quickly before turning on the water to fill the coffee pot, "Oh, no special reason. I was reading about how it's important to backup data, that if there's a crash or something that things are a lot easier if you have a backup to import."

"But the system does that for us," her voice innocent and unassuming.

"Oh, does it?" Peter quickly took the route of ignorance, then changed the subject, "Beautiful morning, isn't it?"

"It is, Peter."

* * *

"Click that," Peter pointed at the file that had been saved to Arthur's desktop.

Immediately after work Peter made the long drive to Arthur's, not wanting to wait around any longer to get him the data. Now, since neither were computer experts, he needed to help him through the process of making the data available.

The resulting window offered options for software to open it.

"Excel," Peter demanded.

Arthur clicked the icon for the program and then *OK* and within a few seconds it opened, displaying column after column of patient names, addresses, phone numbers, dates of birth, and a number of different and potentially sensitive medical information.

Seeing it successful, Peter moved from the chair adjacent to Arthur to the couch across.

He watched as his friend's eyes darted around the screen, and his fingers glided across the trackpad to scroll through the hundreds of rows.

"What are you looking for anyway?"

"A needle in a haystack," Arthur's gaze didn't move from the screen.

After a few minutes he grimaced and leaned back in his chair, moving the lid of the laptop down just enough to not shine in his eyes but without closing it.

"Nothing."

"Nothing?" Peter asked more to get a better idea of what exactly Arthur thought he would find.

"Right, but not a surprise at all. I need to look under every rock."

"Well, that's too bad. I almost got in trouble downloading that."

Arthur tilted his head, "Oh?"

"Yeah, Patrice, my receptionist, actually took the USB out of the computer and saw the message about patient data being exported."

"Do you think she'll report you?"

"Oh, no way. I made up an excuse. Besides, she's great, very loyal and good to my family. She's actually distantly related to Lila's mother somehow."

Arthur sat quietly in thought.

"Perhaps if you tell me what this needle might look like I could help."

Arthur looked at Peter. It wasn't that he didn't trust

Peter, but that he knew the power of words. That speaking aloud is always speaking to the universe, expressing intent. And that could influence not only Peter but also reality. And the risk is that this power would ultimately be working against them.

He resigned to share with his friend just a bit, in order to possibly help with the next step.

"All people are connected, but some more than others. In fact, there can be deep cosmic connections between complete strangers. I'm looking for hints of a connection between your family and another, and ultimately Kacey to another."

Peter nodded, unsure what to think of the purpose his mind didn't even approach looking for any such connection.

Arthur perked up a bit, "Kacey's birthday is November 3rd."

"That's right."

"Transformation."

A moment passed with that word hanging in the air, which Arthur didn't intend and he regretted saying it.

"Does Kacey share her birthday with anyone you know?"

Peter thought for a moment as no one quickly came to mind. "Actually, yes."

CHAPTER TWELVE
2007, Thursday April 5th

The family sat in the quiet waiting area not even pretending to be interested in the few, outdated, and uninteresting, magazines.

Kacey played on the floor moving wooden blocks up and around a series of thin metal pipes that mimicked a roller coaster. The kind of toy, Peter thought, you only found in medical establishments. He had one similar in his waiting area and suddenly wondered why he didn't have anything more fun for the children. *Durable*, he thought as he made a mental note to find something better.

Only one other person, besides the receptionist situated at one of the two check-in stations, also waited. An older woman dressed too warmly for the spring day. She seemed just as disinterested in everything as them.

"Hubbertons?" The nurse who emerged from the door looked right at them.

The couple stood and Lila took her daughter's hand,

"Come on, Kacey."

They walked through the door and it hushed as it closed behind them like a whispering omen.

Lila held Kacey's hand tightly as they followed with Peter just behind the nurse.

"We'll be going down this hall and around a corner for some prep," the nurse said as she half-turned and made a motion to her right.

Lila could feel herself getting emotional, the long walk bringing a realization of the hardship ahead for such a young and happy girl.

"It's okay, Mom," Kacey said as if sensing, "The doctors are going to kick cancer's ass!" She proclaimed it loudly.

"I thought it was 'butt'?" Peter asked more softly.

"No, Dad, this is serious time. This isn't for kids."

That rang through his head, *this isn't for kids*.

Nothing should be truer and he admired Kacey for her strength.

"Right here," the nurse stopped in front of a door leading to the typical examination room with the paper-sheeted exam table, two uncomfortable-looking armchairs, and a small sink and cabinet. "Dr. Cuevas will be in shortly."

The couple sat in the chairs as the nurse closed the door, leaving the family alone. Kacey hopped into her mother's lap.

They sat for a few minutes, Lila and Peter quiet and attempting to keep their energies calm to not alert their daughter of their unease before the doctor entered.

Dr. Cuevas wore the standard blue scrubs, which, for some reason, Peter was not expecting.

"Good morning," he said as he sat on the examination

table, his eyes on Kacey. "How are you feeling today?"

"Okay," she said quietly and confidently.

"Good!" He paused a moment before explaining what would be happening, "We're going to do a quick exam here and answer any questions you and your parents have, then just you and me will go down the hall for the pre-op prep. Sound good?"

"Yes."

Peter and Lila nodded in agreement.

Within minutes the exam ended and he whisked Kacey away, the nurse returning to bring the parents to the waiting area.

It all happened so fast Peter and Lila felt like cattle.

The procedure being a quick one they didn't even bring books or water for themselves. A simple surgery to have a central venous catheter inserted into her chest to make the administration of the drugs, and the taking of blood for testing, easier during her therapy.

They sat alone on the right wall of the surgical waiting area, under the large painting of a traditional Vermont farm with a red barn and a fat Holstein cow. The large windowless area significantly darker than the previous waiting room. Across from them more seats, but also the double doors leading to the operating rooms that only staff could enter.

Under different circumstances, they would have noticed the lack of natural light and uncomfortable chairs.

"She better be okay," Lila looked at her husband as if he controlled the situation.

Peter breathed deeply, "She will be."

Lila took a moment to stress her point, never moving her eyes from her husband's. She didn't know what he could do about it, her rational mind knew this ultimately was out of his control, but she looked to him to solve it. She couldn't go on without her daughter, "Do you understand what I'm saying? She MUST be okay."

He knew exactly what she meant.

Peter nodded and swallowed his saliva, "She will be. I promise."

His second promise.

Satisfied that he said it, Lila turned to face forward and leaned back in the maroon upholstered chair. She would make it through this. It will all be fine.

They sat in silence another few minutes before the double doors moved with that automatic electric whir, someone from the other side had hit the *open* button.

Elizabeth Fuller walked through, in the typical blue scrubs of her profession.

Neither Peter nor Lila, though they always thought of Elizabeth as warm and friendly, felt like chatting. Regardless of how the conversation started, certainly they would turn to the reason they sat here.

"Lila, Peter!" Elizabeth saw them and stopped, "How are you?"

Elizabeth took a step forward, bent slightly, and began to raise her arms. The signal for an embrace.

Lila smiled out of polite habit, stood, and gave in to the hug. Her husband followed suit.

"Hi, Elizabeth."

"Hey."

The couple's voices not quite as energetic as their friend's.

"Oh," Elizabeth realized she got caught up by seeing Peter and Lila, a couple she knew from her husband and although she rarely saw or communicated with them she always enjoyed their company.

She held onto one hand of each of them, "What are you two doing here? Is everything okay?"

Lila couldn't stop the tears and stumbled back to her chair, her husband guiding her down and sitting next to her again.

"Oh no, you guys, what's going on?" Elizabeth sincere as she knelt by them in the otherwise empty waiting area.

Peter spoke for his wife, "Kacey has Hodgkin's Disease. She's in for the CVC procedure now."

"Oh, I'm so sorry."

Lila forced a smile as she wiped her tears away, "She's my baby."

Elizabeth placed a knowing hand on Lila's knee, "Who's your doctor?"

"Cuevas."

"He's fantastic, really." Elizabeth meant it. Though a small, relatively speaking, university hospital, Dr. Cuevas was very well respected nationally. "Kacey is in amazing hands, she'll pull through."

"Thanks," Lila smiled genuinely. The doctor had seemed great through their heart-breaking experiences so far, but it felt good to hear Elizabeth vouch for him.

"How's Henry and Kristin?" Peter changed the subject.

Elizabeth removed her hand from Lila and stood, "Oh, they're doing well. Kristin's 15 and doing great in school. You know, they'd love to see you all. I'll have Henry reach out, whenever might work for you. No pressure at all."

"That would be nice," Lila meant it but grew tired of talking and Elizabeth saw it in her face.

"Well, I'm glad I ran into you both. And Kacey has a road ahead, but you will all get through it. You know how to reach me — if you want to talk about treatment or need any help navigating the system, please please reach out. I will want to help."

Peter smiled, "Appreciate that."

Elizabeth gave a short wave, "Okay, keep us updated. Love to you all."

She continued down the hall leaving the couple.

Lila's head fell to her hands, exhausted. "I wish it were Kristin," she raised her gaze to her husband, "I know how awful that sounds, but I wish it were her instead. I'm such a terrible person."

"No, you're a loving mother," Peter consoled her with a hand on her back, "I know you don't wish it on anybody."

Lila shook her head, "No, I do though. I would wish it on her if it would save Kacey." Tears formed once more in her eyes as she heard the horrific words she spoke.

"Kacey will be fine. She'll come through."

"You promised."

CHAPTER THIRTEEN
2007, Friday June 1st

"Sorry again Kristin's not here, this school project of her's has been consuming her," Elizabeth apologized even though she felt it better Kristin wasn't home. With Peter and Lila's daughter ill, and the couple likely taking the only evening away from her since her diagnosis, a night with adults, though admittedly Kristin was emotionally and intellectually mature for her age, probably was better.

"Oh, no it's fine. We understand," Lila spoke for the two of them.

"Yeah, of course," Peter chimed in any way.

The couples retired to the Fullers' back deck after the relaxing salmon dinner. With the nights getting longer they didn't need the light over the door, but Elizabeth lit a few citronella torches around the railing in hopes of keeping the mosquitoes at bay. Peter never believed those things worked.

Between them, a small table with enough room for

their drinks and a plate of cookies that Henry brought out.

"This is a lovely spot you have."

"Thank you, we like it."

They sat quietly for a minute, listening to the frogs off in the distance.

Elizabeth broke the silence, directing her statement to Lila, "I'm sorry if running into you at the hospital put you on the spot."

"Oh, it's fine. I definitely wasn't in the mood to chat, but please don't take it personally," Lila reached for a cookie.

Elizabeth smiled, "And please, if there's anything we can do. I know the inner workings of the hospital and navigating it can feel complex. Anything we can do, I hope you ask."

"Thank you," Peter took his wife's hand and gave it a little squeeze. "Kacey had a good day today. The doctor said she'd have good and bad days. We're thankful for the good ones."

"Yeah, she's been a trooper through all of this. I swear she's barely fazed by it."

"Kids are resilient, I see it all the time," Elizabeth shared from experience, "and Kacey's strong."

"I'm sorry," Peter looked to Lila and then their hosts, "but my stomach has been bothering me all day. Bathroom?"

"Oh, sorry to hear that. Through the kitchen to the side door, you'll see it."

"Thanks," Peter gave an embarrassed smile before standing and entering the home.

Normally he would never admit to such a thing, having a stomach problem, but he needed to buy time without seeming suspicious. This way they'd hopefully feel empathy and not think that perhaps he was snooping around. His stomach fine, he didn't really need the toilet.

Peter walked as if going to the bathroom, but took a quick look back at the door to make sure he wasn't being watched before ducking into the Fullers' front room that they apparently used as an office.

He quickly but quietly ascended the stairs to the second floor taking two steps at a time. To his right he could see the open door to what he determined was the master bedroom given the fancy armoire he could see.

Just in front of him a bathroom, and two more doors to his left.

One, from the purple walls, he surmised to be Kristin's.

He took the few steps to the threshold and looked in.

It didn't look like a fifteen-year-old's room, in fact it looked much more suited for Kacey. *Perfect*, he thought, *Kristin must not have changed anything in years*.

Peter retrieved the small digital camera from his pocket and glanced at the window that offered a view of the backyard, where the others sat on the deck. He could hear them talking, though not quite clearly enough to make out the conversation.

With it still before dusk, the room was light enough to not need the flash — which he couldn't risk using anyway. If Henry or Elizabeth saw a flash of light from their daughter's room, and then Peter with a camera, they'd probably think him a pervert and kick him out. By then he'd have what he needed anyway but still would rather avoid what could be a messy and embarrassing situation.

He double-checked that the flash was off and took a series of photos, ensuring he covered the entire room. He took four pictures across the walls, then pointed directly at her bed, bureau, and desk.

Mission accomplished he turned and again quietly descended the stairs. Through the office he turned left to the bathroom.

Crap, as he approached Peter realized that the light in the bathroom wasn't on.

If the Fullers were incredibly observant, which most people he felt were not, then they would know that he hadn't actually entered the room yet. That could raise suspicion.

He thought quickly.

Peter entered the bathroom, turned the knob, and with one hand on the door closed it without a sound.

The shade was already drawn, which was a good thing, but it definitely wasn't blackout.

While there was technically enough light to do business, it wasn't enough to do so confidently.

He looked around as if something might offer a solution. Nothing did.

Peter decided to take the chance. He wouldn't turn on the light, and if asked would just say there was enough for his...duty.

Since he was there and felt like not much time had passed, he peed and then flushed.

After a bit to wash his hands, he opened the door and went back outside.

"Are you okay, honey?" Lila stroked his arm as he sat.

"Yeah, I think it was the burger I had for lunch. Apologies, I'm embarrassed."

"I hope it wasn't dinner!" Henry stated with a laugh.

"Oh, no. Definitely not. Been upset since lunch."

"Should we go?" Lila asked on queue, and as they had practiced.

Peter shared a bit more of Arthur's work with Lila

when he realized the odd task that would need to be completed. Though he didn't know all that Arthur was doing either, he kept what he told his wife still at a high level.

With Peter's clandestine charge completed, they had no real reason to stick around.

Peter nodded, "Yeah, probably a good idea."

They stood and went to hug their hosts, "Thank you so much, it was so good to see you both again and catch up," Lila hugged Elizabeth first then Henry, "and please, give Kristin our best."

CHAPTER FOURTEEN

2008, Tuesday February 5th

Fritos, Lays, Snickers, M&M's, the usual things Peter tells his patients to stay away from.

He stood in front of the vending machine, arms at his side, and eyes glazed and staring at something beyond all the junk food.

He thought the machine odd. Not because he found himself at the end of the hospital's long hall of patient rooms, his daughter significantly worse than she had ever been, lying asleep fifty yards away, staring at food considered bad for your health. Not because it was past 9 p.m., with the sun down and only fluorescent lights to illuminate the building, with the brightest being this monstrosity in front of him.

It was something different that he couldn't quite place. Like he was being lied to. He thought of those people he considered conspiracy theorists, who would rattle on about the *establishment*, about how *they* wanted to *distract the masses* from what was *real* with television, video games, and sugar.

He stared at the machine, aware of how ridiculous he appeared, like it might provide a message. Like some fucking fortune cookie it would spit out *Don't worry, be happy* on a thin slip of paper out of its bill slot. *So trite*, he thought, *all the modern-day messiahs just spew the same old sugar-infused garbage.*

A day prior Peter and Arthur sat in Peter's living room discussing the situation, while Lila was still at the Medical Center with Kacey.

"She's so much worse." Peter shared with exhaustion with his friend.

They sat in front of the fireplace, the few logs turning black with veins of glowing red.

Arthur understood better than anyone the complexities of the situation and needed to navigate the conversation delicately.

"I'm sorry, Peter. I imagine this is extremely difficult. I've been…"

Peter cut him off, his eyes leaping up to Arthur's, "Oh, I'm not blaming you, Arthur. Not in any way."

While it didn't really matter in the least, it still felt good to Arthur to hear that.

"It's just frustrating and I want her back to the way she was. I want my family back."

Peter's gaze fixed on the flames again.

"Now is perhaps the time for the next steps."

"Next steps?"

Arthur expanded, "You're probably unaware, but we've really been doing two separate but important enterprises. The goal of the first to simply return Kacey to health."

"And the second?"

"Peter?"

He quickly turned his head to his left, the voice violently pulling Peter from his meandering thoughts of junk food and his discussion with Arthur, to see Dr. Cuevas just through the open double doors looking at him with a clipboard in hand.

"Yes, Doctor?"

"Is Lila in with Kacey?"

"Yes."

"Good, can I speak to you both for a few minutes?"

"Of course."

The two men walked the hall in silence, passed the nurses' station and ten or so rooms until they came to Kacey's.

Inside they found her asleep, her breathing labored and unsteady, in a room barely lit by the small bedside lamp. A Raggedy Ann doll at her side, and her favorite blankie, pink with small unicorns, there too.

Lila sat between her daughter and the closed drapes. She held Kacey's hand up to her cheek, and she leaned on the edge of the bed looking at her. Peter could see his wife trying to take in her daughter in a sort of motherly prayer.

"Honey."

Lila looked up at the men who had interrupted her peaceful moment, as painful as it was.

"Dr. Cuevas would like to talk to us."

"Sure."

She gently placed Kacey's hand down on the blanket at her side, stood, and rounded the bed to meet them by the door. She crossed her arms and smiled, "Hi, Doctor."

"Mrs. Hubberton," he nodded. "Clearly Kacey has a very aggressive form of the disease, and with our lack of progress with our traditional measures, I'd like to discuss with you an experimental drug currently at trial. Kacey does not fit the typical profile, given her age and the aggression, but I did contact the principal investigator and he believes he can help us get a compassionate use exception for Kacey."

Tears of hope came to Lila's eyes.

"There are risks," Cuevas continued, "being a trial the entire safety profile isn't known, and its efficacy in question. That said, you may feel it is worth taking the risk, and certainly the scientists involved, who I've known for years, feel the drug is promising."

Peter looked over to his daughter and Lila followed his eyes.

Hodgkin's Disease manifesting in this way, they were told, was quite rare. Kacey was a member of an unlucky and small club.

"We're grabbing at straws," Peter said it, realizing he had meant it only as a thought for himself, but he vocalized in an angry and pointed tone.

Dr. Cuevas didn't respond. In his many years in the profession he had become used to remaining silent to allow loved ones to vent frustrations and not take them personally.

Lila took her husband's hand, "What else do we do?"

Peter shook his head, let go of his wife's hand, and turned to Cuevas, "Why is this so bad for her? This was curable."

"We don't always have the answer to that question. Immune systems can react differently to disease, treatments can fare better or worse."

Lila rubbed Peter's back gently. The two worked well together because they rarely felt angry at the same time, they balanced each other. "We keep grabbing at the straws until one of them works, honey."

Peter now targeted Lila with darting eyes. She was the one who sat next to him in the waiting area making him promise Kacey would be okay. She was the one applying pressure on him. Lila the one, in not so many words, telling him to make a deal with the devil if that would cure their daughter.

CHAPTER FIFTEEN
2008, Saturday February 23rd

"It's no wonder roads so often are used as a metaphor for fate," Arthur didn't take his eyes off the stretch of pavement ahead as he spoke, "you stay on course and you'll reach your destination. But..." he slowed his SUV and turned right onto a path identified only from years of vehicles driving along what was once grass that quickly weaved into a thickly wooded area, "if you veer off, suddenly you don't know where you'll end up. Now, you could reach that very same destination, that's a possibility, but less likely. You've changed your destiny, maybe it's less in your control now, but there are entirely new possibilities of various probabilities."

Peter, so far sitting quietly in the passenger seat and like Arthur completely decked in camouflage, didn't want to hear it.

He clutched his coffee in the thin paper cup with cardboard sleeve that he got from a convenience store a few miles back. The shaking of the vehicle had the small opening for sipping bubbling a bit.

The feeling of guilt still sat with him. Even now the sun barely welcomed the day, with it planted low behind the trees and darting rays between them, highlighting the evaporating dew. He rose at 4:30 a.m. and kissed Lila before meeting Arthur at the end of the driveway. He hadn't worn his camo in god knows how long, and hated it. He felt self-conscious and uncomfortable — all while feeling he needed to be home. Nothing about this was right.

"Arthur, what are we doing?"

"I told you there were two enterprises. This is the second."

Arthur turned and smiled at Peter, "We're going hunting."

"I realize that, but why are we going hunting when my daughter is incredibly sick and my wife in pieces?"

Arthur tucked the car into a small open spot, just a few square yards, devoid of trees or grass.

"All you do is question," Arthur gave Peter's knee a friendly slap, opened his door, and jumped out. "Come, this is important. This is to protect from the worst-case scenario."

That made Peter pause. *Worst-case scenario*. That would be death. *What did he mean by 'protect' from it?*

Peter did as he was told and exited the vehicle. He hadn't seen Arthur in a mood like this, maybe ever. He seemed...excited. Which was probably why he got away with questioning him.

Arthur raised the SUV's back lid and slid out a rifle, handing it to Peter. "This is yours." He then drew out a large and sheathed machete that he slung over his shoulder.

Peter looked at his old friend, feeling helpless, "I don't

know how to use this, not really. I haven't shot in years."

"Just keep it pointed at the ground until you aim to shoot." He closed and locked the SUV, "Let's go."

Arthur led the way into the woods, the two men trekking along a narrow trail.

"What are we hunting?"

"Moose."

"Moose? I don't think it's moose season. I think that's in the fall."

Arthur didn't answer the question but spoke in a more serious tone than he had been. "We're doing everything we can to get Kacey healthy. But we're off-road now, and dealing with probabilities. We need an insurance policy."

Peter listened between the lines, like he always had to do with Arthur.

"Come, this way," Arthur stepped over a large downed tree and approached what looked to be a clearing ahead as blue sky started creeping between trunks.

After a few dozen yards the men stopped, having reached the top of a small gorge, a shallow and slow-moving stream about thirty feet below.

"Get down," Arthur whispered as he lowered to his belly on the naked rock ledge to watch the open space.

Peter followed, being sure to keep the rifle safely aimed.

They lay there next to each other in silence for a few minutes.

"A moose symbolizes awakening."

Arthur sharing that bit of information, unprompted, and with such a boring tone had Peter's mind swimming. *Awakening? Awakening from what? Who? What the hell was he talking about?*

Suddenly Peter felt a few taps on his shoulder, Arthur

alerting him to what appeared from their right, from a bend in the gorge.

A moose.

Rare to see, Peter just stayed in awe. Even at a good few hundred feet away, its presence was imposing and impressive. And they hadn't even been here long.

It wasn't until he noticed Arthur looking at him with a gaze of direction that he realized he needed to shoot the creature.

Peter looked from it to Arthur and back again.

The large animal's dark brown beard, along with the hair under its belly, dripped from the water it must have been recently drinking. Its antlers looked heavy.

Peter didn't want to kill it.

He took a deep breath as he watched the animal slowly step along the stream below. Kacey came to his mind, that little hand that wrapped around his finger just a few years ago gave him the motivation he needed. He'd sacrifice this animal a hundred times over if it would save her.

Shifting his body to tuck the rifle into his shoulder, and placing it against his cheek for accuracy, he aimed it down.

The men sat in silence, as seemingly did all the creatures of the forest.

Looking down the sight he pointed the weapon just above its left front leg. From basic anatomy, he hoped a vital organ would be there, perhaps lungs or even its heart, but it also offered the best chance of actually hitting his shot given its size.

Peter took a deep breath again, then held it.

He placed his finger on the trigger, held the rifle tightly but gently, and pulled.

The recoil he expected and his body reacted, but the

sound shook him. Peter's nerves erupted at the moment the blast reached his ears and reverberated off and down the gorge.

Birds squawked and fluttered out of their nests and away.

He watched the moose closely.

Dark blood ran from where he had hit, exactly where he had aimed.

The moose took a single step forward, then fell to its front knees. It jerked its head as it tried to use momentum to stand back up, but then collapsed to its right side.

Peter couldn't see Arthur's smile but felt it as his old friend patted him on the back and stood.

"Nice and true. Good shot, Peter."

He didn't move yet, just looked down at the animal. Its head propped up in an odd manner from the antlers jammed into the rocky floor. Its eyes pointed downstream as if in a confused sadness on why he couldn't have just continued on his way.

The creature made no more movements.

"Come, let's go down. No need to be here longer than we need to."

Arthur started down to his right, toward an unseen path he must have already known about that would lead to the gorge below.

Peter shifted back onto his knees, his butt on his heels, and the rifle at his side.

Realizing his mind might start to question what he had done, he shook his head, grabbed the rifle, and stood to follow Arthur. He didn't want to think. Didn't want to consider the moose, the trouble he might be in, or even what this all meant. He needed to focus on what Arthur told him to do. Place his mind elsewhere and become a robot until this was over.

He carefully managed the rocky path to the stream and followed Arthur over the shallow water to the downed animal, where they both stood looking at it. Its large body easily bigger than the two men.

Arthur noticed his friend's eyes. While they pointed at the moose they gazed elsewhere, lost in the gravity of his life.

He spoke quietly and with care, knowing Peter needed to understand, "This a tether. If we fail in saving Kacey and she passes, with it we'll be able to keep Kacey's spirit tied to our plane to prepare for her return. This moose's spirit is now one end of that tether, the end that Kacey will be connected to. Here, in our realm, will one day be the other end."

Peter looked at Arthur, "Another end?"

"That's right. This creature will connect to another, much like people are connected. The living moose acts as the other end of the tether."

Peter thought a moment. "How does that bring her back?"

"The living end of the tether will be tied to someone here, someone alive I mean. We then…well…swap ends."

"Who?"

"That's what we've been preparing, Peter."

Peter stood a moment staring at the animal, thankful he couldn't see its eyes from where it lay.

He thought back to a conversation his father had with him around the age of eighteen. How the Ross family not only played such an important role in the Hubbertons' successes, but that Peter needed to show them respect as they could be dangerous. Bertrand made it clear, don't ever get on their bad side.

Arthur drew the machete from its sheath and positioned the handle in front of Peter as he cradled its edge carefully in his hands.

"Now, cut off his head."

* * *

Peter stood in the doorway to Kacey's bedroom, empty of his daughter as she now stayed at the hospital, and just as empty of light. Seeing it this way made him unbearably sad, like Kacey had already passed. He shook that feeling from him, she was alive and everyone rallying around her to keep her that way. He wouldn't surrender to thoughts of loss.

He made his way down the hall to the master bedroom.

Lila sat on her side of the bed brushing her hair in her long nightshirt, "Today was hard."

"Yeah, I'm sorry."

She looked up at her husband surprised, "Oh, I don't mean because you were gone this morning. I just mean she didn't have a good day. Not that she has good days anymore."

"I wish I was with you both."

Lila returned the brush to the bedside table and tucked her feet under the covers. Peter flipped up the covers from his side of the bed and began pulling the tight-fitting athletic shirt off his body. He had left the heavy camo downstairs to place back in storage.

"I'm exhausted," Peter proclaimed.

"How was the hunting trip?"

Peter didn't know how to answer. Was it good? Not so good? He had no idea.

"I don't even know, to be honest."

"Did you shoot something?"

"Yes," he had difficulty admitting it.

Peter flipped the switch on the wall, draping the room in darkness, then pulled his long underwear off and took his place next to his wife.

"Do you know why?" Lila, even in her naivete of the situation, understood it wasn't really a hunting trip.

"Vaguely."

Lila reached under the covers and took her husband's hand.

They remained quiet until they fell asleep.

* * *

Peter stood on that ridge above the gorge, looking down at the moose he fell.

It lay there with its head still awkwardly propped by the antlers dug into the ground.

The stream flowed over the creature's hooves.

Peter turned to his right to the path down he knew was there. As he walked, carefully, the dark forest floor made him realize the day passed and night had arrived.

He reached the gorge and crossed the slow stream that twinkled under the moon and stars, approaching the massive animal that faced away.

He took steps slowly, behind it, and could see how its right antlers lodged between some rocks which resulted in the strange position of its head.

Along its neck, across the entire wide breadth of it, Peter could make out a thick line of dark blood — clearly from where he had cut its head off.

But Arthur took it, he thought. *We carried it to his vehicle and placed it on plastic in the back. It stunk like hell the entire ride back.*

Suddenly, and surprising Peter, the animal shook its

head free from the rocks and lurched up to its side, still looking downstream. It stayed there, as if waiting, just a few moments before jerking up again, this time to its knees.

Peter noticed the animal's head didn't move as smoothly or in unison with its body. As if it wasn't connected firmly, like someone placed the severed part back on the torso with sticks too weak to hold its weight. It slid, just a bit, from side to side and up and down as the beast moved.

It leaned forward to get its back legs under it, then pushed up to be fully standing.

Peter froze in fear. Perhaps if he didn't move, didn't make a sound, the creature would make its way back down the gorge, never knowing he stood just a couple of feet behind.

But the moose began to turn, its head circling round from the right side, to look down at Peter.

He could see its eyes now.

In the darkness they glowed. But not like a reflection of light from the moon.

It emanated light. Swirling yellows, blues, and reds surrounded by darkness and pricked with pinpoints of white light. Like each a window to some corner of the universe. Nebulae mixed with forming stars and galaxy clusters.

The celestial structures started rising out of its eyes, slowly, toward the sky. The gases and stars drifting up like smoke as the beast towered over him.

It snorted and lowered its head, the cut in its neck making the movement spasmodic and intimidating Peter.

The elements that make up the universe, the filaments, the voids, the black holes, continued to flow from what were the creature's enormous eyes.

The galaxies expanded and stretched to cover the once

clear sky above, then slowly down to surround both Peter and the moose.

Drifting in the great vastness of everything, the moose's eyes now glowed with fury. A deep and angry red aimed right at Peter.

Peter opened his mouth to scream, but no sound came. He forced the air from his lungs, felt his diaphragm tighten, his abs tighten, his chest…but nothing.

* * *

Peter woke with a start, quickly sitting up in bed. He dropped his head to his hands as his heart beat hard against his chest.

He felt Lila's touch on his back.

"You're soaked."

He could feel her hand on his slippery skin, and it felt cold.

"Are you okay?"

"Yeah, yeah, I'm fine. Just a bad dream."

But he wasn't fine, and it wasn't just a bad dream.

From somewhere out there, one end of the tether touched him.

CHAPTER SIXTEEN
2008, Thursday July 17th

On their traditional couch and book-ended by large gold-tasseled pillows, Lila sat on Kacey's right, Peter her left, as she flipped through the pages of *Curious George Flies a Kite*.

Their family room was meant for just that, family — with no television, and just an old-fashioned radio for background music. The furniture all positioned for loved ones to sit together and talk. The focal point of the room being the slightly oversized fireplace, on the mantle above sat two small and ornate Chinese vases and an original painting from a local artist depicting a rotting wagon wheel leaning against an old barn door.

With noon approaching, the silky white drapes of the large windows that look out the front let light in as they danced delicately from the gentle breeze.

Peter, looking over Kacey's shoulder, saw the image of Curious George questioning the family of bunnies caged tightly together. They didn't look overly happy, but from countless readings he knew later the white furry animals would all run back into their enclosure.

She turned a few more pages, to where George, arms out straight, held the string to a kite tightly. Its large white and yellow-stripped fabric stretched by the wind.

The words on the page leaped out at him, *He let the string go a little, and then a little more, and then a little more, and then a little more.*

They echoed in his mind as they did on paper.

George knew the wind was too strong, the Rey's said so on that very same page. But George, curious by name, couldn't help but release the kite, little by little, to see where nature would take it. It was a kite, after all, and built by man to fly.

A small red bird, just above and to the right of the kite, watched while another stood behind George watching secretly. They knew what George did not.

The words made Peter uneasy. He shifted his weight and brought his right arm up and around his daughter, softly placing his hand at the back of Lila's neck.

Kacey seemed none-the-wiser from the past number of months. Just a kid again. Healthy and cancer free. Enjoying a day with her parents.

"What do you say we get some ice cream? Drive up to the islands, get some maple creemees?"

As much as Peter loved the three of them sitting there quietly, just appreciating each other without the concern of disease, he couldn't look at that book anymore. He couldn't logically justify it, nor deny it.

Lila leaned forward to look at her daughter, "What do you think, Kace? Maple creemees?"

"Okay," she said without much excitement, which tore

at Peter's heart. He understood she agreed only because he proposed it.

Kacey closed the book, slid off the couch as kids do, and neatly placed it in the wicker basket that sat on the lowest shelf of their built-ins that surrounded the tiled fireplace.

Lila took Peter's hand and stood, then turned to look at him with her arm outstretched, "Come on, you said."

He stood and kissed her forehead.

Though by all measures Kacey was now perfectly healthy, the pressure of having a sick child hadn't lifted from Peter. Sure, Lila smiled and danced with her daughter as they had before, and no more forced promises came his way. But, he still felt the anxiety and weight on his shoulders. He thought it might pass with time.

Kacey skipped out of the room toward the back door where they could hear her putting on her sneakers.

Lila released him and followed, leaving Peter alone.

He took a deep breath and visualized stress escaping him as he exhaled.

PART FOUR

CHAPTER SEVENTEEN
2021, Saturday June 26th

They all agreed Kristin would go alone. Shelly, her
curiosity too much, stayed at the Fuller's house with Emil
while Kristin took her van to see Betsy. "You better call
once you're out of there," she demanded as Kristin left.

Betsy's was a development typical for the area. She
had a two-story townhouse-style condo in a long row of
identical units, just a few minutes north of Burlington, so
about a half-hour's drive.

She parked in a designated visitor's spot and walked to
her door — as an end unit, Betsy had a nice open space to
the right side.

That morning they tossed around theories of what
Kristin might learn, or what might occur. From the
conspiratorial to the mundane. In the end, none of the
explanations they dreamt up made any sense as none could
account for every particular. If they were transporting
Kacey, who somehow secretly survived, why cause an

accident? If they wanted an accident, why have Kacey there? Was it even Kacey? They couldn't solve the puzzle and hoped they'd learn something from Betsy to put the pieces together.

Kristin set aside, for the sake of conversation with her friends, that she really wanted to meet Betsy to help herself heal. She felt that somehow Betsy was closer to the accident than others were, even though that didn't make sense as her own aunts represented the same relation to her father as Betsy to Peter. She felt that the death of their loved ones together did somehow connect them, and she wanted to hug the woman. She wanted a warm hug back.

Kristin opened the glass storm door and knocked on the closed white wooden front door.

"Coming," she heard a chipper voice from the other side, and seconds later Betsy emerged to embrace her without hesitation.

Kristin fell apart, the emotions running so strong her knees weakened and the older woman tightened her hold to keep her standing.

"Oh my poor thing, you must come in."

Betsy, in the kindest way, led Kristin into her home and shut the door behind.

In front of Kristin a hall led to the living area, to her right a stairway up, and to her left the tiny kitchen. The women walked the short hall while Kristin composed herself by clearing her throat and wiping tears. They passed a couple porcelain feeding bowls on the floor that looked to be for a cat to the living space where they sat together on the sofa.

The condo was small, and though sunny outside, very little natural light found its way in through the glass double doors at the back. Though an end unit, the outside wall facing the couch had no windows. An overhead light and side-table lamp kept the room bright.

The wooden floor was mostly covered by an old Oriental rug, and a number of shelves on the walls held various knick-knacks portraying some holiday scene or representing some location Betsy probably had traveled to.

She wore a blouse you might expect for church and a pair of slacks. She had a little four-leaf clover broach pinned on. Everything about her screamed *Grandmother*.

Kristin dried her eyes, "I'm sorry, I didn't expect that."

"It's okay, dear. You've been through a lot."

"True, but so have you."

"Yes, I have. But I have many years on you. I've been battle-scared."

Kristin chuckled. Betsy's soft voice she remembered well from her eulogy. She felt very welcomed by her and started thinking that Betsy might be someone to continue a relationship with. Perhaps she would be another reason to visit Vermont on occasion.

"So, tell me, what can I do for you?" Betsy placed one hand on her own knee, and another on Kristin's. The gesture made her feel good.

"First, I just want to be transparent. I want you to know that I actually went to Peter and Lila's service."

Betsy lightened in surprise, "Oh did you! That's very nice of you, thank you."

"I heard you talk of course, and what you said was beautiful."

"Oh please. Nothing but words from the heart."

Kristin looked around. The place was one you'd imagine someone working very hard for, but not being paid much for all of their efforts. She felt for her.

She cleared her throat, "Thank you for letting me come visit, I was worried you might be mad or blame me."

"For God's sake, girl. You're at no fault here."

"Thanks, it's nice to hear that." Kristin knew she wasn't to blame, but hearing it brought relief. "I'd love to know more about them…if you don't mind."

"Where would you like me to begin."

"I don't know. What were they like?"

Betsy thought a moment. "Peter had his faults. Everything you heard me say the other day was true, but you don't air dirty laundry. He was human, made mistakes. He could be prideful. Didn't like to admit when he might be wrong. Would even argue a losing point. But, he loved the people he loved with everything he had. To a fault even. When I made the decision to distance myself from our parents, he was all the family I had and he supported me as much as he could and as much as I'd allow it."

"He seemed like a good person."

Betsy laughed, "He could be. He was. One time, I was a Sophomore in high school, and he was…was…well maybe 6th grade, and there was a boy picking on me at a playground we'd go to in the neighborhood we grew up in. The boy, I think his name was Chad," she leaned in close to Kristin, "never trust a Chad…well he was in my grade, a lot bigger than Peter. Anyway, Peter just couldn't let it be. It's not like Chad bothered me much, he probably had a crush is why he was picking. So Peter goes up and clocks him."

Betsy laughed again, slapping her knee and rocking back, "Well, it didn't do much to Chad. Not sure he felt it much at all coming from this little middle-schooler. And Peter got a butt-whoopin'. I had to pull Chad away."

"Oh, my God."

"Yup. He and I had our issues, but if anything happened Peter would throw himself onto a fire if needed."

They sat in silence a moment.

"What about their daughter?"

"Oh so sad, dear. So sad. She drowned, just terrible. They were a wreck, but you know what, they came out of it pretty good. They lifted each other, like I said, and were able to move on."

"Did you go to the funeral?"

"There should never be, on God's own Earth, a service where the church is filled with children." She looked down at her lap, pulling some imaginary little hair from her slacks. "It was beautiful though."

"She was nine when she died?"

"Somewhere 'round there."

The two sat quietly another moment. Betsy lost in memories of the past, her eyes gazing down at the rug, but focused on those visions.

"Kacey was strong. She really gave her parents a run."

"Was she rambunctious?"

Betsy looked back up to her guest, "Oh no, I don't mean that. She…well, she actually had cancer. You know, earlier. Before she passed."

Kristin was taken aback, not thinking that's where Betsy was going by her statement.

"Yeah, she was diagnosed at six years old I believe. It's hard for parents, you know, seeing a kid go through that."

"I can't imagine."

Betsy rubbed her eyes and Kristin looked away for a moment, appreciating the woman's care and willingness to open her home, but realizing it must be hard recounting these tragedies.

"Peter took it particularly hard. She fought it like a champ, kids do that. They don't really know something's wrong because they haven't lived long enough to know. For them, that's just life. That's just what it is. Peter, though, well he wouldn't accept it. He threw everything behind curing her. They did the traditional Western medicine, radiation and chemo, but he also did all sorts of other things. Natural stuff."

Kristin could see how a father might do that, and saw no fault in Peter, "I can't blame him. He was fighting for his little girl."

The woman nodded but without much of a smile. "Anyway, she did recover after a couple of hard years. By the time of the accident she was a happy and healthy girl."

"That's heartbreaking."

A quiet tear formed and Betsy delicately wiped it away.

"I didn't see Peter much for a period after that. Lila would check in, we'd have a ladies' night on occasion, but Peter was a ghost. When I did see him, Lila wouldn't be with him. It wasn't for a couple years that I really saw them together and more regularly," Betsy forced a smile and looked at Kristin, thinking maybe she was over-sharing, "But, they still supported each other through those times. I could see it, could hear it from them. It was just a tough time for them, and odd for some reason."

"They went through something no one should have to. And it sounds like they handled it the best we can hope for from people. They sound very loving."

They sat another moment, looking out to the back patio that faced a thin strip of trees that only partially blocked the busy road beyond it.

Kristin asked the next question only after mustering up the courage, not knowing what sort of emotions it might bring up for Betsy, "You said earlier that you distanced yourself from your parents. Why is that? If you don't mind…"

Betsy looked at Kristin like she needed to examine her intentions, the older woman's expression one of a subtle surprise mixed with needing time to evaluate how much to share while still being honest.

"Well…" she shifted on the cushion so her knees moved from virtually touching Kristin's to now pointed directly at the facing wall, "our parents were different. It's not like they were mean, but they had their ways." She looked back at Kristin, "Look, you know how people are. They have their belief systems, and if you can't live with those, and you certainly can't change people, then you need to do what's right for you. No matter how hard that might make things."

Kristin nodded.

"So," Betsy smiled and happily slapped Kristin's knee, "what else would you like to talk about? Or, perhaps you'd like some tea? I have some cookies too!"

Kristin returned the smile, thankful the awkward question was behind her without any obvious negative consequences, "Actually, I'd love to see any photos of Kacey you might have."

Betsy's growing smile told Kristin she was glad she asked. "You bet. I'm the executor of their will, and I brought the most cherished items from their home here. I have a number of their albums, they loved pictures. Here, let me get one."

Betsy stood and went to a closet by the front door. After just a moment she returned with a large, off-white, photo album which she dropped onto the dining room table that sat between the couch and the kitchen.

"Come, child."

Betsy flipped another switch to turn on the small chandelier over the wooden table.

Kristin went and stood next to the older woman. Both leaned forward as Betsy flipped to the first page.

There two photos of Kacey as a newborn were stuck behind the thin sheet of plastic. The same type of album she had from her parents.

In the first, baby Kacey lay alone in the small newborn bed in what must have been the maternity ward. A little pink cap on, and wrapped in a soft white blanket like a burrito. Her eyes closed, cheeks red, and just a bit of light brown hair poking out on her forehead.

The second, both Peter and Lila held the baby proudly. Smiles brimming from ear to ear.

"So cute," Kristin was being honest, Kacey was a very cute baby.

"Yes, she really was. A little Gerber baby."

Betsy continued to flip through page-by-page, and the two eventually sat at the hard wooden chairs as Betsy recounted a few stories behind some photos.

The obligatory bringing baby home.

The messy dinner-time photo.

Surrounded by stuffed animals.

Baptism.

First day of pre-school, and so on.

Kristin enjoyed seeing the photos, but more listening to Betsy.

Then it happened, taking Kristin's breath away.

* * *

Kristin didn't bother calling Shelly or Emil like she had

promised when she left Betsy's. It took all of her energy not to rush the woman, to be mindful of how she might come across were she to suddenly run out after seeing the photos. Kristin thought she should do yoga more, perhaps that would help settle herself in stressful times.

Betsy continued to be welcoming and entertained all of Kristin's questions thoughtfully. When Kristin asked to borrow the photo album, promising to return it unharmed and to treat it with the utmost care and respect, Betsy did appear curious, even a bit concerned, but allowed it nonetheless.

Kristin did send a quick group text upon her departure from the woman's, *omw. Will talk*.

Emil and Shelly, who had been enjoying lemonade on the front porch, looked at each other in confusion after receiving the message.

"Guess we'll find out what that means." Shelly, knowing Kristin for so long, was not accustomed to communication from her that was anything other than clear.

"Hope she's alright," Emil worried.

Kristin arrived after about a half-hour, driving faster down the driveway than normal and kicking up rocks from the back of the van.

Emil and Shelly didn't move or dare say a word as Kristin emerged from the vehicle clutching a large leather photo album to her chest. She walked quickly down the stone path, up the steps, and right between the two of them to inside the house.

"Come on," she demanded.

They followed curiously.

Kristin went straight to the dining room table where light poured into the open living space. She dropped the album and pulled out two chairs in front of it, directing them to sit.

They did as told, and watched as Kristin left the room.

"What the fuck is this about?" Shelly quietly asked Emil before taking a sip of her drink.

Emil shrugged and shook his head.

Kristin returned quickly with the album they had perused in preparation for Henry and Elizabeth's funeral.

She stood between her friends and plopped the large book down next to Kacey's, and slid them apart to give each enough room to open. Her brown album on the right, and Kacey's white on the left in front of Shelly.

"Look."

She opened each to the first page. The newborn photos of Kacey she had just seen, and her own first page with the photo of just her and her mother.

She pointed as she quickly spoke, "This is Kacey's album from her parents. Betsy had it. I asked if I could take it for a bit, which was super weird but whatever. She let me."

"And this," she tapped it, "is my album." She stated the fact as if it were somehow important.

Kristin flipped to the second page of each, "Normal baby shit." She spoke a little excitedly, but with a hint of frightened anxiety.

Shelly looked up at Kristin, confused by what was happening.

"And more," Kristin flipped to the third, fourth, then fifth respective pages.

"Kristin, what are we looking at? I don't get it."

She turned a few more of Kacey's book until she found what she was looking for, then did the same for her own. Kristin paused, looking at each. On the left, Kacey appeared about six in age and playing with some other kids whom, of course, Kristin didn't know. On the right, little Kristin was playing dress up in her room alone.

"What's going on, Kris?" Shelly seemed nervous, like her friend really had lost her mind.

Emil just sat quietly, afraid to say anything that might not be unquestionably supportive but also feeling a growing concern that Kristin had fallen off the deep end.

"Are you ready?"

Shelly gave a sarcastic affirmative expression including an exaggerated nod.

Kristin turned a page in each book again.

Shelly and Emil remained silent as their eyes examined what now lay before them. They leaned in a bit more closely.

On the left, they could see four photos of Kacey, two on each facing page, still somewhere around six years old. In the first she stood next to a couch where her father, Peter, was sitting. Her right hand in his, her left holding a doll. Peter's expression appeared somber. Across from them, in a winged easy chair, sat someone they hadn't seen in any previous photos, a man that looked older than Peter by a few years. Between the Hubbertons and the man rested a cold red-brick fireplace, and above it a painting that looked to be of a small and old Italian village, a cobblestone and empty road, aligned with stone buildings, meandered up a large hill. Its colors lacked vibrancy.

The second photo depicted Kacey at what was obviously the Burlington waterfront. She was alone on the large lawn that separated the train tracks from the boardwalk and held a small half-eaten vanilla creamee. Her lips covered in ice cream, and hair a general mess.

In the third Kacey danced with her mother in what

may have been their living room, the television in the background off. The two hand-in-hand. Kacey in a pink tutu.

The last looked to be a friend of Kacey's birthday party as another girl wore a *Birthday Girl!* t-shirt. Kacey stood next to her as she sat on a plush carpet opening a gift, Kacey holding a blowout party favor and wearing a small tiara.

On their right, four photos of Kristin.

The first, Kristin stood next to her seated father, holding hands, and in her other hand a doll. Across from them another man. The photo just like Kacey's, including the fireplace and Italian landscape painting. The only real exception being Henry's expression wasn't so somber, he appeared generally happy.

The second she sat in that same spot on the waterfront. Creamee in hand.

The third, dancing hand-in-hand with Elizabeth in their living room. The television off.

The last at a birthday party, just like Kacey's. She wore a tiara and held the party favor.

"Holy fuck," Emil broke his silence.

"Kris, this is weird," Shelly stated without moving her eyes from the pages.

"This is just the beginning," Kristin said solemnly.

She turned to the next page, like before each facing held two photos, four visible in total in each book. And, like the previous, each photo virtually identical, with seemingly only different people — as if they all only played roles in a script unknown to any of them. From the slightly faded colors and different fashion trends, it was easy to see that Kristin's photos were older.

Emil leaned forward, his eyes going from one picture to

its counterpart, examining closely. "Jesus Christ."

Kristin didn't wait, she turned the page again.

The same pattern repeated itself.

She flipped another.

Same thing.

Over the next minute or so Kristin kept turning the pages, giving enough time for Shelly and Emil to see how each held the same photos. What was in each didn't seem to matter, Kacey's mimicked her own.

She got to the last page then took Emil's lemonade, rounded the table, and sat across from them, allowing them to flip back and forth through the books.

Each photo depicted the girls in the same position, wearing similar clothes, and in the same or similar setting. If Kristin's photo had her at home, Kacey was apparently in hers. If they were somewhere public, then the photos were of the exact same location.

Kristin sipped the drink.

Shelly looked at her friend, "I don't get it, how could this be?"

"I don't know. I feel like I'm being fucked with." She felt more than that, in reality. She felt violated, she felt like her life had been stolen or a fraud. But she didn't know why those emotions bubbled up.

"But this is impossible. This literally isn't possible," Shelly's voice emphatic.

"Explain that to the photos, Shell. They're there. They're real."

Emil looked from Kristin to Shelly, "Well something's going on here. These," he motioned to the albums, "are... are I don't know what. But then there's the girl you've been seeing. It must be Kacey, right?"

"Yeah!" Shelly utterly convinced now her friend's

experiences were not derived from some brain damage in the accident.

They sat in silence for a long period, Kristin drinking and refilling the glass, the others still examining the albums.

Emil turned his attention away from the photos and stared out the window across from him, over Kristin's shoulder. He needed a minute to think, and focusing on those images wasn't helping. When he had problems to solve, his mind needed space. He'd look out windows, up at a blank ceiling, or even close his eyes. It helped him process.

He looked at Kristin, "Remember that riddle you told me? The one you said took you two months to solve? I quit after ten minutes because I knew I just wasn't up for it."

"The one about the job interview."

"Yeah, that one."

"So?"

"So maybe this is like that."

"A job interview?"

"No, a riddle."

"It's not a riddle," Kristin became visibly agitated. "Someone's fucking with my life."

"Okay, right, but we need to approach it like that. It's something to solve."

Shelly piped in, "Like a murder mystery."

"Hey," Kristin wasn't amused.

"Sorry, I mean it's a mystery."

Emil rhythmically tapped the table with his fingers, "So what were those tips you told me for solving riddles?"

"Question assumptions."

"Right."

"Examine if there are other interpretations for words or sounds."

"So…" Emil led Kristin on to think about the current situation.

Shelly perked up in her seat excitedly, "Wait a minute!"

She flipped back through Kacey's album to the first photo that appeared similar to Kristin's. The little girl stood next to her father seated on that sofa. That somber look.

She turned to the same page of Kristin's, and there she was also next to her father.

"Look," with the index finger of each hand she pointed to the man that sat across from Henry and Peter. "That's the same person."

Emil and Kristin leaned forward for a better look, but Kristin being on the other side of the table was too far, so, unconcerned with etiquette, she pulled the albums over without a word.

"You're right, it is."

Kristin realized that instinctively she already knew this fact, as the photos obviously had been taken in the same home, but the point hadn't been given appropriate attention until Shelly verbalized it.

Kristin stared at the man as her friend and lover stood and went to her side of the table to look over her shoulder.

In Kristin's photo the man looked pleasant, with an easy and relaxed expression. He appeared to be in his mid-thirties, slender, with brown hair. He wore a red sweater and khakis, his legs crossed with his right arm on his high knee, and his left up by his face. In the picture six-year-old Kristin looked at the man, but the 29-year-old didn't recognize him.

The image from Kacey's album, though similar, had a much different feel. While Kristin's father looked happy, Peter clearly was not — not angry but sad. The unknown man sat again with his legs crossed. This time in jeans and a long-sleeve polo. His hair grayer, and a few more wrinkles around the eyes. Clearly the same man, though this time his expression communicated a pointed focus and not nearly as relaxed. The room pictured was clearly the same — while the sofa had been upgraded since Kristin's, the winged chair, fireplace, and painting remained unchanged.

The three remained on those pictures, to the point where when Emil spoke it slightly startled the women, "So who is it?"

"I don't know," Kristin responded softly.

Shelly didn't want to be rude by touching other people's photos uninvited, "Might the backs say?"

Kristin started with her own, drawing the thin plastic away to pull the photo from the sticky backing.

The reverse of the photo disappointingly blank.

She replaced the picture and did the same with Kacey's. "Nothing, good thought though."

Emil took the seat next to Kristin, and Shelly followed by sitting at the head of the table to Kristin's right.

"So how do we figure out who this person is?" Emil asked.

Kristin knew of two ways. The most likely to succeed was simply to ask Betsy, but she didn't want to go there in case it raised suspicion. The second was a long shot. "Well, he apparently knew both my father and Peter. It's possible he went to both services, and if he did he may have signed the guest books."

"We'd have to compare them," Emil sounded dismissive.

"Right," Shelly added, "how would you get the one for the Hubbertons?"

"Betsy had this," Kristin tapped the album, "I bet she

has the guest book too. Who else would?" While she spoke it aloud she realized the request to see the guest book would raise the same suspicions and she immediately dismissed the idea.

"Yeah but you can't ask her for that," Shelly stated what Kristin had been thinking.

"You don't have to," Emil smiled, "You don't know him, right?"

"No, no idea."

Emil continued, "Then we just start with yours. We go through the list of names one by one. Any names you recognize, family members, friends, whatever, we can eliminate. We can also remove all women. That could narrow down the list to a few, maybe one if we're lucky."

Kristin nodded, liking the idea, "Right. I could text Betsy saying I saw someone at each service but wasn't sure who it was and send her the names. She could check her list."

Shelly's eyes widened, "That could work."

Without any further discussion, Kristin retrieved the book from upstairs — she had placed it in her parents' room as some sort of offering. Like their spirits rested there and would be pleased with the turnout.

She quickly returned and sat back down between the others, turning to the first page.

"Oh," Emil interjected, "If you don't know a name I'll search for them online," he pulled his phone from his pocket, "If they teach at UVM or work at the hospital we could probably eliminate them as co-workers."

"But it might actually be a co-worker." Shelly countered.

"Let's put them on a separate list. If we hit a roadblock we can circle back to them. Can you get a pen and paper from the drawer?" Kristin motioned to Shelly, who did as asked.

Emil held his phone up, "I can also look for photos of the people, may be able to tell if it's him or not."

Kristin went about the task systematically. Each time she came to a non-feminine name she didn't recognize, she wrote it on the paper. This resulted in 33 names, a surprising number that made her appreciate the love people had for her parents.

She then read each to Emil, who performed a quick search, looking for evidence of employment and photos. Anyone found with a photo that looked very different from the man she would gently cross them out. For any working at the University or Medical Center, with either no or questionable photos, she placed a dot on the left side of their names.

Thanks to social media prevalence, this process resulted in three prioritized names. Individuals with male names that Kristin didn't recognize, could not find photos of, and seemingly did not work with her parents.

Jeffrey Abernathy.

Arthur Ross.

Brient Quincey.

"None of those are familiar?" Shelly double-checked with Kristin.

"Not at all."

Kristin rose and went to the kitchen island where she dug into her purse for her cell phone. While at Betsy's they exchanged mobile numbers, each happy to keep in touch. She sent the text as planned, *Hi Betsy. TY again for meeting with me, was so nice to see you and you were so welcoming, can't thank you enough.* She hit *send* and continued with a second message, *I think I saw someone at both services, would love to know how our families might all be connected. I think the person's name is either Jeffrey Abernathy, Arthur Ross, or Brient Quincy. Would you mind checking the guest book for their names if you have it?*

They waited, staring at the phone that Kristin held up in front of her, wondering about what was happening at the other end. Did she get the message? Maybe she's out grocery shopping or something. Does she have the book, or will she have to track it down? Is the request weird? Does she think Kristin is up to something malicious?

Kristin lowered the phone to the table, and Shelly looked at the black screen unblinking, thinking a response would undoubtedly come quickly.

She caught a glimmer of light for just a moment. A quick, star-like, glint of white sparkling and reflecting off the screen. At first Shelly didn't know what it was, in fact largely ignored it as she wanted the damn thing to notify of a message. But then it happened again, and again, until she realized that rays of sunshine were coming in through the kitchen window and bouncing off the white moon around Kristin's neck.

Shelly sat up straight like she had been struck by lightning and turned to her friend, grasping her arm with her left hand, and pointing to the necklace with her right.

"Kris, your necklace!"

Kristin shot back in her seat in surprise, "What?"

"Were you wearing it when the accident happened?"

"Yeah."

"Maybe it's a part of this. Maybe that guy has something to do with it. This necklace is some sort of... well, I don't know what they're called. An amulet or something. Like it has magic powers. It's bringing some evil to you!" Shelly, though embarrassed at suggesting something so seemingly impossible, talked frantically.

Kristin placed the moon in her hand and raised the jewelry up to look at it, "Yeah, maybe."

"That's crazy," Emil spoke matter-of-factly.

"It's all crazy," Kristin lifted the necklace over her head and placed it at the center of the table. All three of them just looked at it for a moment. The white moon still softly glowing from the sun. "Obviously there's something between Kacey and me. Maybe Jim, or this moon, is it. And I'm not taking chances."

After a short minute Shelly stood and went to the refrigerator, "I need some of that vodka."

Emil and Kristin didn't move.

Shelly opened the freezer to retrieve the alcohol and poured just a bit into her glass. She returned it, then topped it off with seltzer from the refrigerator.

She crossed the island, stopping halfway, and looked at the calendar pinned to the closet door. Noticing something odd she called to her friend, "Hey, Kris, what's this?"

"What?"

Shelly turned to face her, wanting to be sure she communicated clearly. She put one finger on the day's square with the little lunar eclipse symbol. "The day of the lunar eclipse, looks like someone wrote 'Peter' on that day."

The air in the room dropped.

Kristin's mind raced. Could that old friend of her father's, the one they were going to watch the eclipse with, have been Peter Hubberton? She didn't remember her father saying the man's name, maybe worse didn't remember even asking.

"Holy shit," Emil broke the brief silence.

"You think it's the same?" Shelly asked as she took a sip of her drink and returned to her seat.

Kristin's eyes went from side to side and back as her mind scanned the events for clues.

"It has to be," Kristin looked at her friends. "Look, throughout this we find coincidence after coincidence. There comes a point they aren't coincidences anymore. I don't know what's going on, but I bet you anything it was this Peter's cabin we were heading to."

"Peter Hubberton?" Shelly asked with dreaded excitement.

"Yes."

Kristin stood and went to the calendar to see for herself. Peter's name clearly represented in blue ink on Sunday, the same day as the eclipse, "That's my father's handwriting." She did a quick scan, but nothing else written on the month seemed related.

Her mind raced as she tried to make sense of the series of revelations they had made. The photos, the man, the moon necklace, the calendar. It all felt like a new puzzle or riddle had formed. She took a deep breath as she calmed, reassuring herself she'd piece them together.

Suddenly her phone rattled loudly against the table from its vibration and Kristin moved quickly to it. But it wasn't a text from Betsy, it was a call as it continued to buzz. A local number, one with no identity saved to her contacts app so *Unknown Caller* appeared on the display.

They looked at each other as the unexpected had them paralyzed on what to do.

"Answer it," Shelly demanded.

Kristin picked up the phone, slid the bar to the green handset icon to complete the connection, and placed it to her ear.

"Hello?"
The male voice responded calmly.
"I hear you're looking for me."

CHAPTER EIGHTEEN

2021, Sunday June 27th

Sunday morning Kristin sat in the small office at the front of the home. She pushed aside her parents' shared laptop.

The antique desk had that smell you'd expect from old wood. Stained decades ago, the dark color had faded, and the soft wood presented thousands of wounds — the small pock marks from pens and colored rings from countless coffee mugs. Her great-great-grandfather, on her father's side, built the desk. She found it surprising her parents had continued to use it given its history.

She caught up on work, responding to emails and catching up with clients and peers. She reminded them to reach out as needed and apologized for the delays in her responses. Kristin sat back in her seat and took a moment to appreciate one email. The subject read "AviCare Confirmation", and in it Ian detailed the status of the biotech transaction. At the end of the first trading week, they had acquired over ten million dollars worth of shares and hoped to complete purchases within the next few weeks.

Kristin began to smile before realizing her parents couldn't celebrate with her. Sure, Emil would be happy, and Shelly too in her own way, but her parents witnessed Kristin's hard work through school and her early career to get where she was today.

They would have been proud.

She cleared her throat and stood, heading upstairs to get ready for the day.

The conversation yesterday with Arthur Ross lasted maybe twenty seconds. It left Kristin virtually speechless, not for its content, but for its simplicity. When she answered, and Arthur introduced himself, she immediately anticipated being threatened or otherwise having her progress in learning what exactly was going on interrupted.

But, at least for now, it appeared quite the opposite as she asked him if he would be willing to meet, Kristin didn't even say what about, and he immediately agreed.

One thing odd, which Kristin didn't so much mind, was that Arthur skipped pleasantries and politeness, though that isn't to say he was rude in any way. After she asked to meet he responded, "Of course. Meet me at my home, tomorrow at 3 p.m." He then gave his address, a house close to Camel's Hump mountain.

"There's no way in hell you're going alone." Emil didn't like the smell of the situation and wasn't about to let Kristin go to some strange man's house who was somehow involved in this strange mystery.

"I'm going too," Shelly jumped in, "Someone's going to have to be there to kick some ass if shit goes south."

"Yeah, that's why I'm going," Emil said to Shelly

offended.

"Love you dearly," Kristin spoke to her boyfriend, "but my money is on Shelly in a fight. You're a self-proclaimed pacifist."

While Shelly chuckled a bit Emil gave a false expression of being insulted.

They debated bringing the photo albums but in the end decided against it. They would take the chance that there's nothing in the pictures that Arthur would need to see.

The group met up again early Sunday afternoon, Joe lovingly asking Shelly when she would return to her family full-time and she had none of it, "When it's done, dear." She responded with both directness and love.

The three piled into Shelly's van at 2 p.m., 30 minutes before they needed to. They wanted extra time to check out the road to his home and get their bearings before walking to his door.

In the driver's seat Shelly sat up straight, her hands at the nine and three positions like she was on a mission. "What are you going to say?"

"Not really sure actually. I think I need to give him very little information at first, just that I saw him at each funeral. See what he says and look for opportunities to ask further questions."

"What if he doesn't offer anything useful?" Emil asked from the back.

"If I have to, then my last resort is to press. Tell him more about what I've been experiencing. See if demanding any answers does anything at all."

"And if not?" Shelly quickly looked over at her friend.

"I don't know, Shell. I can't make him talk if he doesn't want to. Let's hope he does."

They drove past Mountain View Drive, a dirt road with

mostly pine trees aligning on each side, where about a mile up they would find Arthur's home.

"Looks like any old Vermont road," while Shelly spoke it out loud, she did so to calm her nerves. And it did look that way, like a road that had been here since the dawn of the state.

She drove the van a couple of miles further where they pulled into a small gas station's lot. Shelly parked and turned in her seat to face her two passengers. "You guys ready for this?"

Kristin didn't blink, her expression as if this were any other day, "Yes. We have to approach him like we're just curious, just want to know about his relationships with the families." She checked herself, realizing she felt much like she did going into important work meetings with a lot on the line — focus, slow down, think.

Shelly looked at her and nodded, impressed by Kristin's calm demeanor, "You're stone cold, Kris."

Kristin now looked annoyed, "Can we get moving?"

Shelly shifted the van into reverse as she twisted in her seat. With no traffic to speak of, they headed to Mountain View Drive and turned left onto it in just a few minutes.

The van struggled with the incline and she took it slow, the three sitting in silence with only the grinding of the tires on dirt and stone filling space.

Ahead on the right they could see the start of a clearing as sunlight streaked across the windshield and grass replaced trees.

Set back a bit from the road sat the country home. Its classic yellow paint and white shutters, with a covered porch that overlooked Camel's Hump mountain, gave it the look of something you might see in a New England travel magazine. It seemed old, though well cared for. And tucked into the woods as it were, it also felt very secluded.

They pulled into the driveway and parked next to the blue Mercedes SUV.

Kristin opened her door before the van was off and got out, the others meeting her at the edge of the stone driveway.

"Down here," they heard from about fifty yards, past the far corner of the house.

Arthur Ross threw a section of wood onto a larger pile, his hands in thick gloves. "Wood fireplaces are a love-hate thing. I enjoy them in the cold winter, but all summer I just stack wood in preparation," he yelled towards his guests.

He took the first few steps towards them, pulling the gloves off and tossing them on the ground behind him.

With a large circular motion he waved them over, "Come on then."

Arthur Ross' silver hair didn't hide that he was the same man from the photo. More wrinkles, a bit more weight, but it was unquestionably him.

He took the couple steps up to the porch and kicked off his boots, the others following him up. With the gloves and boots off he looked ready for a lecture. His black slacks and brown short-sleeved, button-up, shirt were odd for the chores he had just been working.

Kristin reached him first, as he waited by the front door before going in.

"Hi, I'm Kristin, we spoke on the phone." She reached out her hand in greeting.

Arthur accepted it without hesitation, "Nice to see you again. Been a while I suppose, twenty or so years."

He looked to the others, who stood behind Kristin at each shoulder. "Arthur Ross," he extended his hand.

"Emil."

"Shelly."

They took turns in greeting, the older man polite and smiling to each.

"They came with me, hope that's okay, because they want to learn about the families too."

"Fine by me." He opened the door and motioned them to enter, "Shoes off if you don't mind."

Inside Kristin had to stop before taking another step forward, then caught herself as she didn't want her shock to alert Arthur. She gave quick looks to Emil and Shelly, the kind that say *don't you say a word*.

Along the right wall were two small end tables at each side of a relatively new sofa, and across from it a reclining chair. Between them a fireplace, and above it an old painting of an Italian village.

The room where the first shared photo had been taken.

Kristin could not remember ever being here, ever meeting Arthur, but evidence showed she had. Not remembering what might have been an innocuous event, a one-time visit to someone's house when you were six, certainly didn't surprise her. She just couldn't imagine ever finding herself in this home after seeing those photos.

They took a few more steps in, Arthur moving ahead to claim the recliner.

Shelly nudged her friend and motioned her to look back.

Behind them, on the wall with the door they entered from, hung a large moose head. Its massive antlers taking much of the wall space. She must not have seen it as the door opened inward, in such a way as to block her view of it.

Kristin's eyes darted from the animal to Shelly and back, and finally to Arthur. Her mind raced with questions and fear began to creep into her bones.

Focus, slow down, think, she repeated to herself.

"Please, sit."

All three did as directed, on the couch across from him.

Kristin forced herself to take a deep breath, to take the edge off what might be a slight adrenaline rush from seeing the room and that thing on the wall. She drew her attention elsewhere.

"I love that painting, where did you get it?"

"Oh, I got that when I was a lot younger. From a painter in Florence. That's not Florence, of course, but that's where I purchased it."

"It's very nice," Shelly's voice cracked.

"So," Arthur slapped his knees, "somehow you've found me."

"Yes, and thanks for having us. I actually saw you at my parents' funeral, Henry and Elizabeth Fuller, and at the Hubbertons'."

"That's right, the Hubbertons and the Rosses go back generations. Our families have been close since the old world, some members marrying even. Your father and I, though, met at a business function and got to know him and Elizabeth fairly well. Hadn't seen them in years...But..." Arthur paused, "That's not why you're here."

Kristin, surprised by the man's proclamation, didn't know how to respond. It took her a moment to gather her thoughts, to think of the best way to start without showing her hand — not that she had any leverage at all. The best she could come up with was "I don't know where to begin."

Arthur smiled, "You don't always need to begin at the beginning. Just start somewhere and we'll find our way."

The man exuded wisdom that Kristin rarely encountered in life, and suddenly she felt small, intimidated. Not at all what she was accustomed to.

Shelly jumped in, her frustration with the man growing as he lead on that he knew something without just coming out and saying it. The man's wisdom only made Shelly want to counter it with brute force, "You know why we're here."

"Of course."

Her frustration boiled over, "So fucking tell us!"

Arthur, unmoving, unflinching, his voice unchanging but his tone suggestive of one whom you didn't want to challenge, responded directly to Shelly, "Do not use that language in my home."

Shelly leaned her body back, unused to feeling sheepish but the air about the man suddenly caused her confidence to waver.

He sat in that recliner, his palms resting on the arms and legs square, like Lincoln in his memorial.

"Sorry," Kristin spoke for her.

"But you know what's going on?" Emil asked, wanting to return the conversation to the important point they had left on.

The man heard Emil, even made eye contact, but didn't answer. He just turned his gaze slowly back to Kristin as if she were the only one he had interest in.

"So..." Kristin looked at Emil, testing her thoughts to see if making the leap was the right answer, but Emil's expression gave no assistance. He couldn't think of how to help when his question had just been ignored.

She placed her attention back on Arthur, "So you knew Kacey?"

"Indeed. Sweet girl."

"Yeah, so I hear. Um…" Kristin took another moment to craft her question, "This might sound strange, but do you know that Kacey was in the accident?"

"I do," Arthur revealed the startling news like one might read a mundane weather report, his expression unchanged.

Kristen felt validated and straightened up in her seat, emboldened by an admission of the otherwise impossible, "So she's alive?"

"In a sense of the word."

"How?"

Arthur didn't respond immediately. He took a breath and raised his head just a bit, without moving his eyes from her.

More a moment he paused in thought.

"There are mysteries we may never understand."

Kristin thought a moment, debating on whether to press the question or if the answer was even important. "Why is she after me?"

"She needs you."

Shelly scoffed as, for her, the conversation quickly deteriorated into the absurd.

Kristin didn't expect the answer. In fact, she thought, if she were to list all the possible answers to the question, this may have ranked last in probability.

"That doesn't make sense. What do you mean?"

"You and she are connected. Always have been. Through birth dates, families, and countless other ways."

Kristin hadn't noticed that she had the same birthday as Kacey, but she also wasn't even sure if she had seen it anywhere. She didn't recall seeing her gravestone, which typically would have it.

Arthur continued, "This happens, and if you're looking

you'll find examples. Edgar Allen Poe wrote of a cabin boy named Richard Parker who was cannibalized after a shipwreck. Forty-six years later, the Mignonette sunk and the cabin boy Richard Parker was the victim of cannibalization. Kennedy and Lincoln, each elected to the presidency in '60, have a number of connections. Both were shot in the back of the head on a Friday, before a holiday, by someone born in '39. Lincoln's secretary was John and Kennedy's Mrs. Lincoln. Both succeeded by Johnson."

"Coincidences," Emil concluded.

"But what are coincidences?" Arthur posed to the group. "Because we don't know or understand the thread that connects these people and events, doesn't mean the thread isn't real."

"So?" Kristin's understanding getting foggy.

"So, this thread, an element of our universe, connects and connected you and Kacey. With a bit of a nudge, it's being taken advantage of."

She brought her mind back to the moment, "Taken advantage of?"

Arthur moved his hands from the arms of the chair to his lap, intertwining his fingers and sitting like a professor might while advising a graduate student. "I'm not going to walk you through this, Kristin. Some things you'll need to discover on your own."

"She has, that's what brought us to you," Emil jumped to her defense.

Kristin spoke low, her eyes locked on Arthur's, "She needs me because we're connected. She died, but something keeps her here. And somehow with me she can…restore life."

"What would that mean for you?" Shelly asked

ignoring her host, but Kristin didn't shift her eyes from Arthur.

"Nothing good I suppose," Emil put a hand on the small of Kristin's back.

"That accident," Kristin paused as she fought back emotions from that terrible day a week ago, "that accident was no accident."

"No," Arthur spoke loudly, "no, it had been set in motion years ago. Peter and Lila gave the ultimate sacrifice. Your parents unfortunate victims, but the shared event with lost parents is an important link. You and Kacey are bound by destiny now."

The riddle began unwinding in Kristin's mind. "How do I stop her? How can I break the link?"

"She's between the physical and the spiritual now."

Shelly's discomfort grew. She wasn't one to sit so passively. She wanted to strangle the man.

Emil just wanted to hear it. What had to be done? What was it? He had never been in a fight in his life, and never thought about beating up some little girl, and questioned whether he could bring himself to do something like that.

Kristin's mind sat virtually empty, ready to receive Arthur's words. A course had been set for her as well, it led to Arthur's door, and from there to the unknown until he answered. Whatever it was, she would need to embrace it. Follow the line the universe plotted for her, play it out to its conclusion. Fight like hell.

Shelly spoke, spoke an idea that came to her from somewhere unknown. Without the certainty she's used to, her weak tone came as a whisper, "She's connected to you, but something else keeps her in the in-between state."

It came to Kristin all at once, "The moose."

Arthur nodded, "Her tether." He looked away, hiding something.

Shelly felt rejuvenated, "We need to kill the moose."

The older man returned his gaze to his guests. "We're all just players in this theater. We must give deference to the Universe."

Kristin shook her head, "Earlier you said something about giving it a 'nudge', that doesn't sound like 'deference'. That sounds like imposing your will."

"Kristin, each of us has our place. Some are, well, more influential than others. Your station, your purpose, is set."

"No," Kristin shook her head, "I'm not going out that easy."

"Well, then," Arthur said in that friendly tone that notes a change in subject, "it's time to go." He smiled at the three that sat across from him, "I wish you all love in life."

The man stood and reached his right arm out to point to his door.

The three friends stood and walked in silence, Arthur following.

They quickly forced their shoes back on, and Shelly opened the door and took the first step out, the three stopping as they heard Arthur.

"The Universe seeks balance. You can push it in one direction, which requires an offering in another. You can never set it off course for long though, it always finds its way back."

Kristin, not knowing how to respond, led her friends down the steps and to the van where they all got in. With each not wanting to take much of a second's look away from Arthur, they watched him closely make his way back to the wood pile as he placed the heavy gloves back on.

Shelly turned the engine and backed out into the narrow dirt road before shifting into drive and going as fast as she safely could. She didn't move her eyes from the path and her hands gripped the wheel so tightly they ached. "Fuck him, Kris. We'll get this done."

Kristin, lost in her own thoughts, barely heard her friend's rage.

"This is ridiculous," Emil said quietly from the back of the van to himself. "Can't be real."

They turned a corner and came to the stop sign to the main road. Shelly, wanting to put distance behind them, quickly checked each direction but not coming to a full stop, and turned to head back to Shelburne.

From the front passenger's seat Kristin stared out her window, watching the green of Vermont's grass and trees pass quickly by in a blur. The whole thing so surreal.

She pushed the button to roll the window down, letting in the fresh air. "If she drowned, how's she walking around?"

"Because it's bullshit," Emil proclaimed in anger, realizing he didn't even believe his own words.

Kristin shook her head. As illogical as it seemed, as unfastened from reality, she witnessed enough to know Arthur spoke the truth.

Shelly didn't want to think this through. Her style wasn't to look at it like a puzzle but to drive the van as fast as she could into a moose somewhere. *Brute force and ignorance*, Shelly thought, *sometimes that's how you get shit done.*

Kristin rotated a bit in her seat to speak to the others, but her eyes were lost somewhere like she really was just thinking for everyone to hear, "I know it doesn't seem possible, but it's the only thing that makes sense."

"Where are you going to find this thing?" Shelly asked.

They sat in silence again, with just the sound of the road and rushing air grounding them.

"I think I know where."

CHAPTER NINETEEN
2010, Friday August 6th

Peter pressed his daughter's chest.

She wore the red one-piece bathing suit her mother bought her just a few weeks prior. He hated it. It reminded him of those bimbo Baywatch girls running along the beach. Bouncing.

"Oh stop, it's a normal bathing suit," Lila proclaimed defensively when she first showed it to her husband.

Kacey's skin was wet, not just damp from being in the lake, but spongy from the day in the water. Taking on those prune features that skin does.

Blood trickled down the bottom of his feet from the cuts from the sharp rocks and whatever those clam things were on the lake bottom. But Peter didn't feel any of it.

Nor did he feel the stones digging into his knees and shins as he sat on them at the water's edge.

Or feel cold at all from the chilly Lake Champlain water.

His wife stood to his right, above his daughter, bent at the knees.

She screamed continuously. Relentlessly.

He continued to push, to some beat in his head, applying pressure to get her heart beating again.

But she just wouldn't respond.

He turned her head to her side, thinking perhaps some water might come out and she'd start breathing again.

And he pushed a bit harder, but nothing.

Harder again and he felt a little crack. Unsure if that meant a fractured rib or just that general cracking sensation that bones do, he eased up a bit.

"Breathe! Breathe! Kacey!" his wife yelled virtually in his ear.

God, he was trying.

If she didn't breathe, it'd be his fault, right? Since he was the one doing the compressions.

For hours the family enjoyed the sun, while Kacey splashed and swam, though not too far out. A typical day at the summer cabin on Lake Champlain, he and his wife lay on the long and tattered beach towel, each reading a book and periodically looking up at their daughter.

Then they heard a bit of a shriek and saw Kacey splashing frantically, with her head dropping below the water. Peter jumped up instinctively, without thought, and raced in. He leaped with each step to not be slowed down. Lila stood, her hands over her mouth, speechless and frozen in fear.

By the time he reached Kacey she was fully submerged. Peter stretched down for her, half suspended in the dark and murky water Lake Champlain was notorious for. The water at his chest.

After what seemed like too long a time, he pulled her

up by her left forearm, her head hung back and hair still submerged. Her eyes open, mouth open.

"Kacey?!"

Peter flung her body up to his arms and pushed his way to the shore, where he placed her down on the stony beach.

It would be his fault.

He quickly looked up at his wife, the look on his face a terrifying combination of confusion, powerlessness, fear, and sadness.

Looking back at his daughter he noticed her skin and lips…that purple. A deep and cold purple.

How long had it been? Two minutes? Four? Peter couldn't say, he just kept pushing.

Lila dropped her body to the ground, falling backward. She raised her hands to the side of her head and clutched at her hair. Her wide and glassy eyes accepting what her mind had yet to grasp.

Her daughter was gone.

Lila popped back up, realizing they had wasted precious time. She needed to call 911.

She ran the twenty or so yards back to the towel, where her beach bag rested, and quickly tossed items out of it in search of her flip phone.

She found it easily and as she opened it Lila looked at her daughter and husband, who still administered compressions.

A thought came to Peter, one lodged into his mind years prior. Tucked in a dark recess.

Worst case scenario.

The irony. For Kacey to survive her cancer, to be at the brink of death, only to drown otherwise healthy.

But what of that plan? What of that worst-case

scenario? Kacey didn't need it two years ago, but she did today.

"No, wait," Peter yelled and raised his open hand to Lila to get her to stop.

Lila's eyes grew wide and her expression changed to an angry confusion.

"Call Arthur!"

Lila always thought this whole thing crazy. Arthur doing whatever the hell he did. But her daughter made it, at least through the cancer. And perhaps Arthur had something to do with it.

She made the choice to trust her husband and cycled through her contacts for Arthur Ross.

Peter's left hand still rested on his daughter's chest, he felt no heartbeat or movement from breathing. Her face lifeless and pointed to the sky, he had to turn away.

He looked down the undulating line between beach and lake as the tide came and went. Then, he noticed something. Just twenty or so feet into the lake, its torso and head clearly visible above the water.

Its antlers reached out, dripping, at least eight feet wide if not more, and its massive head looking his way.

A moose.

And above it, a full moon.

* * *

Arthur arrived to Peter holding Kacey, her legs outstretched on the rocky beach toward the water, her torso cradled in his arms as he sat facing the lake.

Lila couldn't bear looking.

Sitting on the beach towel she watched the back of the cabin, her body shaking from the horror of witnessing her daughter pass, her eyes red and raw from the relentless crying.

The sun touches the mountains across the lake as the setting begins.

Arthur quietly made his way to the couple and opened his arms to hug Lila. Out of politeness she stood and obliged. "Bring her back," she whispered to him.

He held her hands and nodded, then turned to her husband. "Peter?"

The man didn't respond but began gently rocking back and forth.

Noticing Kacey in a red bathing suit, Arthur returned his attention to Lila, "Could you get some more comfortable clothes for her?"

"Yeah."

Lila appreciated something to do and headed to the cabin. It made her feel like they were accomplishing something.

Arthur knelt next to Peter and put a hand on his shoulder. "It's getting late. We don't have time to waste."

"I understand."

"Lila's going to come back with something for Kacey to wear, then I'm going to ask you and your wife to go to the cabin."

"Okay," Peter's distant voice sounded robotic, as if not fully present.

"Here you go," with both arms outstretched, Lila presented a white nightgown to Arthur.

He smiled and stood, "Do you think you and Peter could slip that on her, or would you prefer I help?"

She retracted the gown instinctively. She hadn't considered she might be asked to do that, and the thought of touching Kacey's lifeless body broke any defense she had built up from the thought that Arthur could bring her back. It just felt too real.

Her discomfort displayed on her face, Arthur took the gown, "It's okay, Peter and I can handle it. Why don't you go in the cabin? Peter will join you in just a minute."

"Yeah," she turned and walked away.

"Peter, let's slip this on Kacey."

Arthur rolled the nightgown up and placed it over Kacey's head, shifting her pale lifeless body just slightly, as Peter held her, to tuck her arms in and roll it down to the bottom of her ribs.

"Can you help lift her a bit so we can pull it down?"

Without a word Peter brought himself to his knees, lifting Kacey with him, and Arthur pulled the garment its full length, down to her ankles.

"Okay, you can lay her back down."

Peter did, carefully, and looked at his friend as he stood. "What do we do now?"

"Nothing, I take it from here. Lila needs you, and you need her. You can wait in the cabin. It might be a while."

Peter nodded and did as told, and Artur watched him retreat.

Inside, Peter turned off the lights to afford him a view out the window and found Lila sitting on the couch and looking heavy as her weight pushed against the back cushion.

He sat next to her and took her hand, the bright moon giving enough light for him to just see her.

"I don't understand," she said to Peter, not thinking he actually had the answers.

And he didn't, all he knew is Kacey survived cancer, somehow, only to be cruelly taken from them by an unkind universe.

"I don't either."

Peter swung his body around, bringing one knee up

onto the couch in order to look out the bay window behind them.

He could see the top of Kacey's head, her shoulders, and even make out her toes. Arthur, though, he couldn't find as he scanned the scene.

"What do you see?"

"Nothing, actually. Kacey. The lake. I don't see Arthur."

"What?" her voice shared a hint of frustration and concern to the man they were entrusting.

"Wait, no, there he is."

Arthur emerged from the side of the house, walking toward Kacey with a small duffel bag.

"He must have gone to his car for something."

Peter watched as Arthur placed the bag a number of feet away from his daughter's body and unzipped it. He pulled a half dozen or so items out, setting them aside, but he couldn't yet make them out.

"He's doing…something."

Arthur walked around Kacey's body, placing some small object at each of her feet, now outstretched arms, and her head.

He then circled her again, bending at her head first, and with his back to Peter he couldn't make out what Arthur was doing. But when he stood and moved to Kacey's left arm, he saw the small flickering light gently illuminating the top of her head. A candle.

A small spark came from Arthur's hand as his lighter came to life and transferred the flame to the second candle. Peter watched him repeat the process.

"He's lighting candles around her."

Lila sat, listening to Peter's commentary, but not wanting to look. Seeing her daughter laying there, with that man doing what looked like the activities of some teenage goth kid, may result in a rising rage. And she couldn't risk disturbing what little chance this had of working.

"Now he's standing at her head, he has his arms up toward the moon. He's facing the lake, so I can't see his face, but I think he's saying something. Can't hear it."

Arthur lowered his arms to his side and looked down at the girl before him. After a brief pause he quietly retrieved his bag.

"He's coming this way, I think he's coming in."

"What about Kacey?" Lila's tone struggled for hope.

Peter looked for the right words. She hadn't moved, and he had no way of knowing if Arthur had been successful or not. He didn't know what was supposed to happen after the ritual, or if it was even concluded.

"Nothing."

Arthur entered and placed his bag down just inside the door before closing it behind him.

He stood by the couch to watch the scene outside next to the couple. Peter stood and positioned himself next to Arthur. Watching out the large window, Kacey's body rested unmoving at the center of the small dancing candlelights, and under the bright moon.

"What's supposed to happen?" Peter asked just as much for Lila.

"Kacey becomes tethered between our world and the beyond."

Neither Peter nor Lila could make the leap between what that meant metaphysically, and what that meant for their reality with their daughter. Would she jump up dancing and run to them? Would she disappear into the ether?

As her muscles began tensing and pulsing, Lila realized she couldn't take it anymore. She couldn't keep the anxiety bottled up another second as she felt her body might rupture, releasing massive amounts of energy and engulfing everything around her in her anger.

She stood and turned to the window to see her lifeless Kacey, grabbed Peter's upper arm with such force he knew better than to challenge whatever she might say next, and then quickly switched her target to Arthur.

"What the fuck is going on? Is Kacey coming back or not?"

Arthur, remaining calm, didn't remove his gaze from the scene outside, "She will."

Lila released her husband and took two quick steps in front of the men, heading for the door, before Arthur stopped her with a strong outstretched arm.

"You can't go out there."

She looked at him, daggers striking from her eyes, "Why not? My daughter is out there."

"Because her survival depends on it."

Peter reached for Lila, placing his hands on her shoulders to pull her into him, wrapping her in a loving embrace as they continued to watch.

"There," Arthur softly proclaimed without motion.

The couple followed his fixed stare to the left of Kacey, to the woods down the length of beach.

They could just make out the form of a large moose emerging from the trees. It headed in the general direction of their cabin, stopping periodically to look around like animals often do.

As the creature grew closer to their daughter, Peter felt Lila tense. She shifted her weight from one foot to another and tightly gripped his forearms.

He couldn't blame her. Seeing the massive and heavy moose getting closer to Kacey was unnerving. Without trying, or intent, it could trample her.

With little wind, the candles continued to burn, and as the moose took its place next to Kacey, the additional illumination brought a reflection of horror to the animal's eyes. They glowed now, like those from the moose of his dream. The light leaked from its eyes and rise toward the night sky.

The creature looked down at Kacey, examining her.

It then turned its head to the lake, its body following, as it stepped back to the way it came.

Kacey's body sat upright. Not quickly, like shocked to life, but not slowly like Frankenstein's monster. Her movement was natural. An awakening.

Arthur saw Lila push forward as she released Peter's arms, breaking her husband's hug, "Wait, we can't disturb the process."

Kacey leaned a bit to her left and placed one hand on the ground, lifting her body to her knees and then her feet.

Without even a glance at the cabin, Kacey followed the moose just a few feet behind.

"What the fuck?" Lila darted her gaze to Arthur and back to the window.

"She's fully tethered now," Arthur explained.

Peter and Lila watched as their daughter walked the length of the visible beach, before vanishing into the trees.

Lila spun around, turning her back to the window, and squaring her shoulders to Arthur in an aggressive stance, "What the fuck is this, Arthur? You were supposed to bring Kacey back to us. Not living in the fucking woods with some animal!"

Arthur nodded, acknowledging her frustration and confusion. "Please, let's sit," he motioned to the couch, "I'll explain as well as I can."

They sat, Peter in the middle, both his hands clasping Lila's and resting on her legs.

"This is a process," Arthur explained, cautious in his words and tone, "and a long one. She's now safe, nothing can harm her. She's not yet the Kacey you remember, she's…in a sort of holding pattern between worlds. The moose, her tether, keeps her from passing. Kacey is connected to someone here, and if the Universe is to return Kacey to you, we have to give it that person in return."

Lila shrugged her shoulders in anticipation, "Okay, let's do it then."

"We will," Arthur smiled to show Lila his confidence and agreement with her direction, "but it will take time. It's delicate."

"How much time?" Peter asked, his brow furrowed from the disappointing revelation.

"Years."

"Years!" Lila retracted her hands from Peter's and placed them at her sides, propping herself up in shock.

"Yes. I'm sorry, but there's nothing that can change that. The conditions must be absolutely perfect to take advantage of the connection we have cultivated. We need a blood moon, perfectly visible right here. And a sacrifice. Then Kacey will return."

Peter and Lila now sat quiet, focused on Arthur's words and direction.

"Now let's talk about what you do next. It will be important to get exactly right to deal with the authorities, and complete Kacey's return."

CHAPTER TWENTY
2021, Sunday June 27th

Shelly brought them back to the Fuller's where they went right to the computer to research how to kill a moose. From a few different blogs, with photos difficult for the non-hunters to see, it seemed the easiest would be a shot to the lungs from the side. Thankfully, as none of the three had ever actually fired a gun before, moose were huge. And the one Kristin had been seeing was particularly large, otherworldly so. A single lucky shot could do it — but that's all they would likely get. If they missed, or only wounded the animal, it would run off and not be seen again.

Kristin wouldn't even consider the odds. Instead, she focused on the impressive size of the animal. *How could I not hit the lungs*, she kept repeating to herself.

To hasten the process, they also used the Internet to track down a private individual selling two rifles who lived just a town over. Gun ownership common enough in Vermont, this proved easy. And their willingness to pay 20 percent over asking, cash, provided motivation for the seller to transact quickly. They also purchased ammo from the same individual.

They watched more videos, huddled around the laptop together, this time on how to fire a rifle. Kristin worried about how much time she'd even have to get a shot, and the number of things she needed to think about to get as accurate as possible seemed overwhelming.

Feet shoulder width.

Right foot half a step back.

Lean slightly forward.

Cheek on the stock.

Left hand under forestock.

Pull the rifle into your shoulder.

And that was all before just pulling the trigger.

They quickly ate some microwave mac and cheese, and placed flashlights, ammo, and some bottled water into a small duffel bag figuring it wouldn't be a long night and so they didn't need to pack much. Nonetheless, the group couldn't help feel like they prepared for battle.

Emil loaded the rifles and Kristin placed them in the back of the van, muzzles facing out — they thought if the rifles were to go off in the vehicle, it's better to have them pointed away. If anyone even remotely familiar with gun safety had seen them, they would likely have been horrified.

Kristin took the wheel this time, with Emil in the passenger's seat, and Shelly in the back. While Kristin didn't make it to the Hubbertons' cabin that night, she knew where it was. Her father clearly stated it was the last cabin on Salmon Run lane.

As she started the vehicle an unfamiliar feeling came over her. An intense sense of purpose, an overwhelming sensation of impending crisis. She wondered if this is how military professionals felt on missions.

She pulled out of the driveway, heading on the same route her family took a week prior.

The night wasn't even all that different from that terrible evening. The moon high and few clouds. Three people in the vehicle, just like last time. Kristin worried this was some sort of connection too. That Arthur planned for this as well. Maybe she should have left Emil and Shelly, and gone on her own. She wanted, no *needed*, their support. She felt her life was on the line here.

As she pulled onto Route 7 and began approaching the fateful spot, she feared another accident might happen. Every set of headlights she saw coming she braced herself for. She'd let up on the gas and bring the car closer to the shoulder. But they all drove by without incident.

As they passed over the spot, the scene marked by only short rubber marks on the road from the sudden stop, she felt incredible sorrow. Kristin could see the mangled cars in her mind, and of course the brutally beaten bodies of her parents. *Love you*, she sent the thought to her parents as she passed.

They turned on Salmon Run lane and Kristin slowed the car to a crawl.

The street sat quiet. The cabins mostly dark, and no street lights lit the way.

Kristin looked from side to side, hoping for a glimpse of the moose, but none came before they found the end of the road, and the small mailbox and dirt driveway that subtly announced the Hubbertons' cabin from between tall pine trees.

"Here we go," Kristin turned the wheel just a bit to take the soft corner.

After just a few seconds the cabin appeared ahead, a small California-style bungalow that had seen better days, but not without its charm. Sitting in darkness, the small driveway void of vehicles suggested it empty.

The trees became fewer, and none towered over the small building from the backyard, promising a fantastic view of the lake from the rear.

Kristin parked the van in the square dirt patch toward the right side of the house that was made for exactly this purpose.

Emil grabbed her hand before she could turn the key, "Don't worry, baby. We're going to do this. I love you."

He leaned in and kissed her.

Kristin didn't smile, "I know."

Shelly forced her courage to the surface, "I love you too, Kris. And I'll drag that thing by its fucking antlers to the ground and break its goddamn neck if I have to." Inside though, she now doubted herself. Arthur made her uneasy, and this paranormal mumbo jumbo sat far outside her belief system. Though she realized even a small moose would make quick work of her, she would fight one bare-fisted and unarmed over dealing with some ghostly child.

Kristin turned the car off and they exited, circling to the back to retrieve the rifles and duffel, Emil and Kristin both awkwardly holding guns propped against their shoulders.

Shelly grabbed the bag and shut the van's rear door, "Well?"

"Let's go inside first, maybe we'll find something useful," Emil spoke quietly though there was no sign of life.

"Good idea," Kristin took a few quick steps but Shelly moved ahead, her strides long and movement deliberate. She seemed set on punching someone, or something if no one else proved available.

She didn't bother knocking but turned the doorknob to find that it rotated easily. Without hesitation she entered and found a light switch on the wall. She flicked it on, revealing a quaint kitchen.

Emil and Kristin both followed, shutting the door behind, and the three looked around.

To their left the white porcelain sink and countertop, along with a window looking out to the dark walkway at the side of the house and trees beyond. Ahead an open doorway to another living space, next to it a cooking stove, and to their right an old refrigerator and small wood dining table for two.

The room seemed fit for the sixties, with old wood accents, little storage space, and virtually bare of decorations.

"I don't think we're going to find anything in here," Kristin shuffled between her friends and crossed the threshold to the next room.

The light from the kitchen allowed her to see the contents of the rear of the cabin but didn't offer enough for much detail. She found a lamp on a small table to the right and reached under to feel for the knob and twisted it on. It helped little but offered enough to assist their search.

Windows lined the left, right, and facing walls of the living room, which did provide a beautiful view of the water. Kristin could see the moonlight dancing across the gentle waves. To their right, further along the same wall which they passed through from the kitchen, another threshold to a small hallway with a door on each side.

Emil and Shelly entered the room, each taking a moment to just stand and take it in.

Kristin leaned her rifle against the wall to her left and

Emil decided to do the same as the silence indicated it safe.

"What are we looking for?" Shelly asked with a whisper.

"Anything," Kristin responded in her normal tone, "maybe we'll learn something."

Shelly dropped the bag next to the guns and went to a long dresser against the wall between the living room and kitchen and began rummaging through.

Emil started slowly examining everything as he made his way around, starting from their right upon entering.

Kristin took two small steps to the left, her back turning to her friends. Her attention called, for some unknown reason, to the adjacent windows that looked out to the side of the cabin. From the light of the moon and kitchen through its window, she could easily make out the tall trees and brush of the woods. The pines closest to the house were well-lit, but beyond them sat mostly darkness. Just faceless shadows. Shapes of tree trunks, branches, and bushes.

She couldn't turn her gaze away. Something wasn't right out there, but she didn't know what. Couldn't put her finger on what it was, nor why it bothered her. Maybe something didn't belong or found itself out of place. But what could that be? All that was out there was shadow. Only suggestions of shape.

Then a bit of movement, a shadow shifting just enough to get her to squint and take another step forward, but not enough for Kristin to convince herself she actually saw something.

Kristin placed one hand on the sill to support her weight as she leaned closer.

The world outside darkened like perhaps a cloud had begun obscuring the moon. The forms between and behind the tall trees disappeared into blackness. Then those trees followed, and Kristin could see the slow creeping of darkness consume the grasses in front of her window.

She pushed herself away from the windows and took a few steps back to where she had entered the room.

"Guys," Kristin called to her friends without pulling her gaze away from the approaching darkness.

"Yea?" she heard Shelly respond as Emil took her side. "What's..."

Shelly's shoes against the wooden floor echoed as she walked across the room and stood next to Emil, "What's going on?" Her voice told the others that she saw it too. Shelly saw that last bit of light succumb to the dark. The windows framing nothing now. It seemed absent of any color, of anything at all. Beyond that window nothing existed, and any light that escaped from the cabin was consumed violently.

"Look," Emil clasped Kristin's arm and gently directed her toward the large bay window that had provided the view of the lake out the back.

Shelly turned as well, "What the fuck!?"

The lake no longer danced with the light of the moon. Like everything else it had been replaced by darkness.

Each of them began darting their gazes to various windows, from the small one on the door that led to the back, to the kitchen which they could see through the threshold, and those along the right. Outside seemed gone, like the universe had shrunk down to just the size of the cabin.

The three startled as a cracking noise preceded the lights going out, both those in the kitchen and the lamp just a few feet from them, leaving them in complete darkness.

"Shit...guys?" Shelly called out to make sure she was

even still alive.

"Yeah, I'm here," Kristin raised her arms out in front of her instinctively. She reached ahead, then to each side to try and get her barrings, while also hoping to herself that she wouldn't touch anything unexpected.

As she reached something soft to her right Shelly let out a scream.

"Fuck! What was that?"

"Sorry, Shell, it was me." Kristin grabbed her friend's arm with her right hand and drew herself closer.

The two women stood embracing each other, an island of warmth in the abyss.

"Emil?" Kristin called for her lover.

There was a click, then a beacon of light in the black as Emil turned on a flashlight, "Yeah, right here."

"Oh thank God." Kristin released one hand from Shelly and guided them over to Emil, who they could now see digging through the bag.

"Here," Emil pulled out another flashlight and handed it to Shelly, then turned the one he had on over to Kristin. "I'll use my cell."

As Emil fumbled through settings to turn on his cell's flashlight feature, Kristin and Shelly shone their lights around the room to find nothing obviously changed. Everything seemed as it was, with the world through the windows still blanketed in black.

Soon the light from Emil's phone joined the women, "I suggest we keep looking around."

"What?" Shelly turned her light to Emil's face, causing him to turn away, the light too bright, "For what? I still don't get what are we looking for?"

He raised his hand to shade his eyes, "Do you have another idea?"

"No, I just don't even know what the hell we're doing now. The fucking world is gone and we're looking for what exactly?"

Kristin rubbed her friend's arm to try and calm her, familiar with her friend's discomfort with ambiguity, "We don't know. But that doesn't mean there isn't something here. Look at what I found at Betsy's. Maybe something's here. And, as frightening as it is, whatever is going on right now suggests we're in the right spot."

Shelly pulled her arm away, "Yeah, that's my concern, Kris. That's exactly why I'm fucking petrified. We're in the right spot, but for who? For us? Or for…for…for some other fucking evil ass thing? I thought we were going to kill a goddamn moose!"

They stood in silence for a moment, not knowing the answer.

Emil spoke first, "Until there's a reason to do something different, let's keep looking around." He pointed towards the hall, "I'll go explore down there."

Emil could be heard walking away as Shelly and Kristin turned to the living space, deciding what to rummage through first.

Shelly returned to the dresser she had previously been looking through. The top drawer had some placemats, cloth napkins, and some serving plates.

"I'm sorry, Kris. I'm just really scared. I don't want my kids to live without a mom." What really frightened her was the lack of any enemy to target. It's one thing to have a person to fight, but this wasn't that.

"It's okay, Shell, I'm scared too and I should never have brought you guys. Whatever this is it's mine to deal with. If I can get you both out of it I will."

Shelly pushed the drawer shut, and pointed her light

toward her friend, who was flipping through a book she had pulled from a small shelf. "No, that's not what I mean, or want. I'll fight for you, to the bitter end. I'm just scared."

"Ladies…"

Emil called from down the hall, his tone flat.

Shelly and Kristin directed their lights toward his voice, then at each other. They stared blankly, waiting in concerned silence for what he might say.

"Ladies, come here please."

Kristin moved first, crossing in front of Shelly to the hall. Her friend followed close.

Emil stood in the doorway to the room on the left, his cell held up and aimed inside, but looking at the women. The door to the room on the right was open, revealing an outdated bathroom, but Emil directed the girls to the left.

"You need to see this." He took a step back, into the hall, to give Kristin space to enter.

She stepped into the room, Shelly standing with Emil behind her.

She pointed the beam of light to her left and made a sweeping motion across to her right before returning to look more methodically.

Along the left wall a twin-size bed with a pink comforter. A single window straight ahead, with a bureau next to it, and a dreamcatcher on the wall. A small desk sat at the right, a mirror set atop it, along with a jewelry box and some books.

Two posters hung on the wall, both of a young Justin Timberlake.

The room was just like Kristin's at her parents. The furniture, the light purple paint, the plush carpet, the window placement.

"That's my room."

"It's like they copied it," Shelly nudged her way in. "For Kacey."

Shelly looked at the books for some sort of clue before quickly placing them back down as they seemed innocent, like they were selected only because Kristin had read them. Charlotte's Web, Harry Potter, and The Chronicles of Narnia.

Emil followed her and went to the bureau where he opened the top couple of drawers to quickly check their contents but found them empty.

Kristin touched the comforter as if testing reality. She looked around with wide eyes, unable to distinguish this replica from the real thing.

She noticed the framed photo on the bureau, the same one that sat in her own room — her, Shelly, and Wendy in an embrace together.

Then something came over her. Came from deep in her gut, forcing her to the ground with her back arched and mouth open.

She heaved, forcefully. The muscles through her abdomen tensing and leading through her shoulders, neck, and jaw. An airless gagging sound escaped her, bringing Emil and Shelly's attention to her. They saw her lurch again, this time followed by a violent throwing up of water.

"Oh my god!" Shelly called out as they both knelt at Kristin's side.

Emil put a hand on her back, "Kris, what's going on?"

It happened again. Her entire body tightened as water shot from her mouth.

In fear Kristin stood and ran out of the room, her friends calling out for her and quickly following. She wasn't sure why she ran, she had nothing to run to. Kristin felt like she needed to move, to run away, like running from that room might make it stop. But she knew that wasn't the case and that it was all in her mind, this sense that she just needed to escape. No logic or reason propelled her.

She reached the living room in just a few steps, with Emil and Shelly holding her elbows as she collapsed again and vomited more of the clear liquid out onto the wood floor. Her body reacted to whatever it was, whatever was in her. She got the sense that her throwing up was not her way of eliminating something, but rather a process unfolding. Like giving birth.

Emil pointed down the hall as he spoke to Shelly, "Go, see if you can find a bucket, or towel or something. I'll look in the kitchen."

She nodded and quickly took action as Emil turned and entered the kitchen.

With his cell phone light guiding him he flipped open the few cupboards and cabinets and managed to find a large glass serving bowl and a small hand towel. *Good enough* he thought as he returned to the living room.

He met Shelly there, who held two large towels and stood above a large wet spot on the floor where Kristin had been kneeling. Had been. Now she was nowhere to be found.

"Where is she?" Emil asked as he looked around the dark room.

"She's…just gone."

Instinctively Emil ran to the back door. Knowing the only other places inside she could have gone would have meant either he or Shelly seeing her, the only option was outside. He pressed his left hand against the door and grabbed the knob with his right. He tried to turn it, but it wouldn't budge. It didn't feel like a locked door, it didn't have that sensation of something preventing it from turning.

It felt…solid. Like it wasn't just locked, but controlled by some unseen force.

Emil found his face eerily close to the window out to the back, through it the nothingness that looked back.

The rage began in his bones, emanating out to his tendons and muscles, then through his skin and into his mind. He'd never felt this before, this thoughtless fury. Any care he had for his own consequences drowned in the pungent odor of anger.

Something placed that blackness there to hide his Kristin from him, and whatever that was he swore to himself he'd kill it.

* * *

Kristin couldn't remember going outside, but everything had been so odd and such a blur, and now she found herself standing a number of feet from the lake, though with her back to it. She thought maybe it had all become too much and perhaps she blacked out. Some of her hair and shirt were wet, and though she didn't exactly remember why it felt very uncomfortable.

She could see what she thought was the back of the Hubbertons' cabin, though she had never seen it from this angle. Its big bay window held only darkness inside.

She couldn't quite place it, couldn't explain it if she had to, but the spot where she stood felt…important.

The sound of the night's tide she found soothing, and she turned to look out at the water. It wasn't what she expected.

While the waves coming in and out sounded calming, and gave her a feeling of nostalgia and warmth, the sight of the lake was entirely different. Its dark water sparkled red like it held blood. Across the lake, the Adirondacks seemed further than they should be. And darker. It made her feel trapped in a cavern of hell, not standing by a beautiful lake.

Kristin looked up and saw the massive red disk in the sky. The blood moon. In some corner of her mind she knew it couldn't be, knew some law or two of physics wasn't being respected, but whatever reasoning skills she once had took a back seat to a flow of sensations.

Off to her left she heard a rustling, a crunching of earth beneath something heavy.

She took a single step in that direction, wanting to see but not to get too close.

Amongst the tall grasses and trees that lined the woods, she could just make something out. It stood tall, and it stretched out towards the sky.

She took a few more steps forward, and as she did she could see the thing do the same, cutting the distance between them.

The moose.

Still in darkness she could only see its outline. The broad antlers like the wings of the devil.

Mesmerized she moved closer. With no weapon to fight the beast, she could only welcome it. And it moved closer too. One slow step after another, the two drew together, with the sound of the tide starting to roar.

About twenty feet from the animal Kristin could just start making out detail. It wasn't the moose she had seen, or it was…but something had changed somehow. Something looked different.

A couple more feet and it became clear. Horribly clear, and Kristin's mouth opened to scream. Her face contorted in only the ways made possible by true terror. Her body buckled. Her heart stopped a moment.

Just feet from her now, the beast stood under the blood moon.

Impossibly stretched over the moose's long face, was the skin of Kacey's. The right eye of the moose looked through what was the skin that surrounded Kacey's right eye. The moose's other eye lost somewhere behind what was Kacey's left ear. The girl's hair, matted and sticky, lay across its forehead. Her lower jaw hanging on the beast's snout.

No sound came from Kristin. Whether in the terror she just couldn't get the breath for it, or in this new world she found herself in she had no voice, she wasn't sure.

The moose stood there, looking at her with that one large eye.

Kristin couldn't move.

* * *

Emil stood at the center of the room, his arms up and hands on his head in exasperation. Shelly plopped down onto the couch, her weight pushing against the old wooden planks making them creak loudly.

"What the fuck, Emil."

"I don't fucking know. I don't fucking know." He said quickly, his hand clutching his hair to temper his anxiety. Something he was not used to.

Then he saw it.

What was only darkness had been replaced, but it wasn't quite what it had been prior to its appearance. The moonlight's twinkling on the rippling water now tinted a deep red. As was the bit of rocky beach, grass, and trees.

Emil stepped closer to the window, leaned against the frame behind Shelly, and looked up at the sky.

"Impossible."

"What?"

He didn't bother responding, as Shelly turned in her seat and looked up, she would see it. He didn't need to say it aloud.

The blood moon.

"The fuck?" Shelly's voice a whisper.

It went against everything he learned in science classes. The phases of the moon were entirely predictable, by the same principles that governed day and night and the seasons. There was no way a week after a lunar eclipse for there to be another.

But he stood in this cabin, staring out across the lake and into the sky, at a full red moon.

"Emil."

He looked over to Shelly then followed her pointing hand out and to the far left. Just along the edge of the beach with the lower portion of her body obscured by the small grassy decline of the hill, and almost out of sight, he could see someone standing there staring off into the woods out of view.

He felt it was Kristin, knew it was, even though all he could see was a portion of her silhouette in the distance.

"Kristin!"

He ran to the door, the room now dimly lit by the red moonlight, though the electricity apparently still off. Again he tried to open it, but again the knob refused any surrender.

Emil turned to the entrance to the kitchen, where both rifles still stood. "Shit."

Shelly looked at him in hopes he'd find some divine answer.

"That's it," Emil snatched up one of the rifles and took position in front of the bay window. "Stand back."

Shelly stood and stepped to him, placing a hand on his shoulder, "Wait, look."

Outside the scene changed.

The red moon faded, its light shifting to its natural hue, and shape returning to its normal phase.

The lake seemed inviting again, with brilliant reflections.

Somehow the world awoke from a nightmare.

Shelly went to the door and this time it opened without any resistance. She caught Emil's eyes, "It's open."

Emil walked through first, the rifle at the ready. He headed toward where they had seen Kristin like a soldier tracking a down ally. He felt strong. He heard Shelly hustling behind.

He saw Kristin standing ahead, at the water's edge and he started to run, fast with the rifle swinging in his grasp. His heart pounded, he heard it in his ears so loudly he could only barely hear Shelly calling out "Emil!" to him from behind.

"Stop!" he heard at last, and reality set in.

The woman standing just ten yards away now, her back to him, was actually a young girl. She didn't stand five feet tall and wore a white nightgown. Her black hair reached past her shoulder blades. He couldn't see her face, but he had no need to. Emil knew the girl, it had to be Kacey.

Then Shelly's voice came to him again, this time as a curdling scream that sent goosebumps down his arms. "Nooo!"

Emil forgot the girl and turned to his right from where he now saw Shelly running away from him, and toward something on the ground that he couldn't make out.

Emil followed quickly, at first only out of confusion, until it came to him.

Shelly stopped and dropped to the ground, between him and whatever it was.

He quickly shortened the distance and saw his girlfriend laying on her back, her face to the sky with her eyes open, her mouth slightly so.

Lifeless and skin glistening and spongy.

"No!" Shelly called again as she clutched her friend's left hand in hers.

Emil carelessly threw down the rifle and stepped over Kristin's legs to take a position opposite Shelly. He grabbed her upper arm and cupped his left hand under her head, turning it to look at him. "Kristin?!"

Not only did she not respond, but the lazy shift of her eyes as he moved her head told him all he needed to know. Kristin was gone.

The tears came from Shelly as she shifted her butt from her heels to the grass in a gesture of surrender.

"Kristin?" Emil said softly now, a tone more familiar as an apology.

He rested her head back down, his thoughts lost in a moment confused with sorrow, anger, and a need to devise some plan of action.

Emil looked around for answers only to see the dark mountains across the large lake — appearing like the ferryman Charon should be traveling back and forth, which made him wonder which side he was on.

The beach stretched north and south, and off in the far distance a massive moose walked into the tree line and out of sight.

His eyes then went to the girl who now faced them, and Shelly's gaze followed. They recognized her immediately from the pictures lent by Betsy. Her complexion glowed with life. Her eyes sparkled brightly as if just born into the world. A kind smile came to her young face.

The little girl also held an old teddy bear, one that looked homemade with button eyes.

Somehow the innocent-looking girl terrified Emil and Shelly.

"Kacey, come here."

The two friends quickly sought for the distantly familiar voice, to find Arthur approaching the young girl from the side of the house. He walked calmly across the patchy yard, carrying himself with that quiet confidence he exuded at his home earlier that day.

Emil stood, silently, and squared his shoulders to the man. Arthur didn't seem to even notice them. Not that he was unaware but uncaring.

Shelly looked back at Emil to see his eyes fiery like the deadly moon and his fists and jaw clenched. From a few feet away she could feel his muscles flex.

"Good girl," Arthur said to Kacey as she took his side.

Shelly turned back to see Arthur gently guide Kacey, with a soft hand at her back, to continue walking to the front of the cabin.

Arthur knelt down to the girl, "Now, go wait in the car. I'll only be a moment. Is that okay?"

She nodded and they all watched her make her way with a slow walk that transitioned to a skip as she passed the back corner of the cabin and out of sight.

Arthur stood, his attention now solely on Emil and Shelly, and retrieved a small pistol that had been tucked away behind his belt.

"Shit," Shelly stood with an uneasiness, not just at being confronted by this mysterious man with a weapon, but with Emil's expression of one controlled by raw emotion which she felt could lead to an escalating situation and followed by their own demise.

She half-turned and took a step back to better see both Arthur and Emil. The rifle caught her eye, but being easily twenty feet away it held little promise of help.

"It's done. There's nothing you can do, nothing at all. So you should just go. Go home. Put this behind you."

Again Shelly looked across Kristin's body at Emil. That part of him that she despised, the scared and weak man, had been replaced by what now stood before her. His entire body pulsed with angry energy. His eyes so focused on Arthur that she didn't think he held any awareness of anything else around him.

Instinctively she took a step back, her feet moving confidently like they had more than a decade prior when she played basketball in high school, placing herself between the men.

Emil pounced in a swift motion, leaping over Kristin's still body.

"No!" Shelly took one step toward him, bracing her left leg behind her, as she collided with Emil. She clasped her hands behind him, holding him in a tight hug reminiscent of those she'd put opposing players in when intentionally fouling. A common practice in basketball, but she'd always give her opponent an extra and powerful squeeze to intimidate them.

Emil pushed against her, and tried raising his arms but failed against her squeeze.

Arthur raised the weapon, and Emil stared down the short barrel from ten or so yards away.

"Emil, don't," Shelly said it softly, hoping her tone would calm him. But he continued pushing against her.

"Arrrr," Emil yelled at Arthur as if to say *shoot me I dare you*. Under the moonlight, with hate-filled eyes and open screaming mouth, Arthur may have been afraid. But he'd dealt worth worse, a lot worse.

"Emil," she said again tenderly and Emil eased up.

Shelly heard Emil's heavy breathing through his nostrils and felt his muscles relax. With her fingers and wrists aching she released him and turned to look at Arthur ensuring she still stood between the men.

Emil's logical mind returned to him, the visceral lizard brain ducking back into the shadows. Still fearless, still angry, he knew what he was going to do now.

Arthur lowered his gun, keeping it ready at his side. "It's over," he shook his head slightly, "Kacey's here and Kristin is gone. Just go home."

With that Arthur turned and followed the skinny beaten patch back to the front of the cabin.

After just a few seconds the two heard the closing of car doors and the sound of tires against gravel as Arthur drove away.

Shelly turned around to face Emil, hoping to find answers. "What do we do?"

He looked down to meet her eyes, "I'm going to kill him."

"What?"

Emil walked back around Kristin's body, knelt, and now spoke to her. "I'm going to kill him. I'm going to kill Arthur. I'm sorry."

"Emil?"

"What?" he didn't turn his gaze away from the woman he felt so guilty for not saving.

"I mean," she paused, feeling the words sink into her gut like heavy stones, "we're at a stranger's cabin with Kristin's body. What do we do now? Right now?"

Emil thought a moment before standing.

"We wipe down anything you touched, so there's no

trace of you here. You drive me back to the Fuller's so I can get my rental," he shrugged his shoulders like the plan was easy, "you go home and I go kill Arthur. You don't need to be in any trouble here, you have a family."

"Emil..." Shelly said to plead for a better answer.

"It's okay, Shelly. Look, it's my fault. I should have strangled that asshole earlier. Should have manned up. Well, I don't care if I spend the rest of my life in jail for this. I can't get Kristin back then I can at least avenge her death."

"There's got to be a way out of this."

"It's not a discussion. You have kids who need you. Now let's go so you can get home. You may need to talk to Joe so he's an alibi that you were never here."

Shelly didn't like it, but for all the times Emil annoyed her with his passivity, here he stood before her taking charge. She'd be a hypocrite to complain about that. And...well she really didn't want this to impact her family.

"Thank you."

Emil nodded and looked around for what the exact next step should be.

"Let's load up the van with things that I'll need to put in my rental, like the rifles and our bag."

"K, I'll get the stuff inside and meet you around front."

As Shelly walked back to the cabin Emil knelt again to Kristin and took her hand. He gently brushed her hair, "I'm so sorry, baby. I love you so much. I'm going to kill that fucker."

As he said it he realized regardless of how things played out from here, his life was over. And somehow he felt at peace with that.

He stood and retrieved the rifle from the ground and circled the cabin to the van. He popped open the back and slide the weapon in as Shelly emerged with the other items.

As they placed everything in the van and shut the back lid a reflection on the metal caught their attention, and they looked up the driveway to see headlights pulling in.

Someone was coming.

The car came closer, and they could now make out the Volvo insignia. It slowed and turned into the small parking area, stopping short of the open spot next to Shelly's vehicle so the driver could see them through the window.

Emil could just make out a man behind the wheel, one he didn't recognize. But Shelly knew him.

"Hi, Shelly, Emil. Would you like to get Kristin back?"

CHAPTER TWENTY-ONE
2021, Sunday June 20th

Peter sat on the small deck outside their bedroom. He hadn't bothered to put on a shirt or shorts, but had gone downstairs to make a cup of coffee and returned to watch the sunrise. His day would begin and end with a celestial event.

Later, as planned, he'd call up his old friend Henry and act all excited to see him and his family at the cabin. And he'd open that GPS tracker on his phone to know their exact location, as it connected to the device he placed under Henry's car. *A pawn*, he thought, *we're all just pawns to some unknown force.*

His chair faced the corner, which looked directly out at where the sun started emerging from the horizon. His feet planted in front of him, and his hands held the steaming coffee just above his legs.

Eleven years, he thought, *eleven years haunted. Putting on faces for others, that everything was fine, that we were okay.*

People would say things like *Time will help*, and as time went on he heard that less. But, it never really did alleviate the pain, just distanced it on a calendar. Lila felt no better about it, and if anything the passing of time made her pain worsen. Every birthday a reminder. Every Christmas no excuse to buy presents. Missed graduations, celebrations, congratulations...

Maybe time helped those around us, the people that didn't walk the same halls as Kacey, go into the same refrigerator for a snack, sat on the same couch...

Peter took a sip of his coffee.

The sun over the horizon now, with the sky blue and void of clouds, he could tell the day would be perfect for the eclipse viewing later. Not that he would be a witness, God-willing. Peter and Lila would complete the exhaustingly long ritual that evening, under the blood moon, by giving the ultimate sacrifice.

Peter felt ready for it all to be over. He felt it in his bones as he clutched his hot coffee more tightly.

No more missing her. No more glances into her old bedroom wondering how a more mature Kacey would have changed the colors, or what new posters of boy bands she might place. No more passing her old friends in the grocery store and hearing about how they were doing in college, what they were studying, and aspired to be.

An end to trips to the cabin, seeing just in the shadows under the trees the silhouette of his daughter and that damn creature...waiting. An end to quick glances out the window, Kacey outside wandering, a ghost of herself.

And no more of those looks from Lila. The ones where just behind her eyes doubt stared back. Doubt that Peter had done everything he could have that day on the water.

Doubt that working with Arthur wasn't even worse than a waste of time. No more watching her drifting through the halls like she did.

Peter's life over the past eleven years haunted by both the living and the dead.

He took another sip.

But Lila continued to support him, somehow mustered up the courage and trust to move forward. Probably because she was tired of those same things as Peter.

He felt a gentle touch on his forearm as Lila appeared next to him.

She dragged the other chair a couple of feet over to be closer to her husband, brought her bare feet up to the railing, then rested her head on his shoulder.

It will all be over soon.

CHAPTER TWENTY-TWO
2021, Monday June 28th

"Kristin's dead." Emil watched the man as he emerged from his vehicle. For the relatively warm evening, the slender man seemed overdressed with a long-sleeve flannel shirt, pressed jeans that looked expensive, and heavy slip-on shoes.

He cocked his head as he shut the Volvo's door, "Well, you're partially correct."

Extending his hand to Emil, the man presented a welcoming smile, "Jim."

Emil, not entirely sure what to make of this stranger appearing at easily the most frightening moment in his life, cautiously shook his hand, "Emil."

"And, Shelly, nice to see you again," he nodded to acknowledge her.

"You know each other?"

"We met once," Shelly shared, her tone friendly but clear of her uncertainty about the man's intentions. "When

Kristin and I were having lunch." She turned to Jim, "You met her on a flight to Burlington…" it came to her and Shelly pointed at him, her voice gaining in realization, "you're the one who gave her that necklace!"

Emil turned quickly to Jim, expecting an immediate explanation.

"That's correct," he stated calmly and then returned the conversation to the pressing matter, "now, what about Kristin?"

"Yes," Emil said instinctively like his brain had already processed the consequences of various responses and concluded that affirming proved the best option. "But she is dead, her body's out back."

Given the past week Emil understood that *dead* now appeared a relative term, but he felt the need to share the information nonetheless.

"No, it isn't."

"We just came from there, go see for yourself." Shelly felt much less intimidated by Jim and her confidence returned.

Not looking to drag out an argument, Jim conceded, "Okay, let's go."

He started walking to the narrow dirt path around the left side of the cabin and Shelly and Emil followed, their eyes catching each other in a confused thought caught between exhaustion and hope.

As they rounded the corner and began down the small hill to the lake it became clear to the two that Kristin's body was, in fact, no longer lying there.

"What the fuck?" Emil looked around for any sign of his lover, all while convincing himself he shouldn't be surprised by what previously was the impossible.

"Where is she?" Shelly, as usual, got directly to the

point.

"Her body, well, her shell, is now wandering."

"Wandering?" Emil's eyes squinted with the question.

"Look, it would be great to stand here and describe to you what's going on, but hopefully Kristin no longer being here is enough to gain some trust. We just don't have time."

The friends looked at the man, waiting either for some inspiration to know what to do or for Jim to speak again.

Jim broke first, "So, are you coming?"

"Where?"

"We're going to get her back, as I said."

Shelly, anticipating what might come next, shifted her body to reflect her sudden discomfort, "I don't think Arthur would allow that."

"You let me worry about Arther," Jim turned and began heading to the front, his pace quick and determined. "Come, let's go."

Again they followed.

"We'll take my car."

* * *

Thunder rolled and echoed off the mountains, reflecting the anger of the night with the sun still a few hours from rising. The universe did not like being disrupted.

The clouds rolled in to cover the area in an undulating blanket, with its peaks a deep blue and valleys a gray that teased black.

And the rain came down hard.

The windshield wipers pushed sheets of water aside as Jim drove, trying to avoid the large puddles that covered potholes.

Back at the cabin, Emil had taken the front seat only to put himself next to Jim in case he needed to take action.

He resolved to fight through this the best he could, to forever place his pacifism in the past, and even ditch that Gandhi statue once he got back to Dallas.

Shelly sat behind Jim, for no other reason than that was the closest door when she approached the Volvo and saw Emil rounding it to take the front. Regardless, she found herself happy she did as she could see Emil, which made her feel more comfortable.

The three remained in silence, Shelly and Emil literally along for the ride, and Jim not concerned with pleasantries. In fact, he didn't really even need them, only brought them along to reduce contingencies.

The quiet kept its foothold until Jim turned onto a long dirt road with clear views of Camel's Hump on the left, the mountain surrounded by gray clouds across large open farmland.

"Where are we going?" Emil asked, turning to the driver.

"Don't worry about that."

Emil looked at Jim and then back to the road ahead, realizing he might have wanted to ask that much earlier, like before they even got into the car. And as unfamiliar as he was with Vermont, the telltale shape of that mountain had him thinking about Arthur.

Could that be where we were going? He thought and his anxiety grew.

At hearing the question Shelly came to the same realization, and her eyes widened as she looked at Emil. She attempted to somehow psychically impose her will on Emil to get him to turn around and look at her. She needed him to know they were headed to Arthur's. Needed that strength he exuded back at the lake. Needed to know that she, and by association her family, would be okay.

The destination became overtly clear to Emil as they passed the gas station whose parking lot he had been in previously, and then turned onto the road that led to the house of the man that seemed to control the circumstances around Kristin's death.

Emil shifted his body, pushing his legs against the floor and getting his arms into a position where he might grab the wheel, unbuckle his seat belt, or open the door and jump out. He hadn't come to a conclusion on what might happen that would have him react in such a way, but he wanted to be prepared for anything nonetheless.

Jim slowed and stopped the car at the side of the road, just thirty feet or so from Arthur's driveway. In the deep darkness Emil couldn't make out much of the house other than a suggestion of an outline, and the headlights only brushed the mouth of the dirt and gravel driveway.

Shelly's view from the backseat even less impressive, she leaned forward to just see the trunks of trees and glittering rain.

"Wait here," Jim said without looking at either passenger.

Those two words helped the friends relax as they didn't look forward to ever seeing Arthur again. But even in that quick moment Emil caught himself and promised that if he didn't like what Jim did, he'd leave that vehicle and give the man a visit.

Jim reached across the car for the glove box and popped it open, quickly retrieving a revolver. It looked heavy, with a long barrel and polished silver body.

Jim exited and Emil watched him walk up to the driveway, then disappear as he turned into it.

He shifted in his seat to speak to Shelly, "He had a fucking gun in there the whole time." Emil said it like the knowledge would have helped earlier, perhaps he could have grabbed it and dictated Jim's actions. Not that he had any idea what to tell the man to do.

Shelly shook her head, "What's going on, Emil?" She didn't seem to care about the weapon, like so much had piled onto her that this one more thing didn't carry any importance.

"I don't know."

He turned back to face the house somewhere past the trees to his right and he rolled down the window just a bit, hoping to hear something over the patter of the rain against the car and foliage.

Their senses heightened, the LEDs on the dash, the headlights against trees, and the sounds and smells of the rain, all bombarded them.

Time moved slowly, and what was maybe only minutes since Jim disappeared from their sight felt much longer. The darkness outside, the rumbling thunder, and the rhythmic rain only added to the effect.

Emil now kept his eyes locked toward the home, eager to see anything that might indicate what the hell they were doing at Arthur's house — and how exactly that might get Kristin back. He focused so intently that each beat of his heart he felt pushed through his body.

Then the flash of white light exploded from inside Arthur's, which they could only just see between the tall trees, and hear as it echoed from the hills.

"Fuck!" Shelly instinctively pushed herself back, her eyes wide and pointed.

Emil fought back a smile. Sure, he'd like to have shot the man himself, but he'd take it. He just hoped that it was in fact Arthur at the business end and that he hadn't gotten the better of Jim.

A few more minutes passed, the friends not speaking as they kept their focus outside the car.

First they saw signs of movement along the driveway as something broke the beams from the Volvo's headlights. Then, as if just leading a child through errands, Jim emerged with Kacey in hand.

They turned from the driveway and headed to the car, the branches and leaves protecting them slightly from the rain.

Shelly and Emil only watched.

Jim approached the driver's side, and in a spark of realization mixed with fear, Shelly swiftly unbuckled her seatbelt and slid across to behind Emil, where she tucked herself into the corner to not be close to the girl.

The man opened the door and guided Kacey in. "Now buckle up."

Kacey, still in her nightgown and clutching the bear, did as told.

Emil and Shelly examined her closely.

She looked like any other healthy young girl. Her eyes tired for what might have been 4 a.m., but very much alive and non-threatening.

Emil rolled the window back up, no longer needing to hear what might be occurring out there.

Jim returned to the driver's seat and placed the revolver in the glove box, "Okay, let's go." He moved the car forward before backing into Arthur's to turn and head back down the mountain.

"What happened?" Emil whispered to Jim, not wanting Kacey to hear as he didn't know what she might have witnessed.

"Nothing to worry about now."

Emil nodded with satisfaction.

But now Shelly felt intense anger at Emil. *Why did he get the front seat? Why do I have to sit next to this… thing?*

Kacey turned to Shelly, her inquisitive and friendly nature returned from the dead. "Hi, my name is Kacey."

Shelly, supposed to be older and wiser, the adult in the situation, just couldn't deal. She buried her head in her hands and began rocking herself in comfort.

What if that were one of my children? What would I do? How would I feel? What if I spoke to her? Would I then begin to care about her? What would that mean for Kristin? Is this really just Kacey? Just a child looking to live life like every other kid? Are we about to end that again?

The thoughts were too much, the weight of it all just too awesome to bear. She resolved to not think. To replace any and all thoughts with static like that from an old television. *Kacey wasn't real. Arthur wasn't real. None of this was real. Kristin is what matters.*

Emil, on the other hand, started to feel rejuvenated. For him this now made sense. Well, maybe not *sense*, per se, but if Kacey returned when Kristin suddenly passed, then perhaps with Kacey here they could reverse it.

"Where to now?" Emil was on board, bought in, though unaware of the moral struggle occurring just behind him. He didn't even care that he could retrieve the weapon in under a second, he suddenly felt no need for it.

"You'll see, not far."

* * *

Though the sun hadn't begun to break the horizon, the Eastern sky faded to those yellows and blues to announce its nearing. And with the rain stopped, the dew began misting to a low fog as the temperatures rose.

Emil recognized a few roads he'd been on previously but still wasn't quite sure where he was or had any idea where Jim might be leading them. Shelly should have had a much better sense, being from the area, but she hadn't spoken a word since Arthur's.

Emil twisted himself a bit to peek back at Kacey, not seeing his friend pushing herself against the door to create distance. The young girl leaned against the side window, asleep and mouth open, her hands lazily resting on the bear. *She shouldn't be here, be alive,* he thought, *Arthur said something about the universe correcting itself and that's what we're doing.*

After a few more minutes, with adrenaline still keeping the two friends awake, Emil started to realize just where they were. The roads back to the cabin, and his thought was quickly confirmed when they turned down Lakeview Road.

Jim slowed the car and pulled it to the side, with half of it off into the unpaved shoulder.

"What are we doing?"

Jim, a little tired of Emil's questions, turned to look at him as he pressed the ignition button to shut down the engine, "We're here."

Emil didn't quite understand until he heard Shelly.

"The accident."

Then he noticed those absurdly short skid marks just ahead, the lines of rubber-like wounds on the skin of the road.

"Hey, Kacey, can you wake up?" Jim looked into the rearview mirror before turning in his seat to face the girl. "Hey, Kace?" His tone pleasant, loving even.

The girl's eyes cracked open slightly as she stretched a bit.

Emil turned more to get a glance of Shelly, who only looked out her own window at nothing in particular. He whispered to her, "You okay?"

Shelly didn't even look at him, just shook her head subtly, in that way that shares not only are you not doing well but can't bring yourself to even speak it.

Turning his attention to Jim, Emil spoke with an eagerness to get moving. "What do I do?"

"I'll help Kacey wake up and get her out of the car. Go wait for me over there," Jim motioned toward the spot of the collision a week ago.

"Okay." Emil took another moment to look back at Shelly, who hadn't budged. Deciding to just allow her to be, he opened the car door. Careful not to slip down the short embankment, he stepped back to close the door and then made his way to the spot.

He kept his focus there until he stood just outside the white line of the road, where he tucked his hands into his jeans' pockets and turned to see Jim now standing beside the Volvo helping Kacey out.

With Buttons in tow, Jim led her to the center of the spot.

Kacey's seeming willingness, or lack of questioning, made Emil curious as he looked at her holding the man's hand. *What the heck did she think was going on*?

Emil also noticed the revolver now tucked into Jim's side. He figured if Jim wanted him dead, he'd be dead.

"Now we just wait," Jim said to Emil as he held Kacey's hand like one might hold the handle of a piece of luggage.

The sky began to brighten more, and the rays of first light burst through treetops, causing the fog to sparkle as it began to dissipate. But, it wasn't long before they heard the rustling from the woods.

Emil, pivoting completely to the forest behind him, could just see the face of the moose between tall tree trunks.

With each step the beast hesitated a brief moment, looking at the humans awaiting it on the road. But the creature's drive came from elsewhere, its nature to avoid humans overpowered by a force immeasurably greater. Its eyes taking in light and passing it to the megacosm, the all-seeing and all-being.

With its wide hooves it emerged from the tree line and stepped up the small embankment to the road.

Towering over the three people it looked down at the familiar girl, the one that had followed him for so long.

He did understand that he had a new companion, another shadow. And that that's who these people truly waited for.

Emil, being overtly aware of the power an animal like a moose possessed, kept his eyes cleanly on it. If he reached out with his right hand he could touch it, or with his left he could do the same to Kacey. The four beings stood at that spot, the one he had come to realize was an important connection point between Kacey and Kristin.

Shelly, though, still sat in the car. Refusing to even glance at the girl in fear of seeing her resulted in a swelling of compassion that might risk the return of her friend.

Her eyes locked on the animal in awe of its size, until the movement at the corner of her eye called her attention.

With Shelly's attention so focused on the scene, she didn't notice Kristin come from somewhere behind the car. Didn't see her friend until she appeared through the windshield.

Kristin slowly made her way down the center of the

road, her gaze lost and eyes unblinking, like in a trance or sleepwalking.

Kristin approached the group, and stood between Kacey and Emil, the moose looking at her as if offering an introduction.

Emil took her hand, but Shelly couldn't tell if any words were spoken.

She couldn't move. Then thought, *shouldn't move as not to disturb whatever this is.*

Pulling herself between the front seats for a better view she saw Jim dig into a front pocket. He retrieved something that he held tightly in a fist, and releasing from Kacey's grip, he delicately held the necklace up with both hands. The white moon sparkled in the early morning sun.

Jim took a short step to Kristin and slid it over her head, gently moving her long blond hair so it rested nicely on her neck. Though Shelly couldn't read lips, she was able to make out a few words Jim mouthed, specifically *moon, magical, rain,* and *tomorrow.*

With that, the moose raised its massive head and let out a howl, a long, deep, and guttural sound that evoked immense pain and finality. A cathartic celebration.

Shelly watched as Kristin stumbled, her left hand moving quickly to her head, and her right tightly grasping her lover.

At that moment Kacey stumbled as well, and Jim instinctively caught her and eased her to the ground where she then sat on her knees dazed.

Jim straightened, gently releasing and turning his back to the girl. He spoke something unheard to Emil, ignoring Kristin altogether. He then pulled the revolver from his hip and handed it, butt-first, to Emil.

Kristin, whose face Shelly desperately wanted to see,

turned her attention from one of the men to the other.

Emil just nodded, as if taking direction.

He raised the revolver to the moose, positioning it what appeared to be just short of its skull and right between the eyes.

Without hesitation, he pulled the trigger.

The gunshot collapsed the animal violently, its weight an unstoppable force as it fell to its side, one large antler cracking as it slammed against the pavement. The flash lit the morning, and the sound reverberated off every tree sending chills up Shelly's spine.

Calmly Emil handed the weapon back to Jim before embracing Kristin, and Shelly could see her raise her arms to hug him back.

Then she noticed, as Jim turned to look down, that Kacey had collapsed completely as well. She lay on the ground, unmoving.

She turned her attention away from that, Shelly couldn't let herself begin thinking about the now-deceased girl.

She wanted to get home.

CHAPTER TWENTY-THREE
2021, Tuesday June 29th

Jim took the steps up Arthur's deck and then leaned against the long wood railing to appreciate the majestic view. The busy night made him feel heavy, but the morning's sun energized him as it sparkled off the dew. *The mountains are so pretty here*, he thought.

Arthur emerged from the door that led into his home, a steaming coffee in hand, and sat cross-legged just behind Jim. Once settled he didn't move his gaze from the mountains he could see between cedar boards, and he admired the soft cloud that clipped the peak of Camel's Hump.

Jim didn't bother looking back at Arthur.

The men remained silent for a moment, both relishing in the calm after the storm.

"You know," Arthur stated before taking a quick sip of his coffee, "when we talked about you shooting into the woods I never thought you'd hit my birdhouse."

Jim looked at Arthur and smiled proudly, "No shit?"

Arthur tilted his head quickly before returning it upright, "Figures. I liked that birdhouse."

They returned their gazes to the view of a valley below and the undulating mountains across the horizon.

"I still remember what Dad said to us at Mom's funeral."

"He said a lot to us that day," Arthur replied tiredly.

"He said, 'Happiness lies in a small world; success thrives in a large one.'"

Arthur nodded, "Well, Texas *is* larger."

Jim took the chair behind Arthur, "Flight to Dallas Thursday."

"How's Melissa handling the move?"

"Oh, yeah she's been great. She understands that I need to be closer to Kristin to continue the work. And since we're keeping our Vermont home we'll still be up here a lot."

Arthur watched the steam rise from his coffee mug that rested on the arm of the Adirondack chair, "It's strange, the Hubbertons gone feels like the end of an era."

Jim frowned slightly in recognition, "Not strange at all, it is the end of an era for our family."

And it was. The Hubbertons' rise in Vermont, thanks to the Rosses, brought them honor and some wealth. It just so happened that, in comparison, Kristin Fuller as the future head of a quickly expanding and influential bank, showed much greater promise. With their help, of course.

ABOUT THE AUTHOR

Dan Durick lives and works in Vermont with his family. While Tether is his first novel, Dan has enjoyed writing screenplays, short stories, and poetry since he was young. When not writing, Dan explores Vermont in his Jeep with his family and contemplates the mysteries of our universe.

CPSIA information can be obtained
at www.ICGtesting.com
Printed in the USA
BVHW072238170523
664183BV00004B/9